Hall *of* Small Mammals

Hall of

Small Mammals

· Stories ·

THOMAS PIERCE

RIVERHEAD BOOKS
New York
2014

RIVERHEAD BOOKS
Published by the Penguin Group
Penguin Group (USA) LLC
375 Hudson Street
New York, New York 10014

USA · Canada · UK · Ireland · Australia
New Zealand · India · South Africa · China

penguin.com
A Penguin Random House Company

The following stories have been published previously, in slightly different form:
"Shirley Temple Three" (*The New Yorker*), "The Real Alan Gass" (*Subtropics*),
"Grasshopper Kings" (*The Missouri Review*), "Why We Ate Mud" (*Oxford American*),
"Saint Possy" (*The Coffin Factory*, now *Tweed's*), "Felix Not Arriving" (*VQR*),
"Ba Baboon" (*The New Yorker*).

Library of Congress Cataloging-in-Publication Data

Pierce, Thomas, date.
Hall of small mammals : stories / Thomas Pierce.
p.   cm.
ISBN 978-1-59463-252-5
I. Title.
PS3616.I3595H35   2015   2014017324
813'.6—dc23

Printed in the United States of America
1   3   5   7   9   10   8   6   4   2

BOOK DESIGN BY AMANDA DEWEY

Contents

for c & e

Shirley Temple Three

Mawmaw's throwing the party, and her own son is three hours late. Already he's missed his cousin's goshdern wedding ceremony and the grape-juice toasts and the cake-cutting, and now he's about to miss the couple's mad dash to the car too. All the tables are decorated with white flowers in beakers, since the groom, new to the family, is a chemist for a textile company, and in the foyer she's put out enlarged photos from when the bride and groom were babies and total strangers to each other, and overall Mawmaw would give her reception an A-plus if not for this business with Tommy.

Tommy is supposed to be driving in from Atlanta, where he works as the host of a popular show called *Back from Extinction*. On each episode they actually bring back long-dead, forgotten creatures—saber-toothed tigers, dodo birds, and all the rest. The show is a little controversial, but people seem to enjoy it. Tommy always looks so handsome in his khaki safari vest.

The happy couple is about to depart when the phone rings.

One of the uncles holds it out the door saying it's you-know-who on the line. Mawmaw swats it away, because she doesn't want to hear it. Not a word of it. Tommy is always full of excuses. She gives all the guests baggies of rice, and they go out front and shower the bride and groom with kernels as they dive into the back of a Plymouth decorated with shaving cream and condoms, and then they're gone and the party is over, and Tommy has missed the entire thing.

What's crystal clear is that he doesn't give two hoots about anyone but himself.

House empty again, Mawmaw steps onto the back porch to smoke a menthol and feel the cool night air on her freckled skin. The night air is a natural force, and natural forces help you remember how small you are, and when you remember how small you are in the Big Picture you see how silly it is to be upset at almost anything. It's a technique she picked up from a woman on television, and even though the woman was talking specifically about money trouble, Mawmaw finds it works in most situations. The technique helps you to remember that you have to surrender control to the universe. She can feel the breeze tickle her skin. She can recognize the breeze as a natural force much larger than her little old arthritic self. And she understands that one day—who knows, maybe even tonight in her sleep—she will die and enter God's eternal golden Kingdom and feel His Love, and when that happens all her frustrations and concerns will be like dewdrops on the windshield of a fast-moving car, the glass streaked clean and clear of all blurriness. That thought is a true comfort to her, and she's close to letting go of her anger, but then she allows herself to picture Tommy with that boyish look on his face, the one

2

he puts on when he pretends to have absolutely no idea why anyone could possibly be mad at him.

Mawmaw stubs her menthol out on the steps and goes inside to stack the dirty dishes and glasses. The real clean can wait for the morning. Upstairs, she changes into her nightgown and takes her pill. She is on the edge of sleep when she hears the truck in the driveway.

The porch lights hum with a new electricity. If the moon could radiate more light, it would. Tommy is home. She wants to sing. She wishes the party wasn't over, so everyone could see her son. When she greets him out front, he pulls her into a deep hug. "You look thin," she says. "How about some coconut shrimp or wedding cake?" His eyes are bloodshot, his brown hair ruffled. He's wearing suit pants and a white undershirt. She hasn't seen him in eight months and six days. She's already forgiven him, already forgotten how mad she was an hour ago.

He pulls her into a short waltz across the asphalt. "I promised you a dance," he says. "Don't think I forgot."

"Your uncle asked me if you'd fallen in with the wrong sort of people," she says, teasing him. "That's code for drugs, in case you're wondering."

They stop dancing. "Did you set him straight?"

"I wasn't sure *what* to tell him," she says, eyebrows arched, looking away but smiling. Sometimes she feels like a different person around Tommy—carefree, lighthearted.

"Well, Maw, I've got a good reason for being late," he says, and pats his truck, which has a BACK FROM EXTINCTION magnetic decal on its door. "Something I need to show you. Pour us both a drink and meet me around back."

She pours him some grapefruit juice in a tall Daffy Duck glass. Tommy comes into the house through the back door. She hands him the glass and he takes a swig, then looks at her, confused. He pulls a flask out of his pocket and tips it into Daffy Duck. "Follow me," he says, and leads her into the backyard, both of them swatting their way through a veil of mosquitoes and moths attacking the overhead floodlight. There, in the freshly mowed grass, Tommy has something hidden under a quilt. It's moving.

"What I'm about to show you," he says, "you can't tell a soul about it. If you did, it would be major trouble. Trouble with a capital T." He sips his drink and tugs the quilt away.

Mawmaw takes a step back. She's looking at some kind of elephant. With hair.

"Don't worry. She's not dangerous," Tommy says. "Bread Island Dwarf Mammoth. The last wild one lived about ten thousand years ago. They're the smallest mammoths that ever existed. Cute, isn't she?"

The mammoth is waist-high, with a pelt of dirty-blond fur that hangs in tangled draggles to the dirt. Its tusks, white and pristine, curve out and up. The forehead is high and knobby and covered in a darker fur. The trunk probes the ground for God-knows-what and then curls back into itself like a jelly roll.

"What's a goshdern Bread Island Dwarf Whatever doing in my yard?" Mawmaw asks.

"Listen," Tommy says. "This is very special. Other than the folks at work, you're the first modern human to ever lay eyes on such a creature. Her episode hasn't even aired yet. Go on, you can touch her. She's friendly. Practically tame. Her name's Shirley Temple."

4

"Shirley Temple?" Mawmaw asks. "You can't name it that. Shirley Temple was Shirley Temple." She points to the dog pen, under which Shirley Temple the Great Dane is buried. The dog had tumors that couldn't be removed. The vet wanted to put her to sleep, but Mawmaw couldn't bear it. One night she left the pen open by mistake, and three days later she found the dog curled and cold under the porch.

"All right," Tommy says. "I meant it to be honorific. Call this one Shirley Temple Two, if you'd like." He puts his hand on the mammoth's tusk. "Or maybe we should call her Shirley Temple the Third? Since, you know, technically, the first one was the 'Good Ship Lollipop' Shirley Temple. This one's about as dangerous as the little girl."

He runs his hand along Shirley Temple Three's back. The mammoth looks up at him with dark, mysterious eyes. It doesn't seem to know what to do in this new setting.

"Is it full-grown?"

"That's what they tell me. Isn't she amazing?"

Mawmaw nods because the mammoth really is a scientific miracle, a true marvel, but then again, it's getting late. She's been awake since four a.m., working on final preparations for the reception, and she's already taken her pill. The moonlight shines down on the three of them. They decide to keep Shirley Temple Three in the dog pen for the night.

Not all of Mawmaw's friends like her son's show—especially her friends at God's Sacred Light. When the show debuted, she had not yet retired as the church's financial administrator, and Pastor

Frank pulled her into his small, warm office and asked if she was concerned about her son. She hadn't been until that moment. Pastor Frank knows everything there is to know about Mawmaw and Tommy. They joined the church two months after she gave birth. She wasn't married, because Tommy's father was already married to someone else. Kyle Seevers was a CPA in another town and had given a talk in Mawmaw's night class in business administration. Kyle couldn't leave his wife, but he was a real gentleman about all of it and mailed regular checks until the day he died of a heart attack. Mawmaw thought it best not to attend the funeral.

Tommy knows the name Kyle Seevers. Mawmaw doesn't like secrets.

Her son comes into the kitchen the morning after the reception and asks if he can have scrambled eggs and grits. She can't refuse him. His hair sticks up in the back. He's forty-two but could be twelve. Up on her toes, Mawmaw reaches for a pan on a high hook, then down low for a whisk in a bottom drawer. She's feeling more energetic than she has in months. Her knees are hardly bothering her at all. Tommy sips his black coffee and reads the newspaper. The eggs crackle in the bacon grease.

"And how's Shirley this morning?" Tommy asks.

All morning Mawmaw hasn't let herself look out the window above the sink.

"Don't see nothing out there," she says.

"Don't see it?" Tommy is up in a flash and out the back door. She watches him scurry across the grass in his boxers. He goes inside the pen. The mammoth emerges from behind the oak tree in the far right corner. From a distance it's almost doglike. But that long probing trunk. Those tusks! Tommy squats in front of the mammoth and runs his fingers through the dirty-blond coat.

"Wash your hands," Mawmaw says once he's back inside. "Could have diseases."

"Maw, it doesn't have any diseases," he says. Yet she can't help but notice how thoroughly he scrubs his hands in the sink.

She puts his breakfast plate on the table and sits down to watch him eat.

"How come they let you take this elephant?" she asks. "Isn't that against the rules?"

"It's not an elephant. Listen, Maw, I'm going to let you in on a dirty little secret. You know about the Back from Extinction Zoo, right?"

"It's where that cute little zookeeper takes all the animals to live at the end of every show."

"Right. Her name is Samantha. Only, she doesn't take every animal to the zoo. We never say this on the air, but sometimes we clone twins by mistake, and that, legally speaking, is a bureaucratic nightmare. There are so many fucking laws that we—"

"No *f*, please."

"Sorry, but it's true. You'd think we were trying to make nuclear weapons. We're allowed to keep both twins alive until we've filmed the episode, so we can use each one on camera. But then we have to get rid of one. Samantha is the person who has to euthanize them. It's awful."

Tommy scrapes the grits into a small pile and takes another bite.

"Why are you telling me this?" Mawmaw asks.

"Because," Tommy says, "we had two dwarf mammoths. Twins. Only, this time Samantha couldn't bring herself to do it. She took Shirley home instead. Not the smartest move, but it's not like she could just set a mammoth loose in the woods, you know? Anyway, the show suspected something was up. She needed it out of her house for a few days in case they came snooping around, and I told her I would help."

Mawmaw goes to the window. Shirley Temple Three is using its tusks to root up the dirt. She wonders what it eats. If it would eat eggs. Shirley Temple the dog used to eat eggs.

Tommy plans to be in town for less than a week, but his friends want to see him. One night his high school buddy Mitch Mitchells comes over to take him out like old times. Mitch is recently divorced, and Tommy says he thinks he's lonely, which is enough to make Mawmaw laugh. What does Mitch Mitchells know about loneliness? But, standing in the foyer, Mitch gives Mawmaw a long, sad hug. She hasn't seen him in probably a decade. Unlike her son, he hasn't aged well. He has an extra chin, thinner hair. He's clearly in awe of Tommy, a real celebrity, and is full of questions. Has Tommy met many movie stars? Is he dating anybody special? Have any of the animals bitten him or stung him or stabbed him or done him any sort of bodily harm as yet unimaginable? And how do the scientists bring back all those animals, anyway?

First of all, Tommy says, he hasn't met many movie stars, since he lives in Atlanta, not Hollywood. And he's not dating anyone special, certainly not anyone famous, and thus far, knock on fossil, he hasn't suffered even a single scratch from the animals, and as for the science, well, to be perfectly honest, he doesn't have a clue how they do it. He's just the talent. He reads the cue cards. He doesn't have to handle any pipettes, let's put it that way. Mitch Mitchells thinks that's just hysterical.

"You'll look after the dog?" Tommy asks on his way out, a glint in his eye. Mawmaw nods, but once he's gone she wonders what she's supposed to do. Walk it? Give it a treat? Earlier that week, on the computer, she learned that prehistoric mammoths ate grasses, fruits, twigs, berries, and nuts. In the pantry Mawmaw has a tub of mixed nuts. She pours some cashews and almonds and pecans into a metal bowl and takes it outside, to where the mammoth has stuck its trunk through one of the squares of the metal gate. The trunk recoils when she places the bowl in front of it. It doesn't seem very interested in the nuts.

"Take it or leave it," Mawmaw says, and abandons the mammoth for her nighttime ablutions: her face cream, her electric toothbrush, and, just before sliding into the faded red nightgown, her sleeping pill. She sleeps hard until midnight, when a car in the driveway pulls her awake. She realizes she's not in bed anymore but at her desk in the office, half her toenails painted dark red, the computer printing a ninety-two-page document about the dangers of lead-based paint. Her pills can have that effect sometimes. They turn her into a zombie. She goes to the window, but it's not Mitch's Bronco outside in the driveway. It's a taxicab. Tommy shoves a wad of cash through the driver's window and stumbles toward the house. Mawmaw creeps back into her room and shuts her door. She considers taking another pill but turns on the television instead.

An hour later, her son's show comes on. It's a rerun about the Glyptodon, a prehistoric armadillo thing with a spiky tail shaped like a mace. The Glyptodon is the size of a small car. They name him Glypto-Donny. Tommy narrates Donny's reentry into the wild, in this case a reedy riverbank, the water brown and slow. The camera follows Donny through the reeds. Through the trees on the opposite bank, only for a moment, Mawmaw sees what looks like the top of a condominium. Donny doesn't do much except nose at the reeds. Tommy enters the scene and walks right up to the beast. Her son looks so small in comparison. He knocks on its hard shell. Donny doesn't seem to notice. The show ends with the Glyptodon in the back of a truck headed for the zoo. Samantha, a sturdy, petite woman with curly blond hair, gives Tommy a thumbs-up, and then there's the quick stream of credits.

No light outside yet, but she goes downstairs to put on the coffee and check on Shirley. All the mixed nuts are gone from the bowl. The mammoth makes a squeaking sound in the back of its throat.

Later that morning, Tommy appears, disheveled and quiet. They're eating breakfast when his phone screeches noisily—a pterodactyl ringtone?—against his cereal bowl.

"Not at the table," she says. "Please."

But Tommy takes the call. He goes into the living room. She can hear that he's upset.

"Of course, yes, she's safe here," he says. "She's holding up well. I told you everything would work out fine if we just—" He paces. "Okay, well, we knew that was a possibility. But listen, please don't do anything drastic. Just take a deep breath. Have you had breakfast? Go get one of those egg sandwiches you like and take a walk. I'll be back soon. We can sort this out together. One step at a . . ."

Mawmaw goes out back for a menthol. She smokes two a day—one after breakfast, one after dinner. A self-imposed rule. It's been this way ever since she was a teenager. No one called her Mawmaw back then. She was Louise Baker, the dark-haired beauty who scooped ice cream at the drugstore after school.

A crow lands on the top rail of the dog pen, and then flies away. The little mammoth hardly moves. It's almost like a mannequin. Why isn't it moving? It moves. Mawmaw realizes she's been holding her breath. The mammoth shuffles to the back of the pen, on the other side of which is a stretch of woods. Sometimes the deer emerge from those woods to eat the small green apples when they fall. Shirley Temple Three might like to see that, she thinks, and then takes a final drag of her menthol. Tommy says that the mammoth is from the late Pleistocene. It's been yanked out of its own time and lives outside God's natural laws.

God created the world in seven days, but those days weren't necessarily twenty-four-hour days. Each one of His days might have been a million years long. Human time means nothing in the realm of Heaven, where the clocks probably don't have hands but golden arms, and the arms belong to God. On which day did the mammoth get created? It wasn't on the seventh day, since that was the day of rest. Quite possibly it came into the world on the morning of the fifth and went back out again that same afternoon.

She is grateful to have been included at all in the grand parade of Creation, but thinking of entire creations already come and gone, it's hard not to feel a bit lost in the procession. Mawmaw has experienced this anxiety before. "The anxiety of smallness," her pastor called it once and advised, in these situations, that she imagine a zipper running down the length of her back, a flesh-colored set of teeth that when unzipped split apart to reveal a dazzling white vastness as big and deep as the universe itself. But to have invested something so big in something so small and limited, it often seems to her, was probably unfair—or even dangerous.

When she goes inside, the plates are still on the table. She finds Tommy upstairs, packing his bag. She asks if everything is okay, and he says of course it is, then adds, "But I have to leave a little earlier than expected."

"Is everything okay with Samantha?" she asks. "I assume that was Samantha?"

He gives her a curious look, then continues collecting clothes off the armchair and floor.

"Are you dating the zookeeper from your show?" she asks.

"Dating her? I don't know," he says. "Does it matter? Listen, Maw, I'm sorry, but I need to get back to Atlanta for a few days. I'll come back once things get sorted out."

"What about . . ." She motions out the window to the other houseguest.

"Don't hate me, Maw. Please don't hate me, but Shirley has to stay here for a while. Not for too long, I promise. It's just that, well, if you want to know the truth, people are asking questions. Samantha's in some hot water. They want proof of death. Someone at the zoo must have made a call."

"And you're helping her because why?"

He grimaces. "What do you want me to say, Maw? That I'm doing it all for love?"

Mawmaw is quiet. His doing it all for love certainly wouldn't make the situation *less* palatable.

"Fine," he says. "Sure, Samantha and I might have something. Maybe. And so that's why I have to leave and sort this all out. She might have broken a few laws."

Mawmaw doesn't bother to ask him how many laws are currently being broken in her own backyard.

"Whatever you do," he says, pulling up the handle of his roller suitcase, "don't tell anyone about the mammoth. Once this business with Samantha settles down, we'll figure out what to do next. I promise."

She's been babysitting the mammoth for not quite a month when it starts losing hair. Mawmaw sits in front of the pen on a kitchen stool. The days are getting warmer, and she doesn't know what to do. Clumps of the mammoth's blond tangles are spread across the ground, and its exposed skin is red and irritated. It rattles the gate with its curvy tusks.

"I'm not going to lie to you. I'm worried," she says to Shirley. "Tommy's not returning my phone calls. Don't look at me like that. I know exactly what you're thinking. Tommy's not calling? What a surprise, right? You got fleas, is that it? Or are you molting? Is this normal? You're probably not used to this weather, are you? Eighty-eight degrees today, and it's only going to get hotter. What happens then?"

Mawmaw wonders if the mammoth might be scratching it-self raw along the fence, but over the next week, looking out the back window, she never catches it in the act. Mostly it just stands there in the heat, breathing heavy. But the hair continues to fall out. One patch of skin looks so rough that Mawmaw takes out her lotion and rubs some on the spot with two fingers.

"Just so you know, this is expensive lotion. I have to order it special. I use it on my face—otherwise I get dry between my eyes. Does that feel better?"

She calls Tommy and gets his voice mail. When the tempera-ture hits ninety, she brings Shirley inside the house to cool off for a little while. Guiding the animal down the hallway is a challenge. The mammoth comes up only to her waist, but it is a hefty crea-ture, much too heavy to lift or shove. Mawmaw steers it toward the laundry room, where the dryer is tumbling a load. She moves some cleaning supplies and boxes onto the shelves along the back wall, clearing a space on the floor. She spreads a plastic tarp and cranks up the air-conditioning. She fills the mammoth's bowl with beans and orange peels and mixed nuts—always nuts—and a little hay that she picked up at the garden-supply store. With some old bath towels she creates a nest beside the washing ma-chine. She tells Shirley good night and closes the door.

By the time she climbs into bed that night, the house is nearly an Arctic tundra, and she needs four blankets to keep warm. In the morning she puts on a sweatshirt and a jacket. The laundry room smells like the circus. She shovels the dung into buckets and dumps the buckets in the woods behind her house. She burns citrus candles to mask the scent.

. . .

Tommy still hasn't returned her phone calls by the time Shirley has her big television debut on *Back from Extinction*. It's been on the calendar for weeks, and Mawmaw lets the mammoth come into the living room as a special treat. She offers Shirley a small bowl of milk and sinks into the couch just as the episode begins.

Mawmaw knows the theme song by heart, the horns and jungle drums that float above a highly scientific electronic beat. Tommy narrates a few basic facts about woolly mammoths. How they haven't walked the earth for thousands of years, how in some cases they were overhunted by early man. The show is very protective of the technology that gestates the mammoth, and so it skips ahead to post-birth with a montage of Shirley's first year, as her legs and trunk elongate, as her coat thickens, as her tusks sprout outward. Then Tommy enters the action. He asks one of the scientists what mammoths used to eat, and the scientist, a limp smile on his face, informs Tommy that frozen mammoths have been discovered with bellies full of leaves and grasses. They also like fried eggs and grapefruit rinds, Mawmaw adds, not to mention M&M's.

"Look at you, Shirl. You see yourself? Pretty impressive."

In the next scene, Shirley is loaded into a truck and dropped off in the middle of the Canadian Arctic, in an area that approximates conditions on Bread Island thousands of years ago. In the back of the truck, with a fur-lined hood pulled tight around his pinkish face, Tommy explains that Shirley has been wired with cameras and a tracking device and that now, for the first time in thousands of years, we're going to get a glimpse of a mammoth in the wild. Mawmaw knows that Shirley will survive, but still she grips her armrest.

The mammoth loses interest and wanders into the kitchen.

"You're missing it," Mawmaw calls. She can hear its tusks knocking against the walls as it migrates to the back of the house.

Shirley stops losing hair. Gray scabs form a light crust over the bald patches, which break apart under a wet washcloth. But Mawmaw is still concerned about her patient. Shirley isn't drinking enough water. She seems lethargic. She comes down with diarrhea. Mawmaw discovers it, the dark green puddles across the tarp. She leads Shirley back to the dog pen so that she can clean up the mess. She tosses the whole sheet of plastic in the trash and lays out a new one.

"What can I do for you?" Mawmaw asks, leading Shirley back inside. "Would Pepto help? More sunlight?"

The next morning Mawmaw wakes up to find even more diarrhea. The mammoth is trying to hide behind the washing machine, her tusks tapping the metal side.

Mawmaw gets on the computer and searches for "elephant + flu," but the sites aren't especially helpful. She dips her fingers in the water bowl and presses them to the mammoth's wrinkled gray lips beneath the trunk.

"Come on. You can do this. Just a little. You need this."

She wets her fingers again and this time the mouth opens a little to receive them, but when the water drops pass Shirley's lips she shuts her mouth tight again, as if the liquid were toxic.

Mawmaw strokes her tusks and knobby forehead, brushing loose strands away from her dark eyes.

She calls Tommy's cell, but gets his voice mail again.

"Tommy. Shirley Temple is dying. I just thought you should know. I'm doing the best I can, but I don't think it's going to be enough. Maybe Samantha should have put her down like they asked her to. Maybe something really is wrong with her. I don't know why you brought this goshdern thing to my house."

Mawmaw imagines finding the mammoth dead, its blond hair stiff with dried excrement, its eyes white and milky. She won't be able to lift it. She'll have to carve the mammoth into chunks to get it outside again. She imagines the jagged saw blades, the mess.

This is all Tommy's fault. What kind of a fool son did she raise up? This mammoth doesn't belong here, or anywhere. *Back from Extinction* is a cruel television program. The cruelest. Shirley is a clone, and that means ten thousand years ago her exact copy walked the earth. The original Shirley had parents, and maybe even children. The original Shirley probably died in some kind of ice pond or avalanche or tar pit. Ten thousand years from now scientists could make a Mawmaw clone. What would the world be like then?

Then a terrible thought: What if today is still God's seventh day and He still hasn't woken up yet from His rest? That would explain why He's been so quiet lately. What if, when He wakes up on the eighth morning, He decides He doesn't like what we've been up to down here? Maybe He'll be grumpy with us and stamp out all the lights again, return the world to darkness. In ten thousand years, the earth could be cold and barren, an endless frozen wasteland more suitable for mammoths than for humans.

If they—whoever they are—do grow a new Mawmaw out of a petri dish, she can only hope that someone will set her up in a nice warm room. And if that Mawmaw gets sick she can only hope that they'll do what's right and call a doctor.

She finds a vet in the yellow pages. His name is Dr. Mark Sing. She promises to double his fee for a house call, and he comes over that evening. His hair is dark and shiny. He has a leather bag that she hopes is full of instruments and medicines. He takes off his tan blazer, then puts it on again. The house is still cold. Mawmaw's last electricity bill was astronomical. "You have to swear to me that you won't tell a soul what you see here," she says, and he shrugs like he's heard this all before.

"I'm serious," she says, and across a blank sheet of paper writes, *I won't tell a soul.* "Sign this. I want to have it in writing."

The man looks tired. He removes his glasses and rubs his left eye with the palm of his hand, the gold watch snug around his wrist. He signs the paper, and she leads him down the hall and opens the door. The mammoth is nested in the bath towels. Mawmaw has done her best to clean the room. Vanilla candles burn on the washer. The plastic tarp crinkles under their feet. Dr. Sing opens his mouth but doesn't say a word. He kneels down by the mammoth, runs his hand through the hair, caresses its knobby forehead. Shirley doesn't seem to mind, and Mawmaw considers this a good sign.

"Can I ask you where it came from?" he says. "How long you've had it?"

"I'm sorry, but no. She going to be all right?"

He opens his bag and removes an electronic thermometer. He taps it a few times against his palm, as if uncertain whether he should proceed. Finally he lifts the mammoth's thin hairy tail and inserts it quickly. Shirley's head jerks around and the tusk collides with the doctor's left shoulder, almost knocking him over. The thermometer beeps. He looks at the reading. Mawmaw asks if it's high, and he says he's not sure exactly, because he doesn't know what's normal. He says what he really needs is a blood sample, to run some tests, but Mawmaw can't permit that. He gets up off the floor and goes into the hall. On the wall he sees a framed picture of Tommy in his khaki duds.

"He's the one from that show."

Mawmaw doesn't answer.

"Could be a mammoth flu, for all I know," he says. "She definitely seems dehydrated. I suppose I could give her fluids intravenously."

Mawmaw agrees that he should, and that's the plan. Fortunately, Shirley doesn't protest when he inserts the needle. Mawmaw pays Dr. Sing triple his usual fee and shows him the piece of paper again. "Who would believe me anyway?" he says, and takes the check.

The next morning the mammoth has her appetite back. Mawmaw cooks her rice and yogurt. She lets her out into the yard and runs a stiff wire brush through her matted blond coat. The mammoth seems to like being brushed. Then she wanders to the edge of the property to root around. Mawmaw pulls the excess hair out of the brush, stretching and curling the strands between her fingers.

"I could make a Shirley sweater. I bet it'd be warm."

That night Mawmaw is in her bed when she hears the first wail. She's taken a pill, but she's wide awake now. The mammoth

19

lets out a long guttural cry that almost shakes the house. Maybe her cries are a reaction to the vet's visit and the fluids he administered—or maybe the fever and the dehydration were only early symptoms of some deeper crisis. Mawmaw waits for another, but it doesn't come. She might have dreamed it. She's on the verge of sleep when it erupts again, that slow mournful bellow. Pulling the top blanket over her shoulders, she sticks her veiny feet into her Goofy slippers and flips on every light switch on her way downstairs. In the laundry room, Shirley is staring at the floral-print wallpaper, as close to the wall as her tusks will allow.

"What's going on in here?"

The mammoth doesn't move.

"You need to drink more water. That's all it is. You've got some kind of flu. You need sleep."

Mawmaw has an extra pill in her pocket. She takes it into the kitchen and coats it in a gob of peanut butter. The peanut butter sticks to the food bucket when she brings it out to Shirley. The mammoth's trunk grabs the gob and tucks it into its gray mouth.

"Whatever's bothering you, we can talk about it in the morning."

She gets back in bed and nestles under the weight of the blankets. A few minutes later, the mammoth repeats the sound, but this time, instead of trailing off into nothingness, it ends with several shrill, trumpetlike staccato bursts. Mawmaw considers turning on her television but doesn't. She's worried. Maybe it's mating season. If so, how tragic. Shirley is separated from her closest mate by ten thousand years. Then comes another wail. The mammoth lets up only at the first hint of sunlight.

. . .

The mammoth's night terrors have been happening for a week when Tommy finally calls. She can hear street noise behind him.

He says he's so sorry she's had to deal with Shirley these past few months, but if the mammoth dies of its sickness, maybe it's for the best. For everyone. He says the network still hasn't figured out that Samantha took the mammoth, but they've been keeping an eye on her. And on him. That's why he hasn't been able to bring Shirley back to Atlanta. "I was actually beginning to worry I might have to come down there and euthanize her myself," he says.

"And how would you do that exactly?"

"God, I don't know. A shovel, I guess. Or maybe I could poison it."

"And what would Samantha have to say about that?"

"Why, you plan on telling her?"

Mawmaw is quiet. So, her son would protect his girlfriend from that tragedy but not his own mother. No doubt they'd bury Shirley in the backyard, and every time Mawmaw walked across the grave she'd have to remember what her son had done.

"Thankfully, I don't think it's going to come to all that," he says. "Not if she's sick. Right?"

Mawmaw doesn't mention Dr. Sing's visit. She doesn't mention the wailing. She doesn't tell him that Shirley's problem might not be physical but spiritual. She lets him think she wants it dead too.

Calling Pastor Frank is a risk, but Mawmaw is desperate. Three years ago Pastor Frank prayed over the body of a young girl with brain cancer, and despite the doctors' dire prognosis the girl survived for another two years.

He arrives five minutes early and, without being asked, removes his large black sneakers at the door. He pulls her into a deep hug and pats her back. In the living room, she offers him coffee.

"No, thank you," he says. "I get jumpy."

He's examining the items in the spacious living room: the oil portrait of baby Tommy on the wall, the antique tea cart with the porcelain teacups, her mother's old electric organ with the thin black pump pedals. Possibly he's wondering how Mawmaw could afford such a nice living room with what had been a modest church salary.

"My son bought me this house after I retired," she says. "A total surprise, believe me. I didn't ask for it."

"It's lovely," he says. "You look exhausted. Everything okay?"

"My dog is dying. I haven't been sleeping well."

"I'm sorry to hear that. Never easy. I still get teary-eyed thinking about our Pomeranian that died two years ago. Copperhead bit him."

"Did you pray for him?"

"For the dog? Well, it happened so fast. He was dead within hours. Do you have any tea? Noncaffeinated?"

"Of course," she says, and goes into the kitchen. As the water heats, and then as the tea bag steeps in the Mickey Mouse mug, she imagines what happens next, the moment of first contact. She tries to picture Pastor Frank, the tarp crinkling under his knees as he places his warm hands over Shirley's tangled hair. She imagines his words as a light, almost liquid, that forms an amber-like shell around the mammoth's body.

She takes the tea into the living room. Pastor Frank is leaning over the electric organ, tapping the keys. He hasn't turned it on, so it produces no sound. She offers him the tea.

"You know, my wife and I don't have cable," he continues, "but we've been hearing an awful lot about your son's show recently. Is it true they brought a Neanderthal back from the dead? Two ways of thinking about these things." The pastor's thin brown hair is brushed back with pomade. He has one finger on a low B-flat and another on a high one. "Two scenarios. In scenario one, God killed off the Neanderthals because He wanted it that way and therefore we're going against His will by bringing one back. In scenario two, there never was such a creature as a Neanderthal, and the so-called fossils were put there by the Devil himself. The second scenario is frightening, of course, because that would mean we're breathing life into the Devil's creations."

Mawmaw can feel the pulse in her temple. "They never brought back any caveman," she tells him. "Only animals."

"Still," he says, as if that settles it.

They sit down in the wingback chairs, facing each other. Mawmaw isn't sure whether or not to proceed with her plan. After a long silence, he asks her if she'd like to pray for her son.

Pastor Frank reaches out for her hands. How many times over the past thirty years has she put her hands in his and said the words? How many times has he shined the light into the shadows of her heart? He knows all there is to know: about every sordid encounter she ever had with Tommy's father; about her visit to the clinic and what she almost did there, the blue gown and paper-thin slippers, so thin they barely existed at all; about every dark dream, every dark thought; her doubts about God, about Hell, about what happens next.

Pastor Frank is praying for her son. He's asking God to bring Tommy home again, to protect him from evil forces at work in the world, to reveal to Tommy the path back to God. His words hover in the space above her head, a wispy cloud in a night sky, breaking and re-forming in the high atmospheric breeze. From below, her feet planted firmly on the ground, Mawmaw could reach out for those clouds if she wanted, poke her fingers through them, but she doesn't. She recycles Pastor Frank's words, borrows their power. She recites a silent prayer of her own, this one focused on the creature in the next room, their two prayers, she hopes, working in tandem.

"Can you add my dog?" she interrupts.

"Of course," he says. "Do you want to bring her out?"

"She's at the vet."

Pastor Frank smiles and gives her hands another squeeze. He speaks softly, almost in a whisper. He asks God to keep watch over sweet little—what's the dog's name?—to watch over sweet little Shirley Temple. "Lord," he says, "we praise all the beauty in Your creation, the fish and the birds and the turtles and the squirrels and the cats and the dogs and even the possums."

The wailing at night does not stop. A neighbor calls to complain about the noise, and Mawmaw blames the television, her bad hearing. She tries a night-light in the laundry room. She tries stuffing towels under all the doors to muffle the sound. She prints out pictures of the tundra and other mammoths and tapes them to the walls. Some nights, half asleep, Mawmaw worries that the noise is emanating from within the catacombs of her own body. Opening her mouth she half expects the cries to amplify. She is able to sleep only in spurts. She dreams that Shirley is her guide through a world of snow and ice and unidentifiable landscapes. Every direction looks the same, but Shirley knows the way. Where they are going is important, but in the morning Mawmaw can no longer remember why.

One night, she gives the mammoth three pills. The next night, four. But, no matter the dosage, they don't seem to have any effect.

"What is it?" she asks, downstairs again, desperate, the lights flipped on. "What do you need from me? Is this mating season? I'm sorry to tell you this, but you got no one to mate with. You're on your own. You got to hush up. I've tried everything I know to try. I'm going out of my mind." She steps backward into the hall, the door to Shirley's room still open. "Is this what you want? You want out? Here." She opens the door to the backyard. "Do whatever you need to do."

She stomps back up the stairs and climbs into bed. A little after midnight, thank God, the cries downstairs finally stop.

What wakes her in the morning isn't a noise but a light. Bands of gold and yellow sunlight crawl slowly across the end of her bedspread. She's quite certain no morning has ever gleamed in this particular way. She feels like she's been asleep for a thousand years.

Only once she's on the stairs in her bathrobe and slippers does she remember leaving all the doors open for Shirley. The mammoth isn't in the laundry room—or anywhere else in the house.

"Come on out, wherever you are. Don't play tricks on me."

She steps outside into the sunlight and peeks under the edge of the porch, just in case Shirley managed to squeeze herself underneath. The far corner is where the dog went to be alone in the end. But the mammoth is not there. Nor is it anywhere in the yard or the dog pen. Shirley has escaped.

Of course, there's no one to call for help but Tommy. His voice mail picks up after a few rings.

"Call me back. It's about Shirley," she says vaguely.

As soon as she hangs up, she regrets the message. Her son doesn't need to be involved, not if his solution is poison-laced candy or a bop on the head with the shovel. An unsettling image begins to take shape: her Tommy, no longer handsome but totally devolved, a swollen caveman's brow, hunting spear in his grimy hand, bits of broken leaves in his long and matted hair.

She climbs into her car and drives up and down the block, too afraid to actually yell out Shirley's name. Two streets over she spots a hulking shape beside a brick house, but when she gets closer the shape is only some yellow pampas grass. On a cul-de-sac, a white-haired man in a blue tracksuit is walking his Jack Russell terrier. The sight of the man with his dog, the parallel rhythm of their strides, almost brings a tear to Mawmaw's eye.

When she pulls up alongside the man, he leans down to her open window.

"Something wrong?" he asks.

"Sorry, but you seen anything kind of odd this morning?"

"Like what?"

She's not sure what to say. "I lost my dog. A real big one."

"Sorry to hear that. You tried animal control?"

"I will," she says. "Good idea."

She drives home again and gets on the phone.

"Listen," she says, once she has a woman on the line. "Have you gotten any of what'd you say were 'odd calls' this morning?"

"Like what?" the woman asks.

"Like, for instance, about a real big and sick hairy dog?"

The woman breathes deep. "Ma'am, are you calling to report a big and hairy sick dog?"

Mawmaw hangs up. She opens a cabinet for breakfast but isn't very hungry. Next to the cereal boxes is a tub of mixed nuts. Upstairs she flips on the television in her bedroom. She waits for Shirley to show up on the morning news, then the afternoon news, then the evening news.

She goes outside to smoke a menthol, but can't remember which end is which. The ash flakes on the brick at her feet. She pictures Shirley in the oncoming beams of interstate traffic. She pictures her in a hunter's crosshairs, then her head stuffed and mounted *as a trophy*.

She is on her fourth menthol when she hears a car in the driveway. A few minutes later, Tommy comes around the corner of the house, his face gaunt under the porch light. He looks out to the dog pen and seems relieved not to see a mammoth there. If Shirley knows what's good for her, Mawmaw thinks, she won't come anywhere near the house tonight, not with Tommy here. She'll wait until he's gone again before coming home.

"I was knocking out front," he says, his hand up to shield his eyes from the light. "Guess I should have called first."

Mawmaw takes another drag of her menthol. In this light, he is only the outline of a man. "What's the matter?" he says, stepping toward her. "It's me."

The Real Alan Gass

He's been living with her for not quite a year when Claire first mentions Alan Gass.

"I think I need to tell you about something," she says. "About *someone*."

Walker turns down the stereo above the fridge and readies himself for whatever comes next. They are in the kitchen—formerly her kitchen, now their kitchen. The butter crackles around the edges of the potatoes he is frying in a big cast-iron pan. He runs his hand through his dark hair, as if exhausted. If she confesses an affair, what will he do? First, switch off the burner. Second, grab his jacket and go without a word. The third step could involve fast walking, tears, and possibly a stop at the liquor store. Beyond that, it's hard to say.

Claire is on the other side of the kitchen island with her laptop open, an old black T-shirt sagging down her left shoulder, a turquoise bra strap exposed. Until now, she's been quietly at work. She no longer takes classes, but when she did, they had titles like

"Advanced Topics in Sub-Subatomic Forces." Thanks to a graduate fellowship, she spends most days on the top floor of the physics building at the university, thinking about a theoretical particle called the daisy.

The daisy is a candidate for the smallest particle in the universe, but no one has devised a way to observe or prove the existence of one. Doing so would probably require re-creating the conditions of the Big Bang, which everyone seems to agree would be a bad idea. The wider academic community has not fully embraced Daisy Theory, as it's called. Claire's advisor came up with it, and, like him, Claire believes the mysterious particle is forever locked in a curious state of existence and nonexistence, sliding back and forth between the two. Daisy Theory has helped put Claire's physics department on the map.

"I haven't mentioned him until now because"—she scratches her chin with her chipped electric-blue fingernail—"I was embarrassed, I guess."

"Just tell me," he says, wanting this over with quickly.

"All right, here it is. Okay. I'm kind of married."

"Kind of?" He doesn't understand. Typically, one is or isn't married. He races through the possibilities: she's separated from someone and failed to mention it until now; or rather, she met and married a mysterious man on the sly; or, not a man, but a woman, and what she wants to propose next is an open relationship. No, more likely this is a new and clever update on the same old fight they have about time and priorities. She's married to her *research*, and he just needs to get that through his head.

"No, what I mean to say is, sometimes at night, when I dream, I dream I have a husband."

"A dream marriage," he says. "Okay." He kills the burner under the pan and scrapes the potatoes onto the plates where already the green beans have gone cold.

"Tell me what you're thinking. Does this bother you? You're not the man in the dream."

"Just so I'm clear," he says. "This isn't you telling me that you're cheating on me?"

"I'm not cheating on you. Not unless you count dreams as cheating. Do you?"

Walker wonders if this is an elaborate test; if, maybe, he muttered some other woman's name in his sleep the previous night. Although he sometimes dreams about sex, in the morning the details of his encounters are usually hazy and impressionistic, with floating parts that don't connect to a specific face. He doesn't mention this now. A dream marriage, if that's really what this is about, should probably not bother him. He tells her so.

"So it doesn't concern you that I'm in love with someone else in my dreams?" she asks.

"You didn't mention love."

"Well, I married him, didn't I?"

"Do I know the guy? Have I met him? Please don't tell me it's your advisor."

Whenever she talks about needing more time for her research, Walker knows, that includes more time alone with her advisor. She reaches across the island for Walker's hand, a gesture that makes him suspect he's about to get more bad news.

"It's not my advisor," she says. "My husband's name is Alan Gass."

Alan Gass only exists in her dream, she explains. He is an

ophthalmologist, a tall man with bright blue eyes and a lightly bearded face. His favorite meal in the world is barbecue biscuits. He is allergic to shellfish. Years ago he played college football, but he's put on a little weight since those days. On Saturdays he plays golf, but professes to hate what he calls clubhouse culture. He just likes the wind in his hair, the taste of a cold beer on the back nine. Claire has been married to him for almost a decade.

"Wow," Walker says. "You have incredibly detailed dreams."

"That's what I'm trying to tell you. They're super-realistic. Sometimes I dream that we're just eating dinner together, kind of like this. We tell each other about our day. Or we don't talk at all. We've known each other so long, silence is okay at this point, you know?"

Walker takes a bite of the potatoes. Claire hasn't shut her laptop.

"You writing Alan an email over there?" he asks, and expects a full assault of noncommutative geometry, U-waves, big gravity. But when she turns the screen, he discovers that she's looking at a website with pictures of celebrities eating messy sandwiches and picking out shampoo at the drugstore.

"So is Alan Gass better-looking than me?"

"Silly duck," she says, a recurring joke about his outturned feet. She shuts the laptop and comes around the island. "Silly duck with big sexy glasses." She plucks the glasses from his face. "Silly duck with snazzy shoes." She taps his black shoes with her socked feet. "Silly duck with perfect duck lips." She kisses him.

He stands and wraps his arms around her waist. A former high school volleyball star, Claire is a few inches taller than Walker, and even more so right now with her blond hair up in a

32

high, messy bun. He doesn't mind her height, but whenever they ride an escalator together, he claims the higher step to see what it's like.

Admittedly, her dream is a strange one—so visceral, so coherent, so consistent—but he can see no reason why Alan Gass should come between them. After imagining a real affair, he feels somewhat relieved. It isn't as though she is actually married and actually in love with an actual ophthalmologist. What counts is that the real Claire—the waking Claire, the part of her that matters—wants Walker and only Walker, and that is the case, is it not? She says that it is most definitely the case. She kisses him, tugs his hand to her cheek. She is relieved, she says, that he finally knows her secret, a secret she's never told anyone, not even her parents. What a weight off her shoulders. Anything he wants to ask, he can ask. She will hide nothing from him.

Over the next few weeks, new details emerge. Claire's dreams began when she was in high school. Walker can't help wondering about the subtle differences between himself and Alan. Alan grew up Baptist in a small town and doesn't drink. Walker grew up Episcopalian and drinks a glass of wine every night. Alan regularly wears suits. Walker prefers tight dark jeans and designer T-shirts. Alan volunteers at a free medical clinic. Walker can't remember the last time he volunteered for anything.

But Walker tries not to dwell on Alan Gass.

Walker is the artistic director at a theater downtown. He met Claire there when she volunteered to help at the box office one semester. He was in that particular production. It was a German play about a ghost that wreaks havoc on a town by possessing prominent citizens and causing them to behave strangely. The town believes the ghost is that of a young woman who recently drowned herself because of a broken heart. The townspeople set out to find her body, thinking that will satisfy her, but it does not. The ghost responds by taking over the body of the town mayor and hurling the man off a tall building. To try and appease the ghost, the townspeople gang up on the man responsible for the woman's broken heart. They tie weights around his ankles and drop him in the ocean. But that doesn't solve the problem. This man also returns as a ghost looking for revenge. It was a gruesome play. Walker played the second ghost, the heartbreaker. Despite the white gunky makeup, Claire told him he was handsome.

Alan Gass is a ghost, and Walker knows you cannot fight ghosts. They are insidious. You can't punch a ghost or write it a drunken email. You can only pretend the ghost is not there, hope it loses interest, evaporates, moves on, does whatever it is that ghosts do when they disappear completely.

They are sitting in the back row of a half-packed lecture hall on campus. Thanks to Claire's advisor, their university is home to a conference dedicated entirely to the daisy. He is on the stage, pacing before a giant screen of exploding charts and graphics, a headset microphone curled around his ear, a scientific evangelist with brown curls and a bright, boyish face. Daisy Theory is under attack, he warns, from all sides.

Planets, hearts, even the parts of our brains responsible for dreams—everything in the universe is made of daisy particles. The daisies come together to form larger particles by interlocking in a chain formation. No one is entirely sure what holds the chains together, but Claire's advisor imagines them like the daisy garlands that children wear as crowns.

In theory a daisy chain could pop in and out of existence, just like the individual daisy. In theory your entire body—since every atom in it is nothing but a complex collection of daisies—could also pop in and out of existence.

"Isn't that amazing?" he asks the crowd.

On the top of the conference program, Walker draws two flowers and gives them arms and legs and hands to hold. The figures are like cave paintings. Me, man. You, woman. This, love.

He writes, *Want to be in my chain gang?* and slides the program across his knee to Claire. She smiles and grabs the pen. She doodles a penis on one figure and breasts on the other. They have to avoid eye contact or else they'll lose it.

After the lecture, a handful of people gather in a small white room with mahogany tables, where they quietly sip red wine in groups of two and three. Claire's advisor meanders over with a barely suppressed grin on his face.

"And?"

"Brilliant," Claire says.

Within only a few seconds, the two of them are lost in daisy revelry and Walker can only nod and smile. "We're stretching math to the breaking point," her advisor says, turning to Walker. "It's almost unmath. One and one aren't two, but onetyone." Her advisor has his hand on Claire's elbow, cupping it, as if propping it up. If he lets it go, her elbow might go crashing to the floor like a satellite from space. But when he walks away again, at last, Walker is pleased that her elbow stays put at her side.

"He's got a thing for you," Walker says.

"This again?"

"Not that I can blame him."

"Even if he did," she says, "it's not like I've got one for him."

On the way home, because of construction on the bridge, they have to take a detour through another neighborhood. Claire knows these streets better than him but, against her advisement, he takes a left turn. The road dead-ends in front of an old farmhouse, its giant gray shutters flapping in the wind like moth wings. It is early summer, perfectly warm, and they have the car windows rolled down. To turn around he backs their Jeep into the driveway, the brakes squealing. Another car has turned onto the street behind them. They pass it on their way back to the main road, a pearly gray Lexus. The driver's face is obscured by lights across the glass, but Walker can see that he has a military haircut, the gray lines sharp around his ears, the seat belt tight against a white oxford shirt. But his features are blurred. He could be anyone. Even Alan.

Walker waits until they are back on the main street before asking what he wants to ask. Has she ever wondered if Alan is really out there somewhere? That's he not just a dream? What if he's real and dreams he's married to a woman named Claire?

"Very funny," she says. "I don't think so."

"You should ask him. What do you normally talk about?"

"The usual stuff. Books, movies. What to fix for dinner."

"So in the dream, you're definitely still you?"

"Who else would I be?"

"Anyone. A prairie wife, a criminal, whatever. One time I dreamed I was the king of Europe."

"There is no king of Europe."

"Right, but the point is, some people dream about being someone else. And apparently you don't. You're you, and Alan is Alan."

She shrugs. They've reached the house. He parks the car along the curb, lined with tall shapely pear trees, their wilted white blossoms pressed flat into the sidewalk that leads to the front door. Claire inherited the house from her great-aunt. Her parents were both engineering professors at the university. She went away for college but came back for graduate school. Inside, Walker leans over Claire's blue bicycle and flips the light switch on the wall.

"Okay, I have to ask something else," he says, dropping his satchel on the hardwood floor. "Do you have sex with Alan in your dreams?"

She is ahead of him, halfway up the stairs.

"He's my husband," she says.

Walker knows that Claire has been with other men. He thinks about this fact as little as possible, though he knows that before him there was another student in her department, and before that a Swedish guy named Jens who actually proposed, and before them a couple of college mistakes and a backseat high school fling. She never mentioned Alan in the list.

"How often?"

"Do you really want to do this?"

"Just tell me once, and then we won't have to talk about it again."

She's pasting their toothbrushes.

"If you must know, probably a few times a week. But it doesn't often happen in the dream itself. It's kind of offstage action, you know? For instance, the other night, we were on our way to a friend's house for dinner, and the car ride took up the entire dream. But I knew what I'd done over the course of that day. I'd run some errands, picked up the dry cleaning. Baked strawberry brownies for dinner. The dessert was on my lap in the car."

"I can't get over how detailed these dreams are," he says. "I hardly remember anything from mine."

They both brush and spit into the sink.

"Do you remember me in your dreams?" he asks. "Does it ever feel like cheating when you're with him?"

"Don't get weird on me. They're just dreams. I'm not cheating on anyone. You or him."

They turn off the lights and climb into bed. She tickles his back until he flips toward her. She's naked. He wiggles out of his boxers quickly, shoves them to his feet.

"You don't need to worry," she says, and climbs on top of him. He doesn't need to worry. He knows that. Sort of, he does. She's moving faster now. He has his hands around her waist, the way she likes. He mutters her name, and, thankfully, she mutters his, *Walker*, and when it's over she tugs at his chest hair playfully, smiling. Then she goes into the bathroom. He can hear her peeing, and then, seconds later, she's back in his arms, skin hot, nuzzling under his chin until she's asleep.

He lets his breath fall in line with hers and keeps his arm

draped over her side, inhaling the conditioner in her hair. He can feel her heartbeat, soft and far away. Is she with Alan now? He wonders what it must be like for her, this double life, if she closes her eyes in this bed and opens them in the one she shares with Alan. Maybe her life with him mirrors this one. At that very moment, it occurs to Walker, she could be waking up and brushing her teeth all over again, discussing the upcoming day with her husband. She could be straightening his tie, pointing out the spot on his chin he missed while shaving. She could have her warm palm flat on his chest as she kisses him goodbye, the same way she sends off Walker most mornings. The idea of her repeating these private routines with another man, even one who doesn't technically exist, is almost more unsettling than the thought of her sleeping with him.

The phone book contains two listings for Alan Gass and one for A. Gass. Walker scribbles down all three on the back of a take-out menu. He carries the take-out menu in his satchel for two days before pulling over on the side of the road one morning on his way to work. The sky is cloudless, and across the street a long green field unfolds between two wooded lots. A row of ancient transformer towers runs down the middle of the rolling field.

He dials *A. Gass* first, and a woman answers. Her voice is so quiet and shaky that she has to repeat herself three times before Walker understands that her husband, Albert Gass, passed away the year before last.

Walker gets out of the car. The road is not a busy one. He dials the next number, but the Alan Gass who used to live there has moved to Columbia, the city, or possibly to the other Colombia, the one with the drugs. The man on the phone can't remember which it was.

He dials the last number. The phone rings and rings. Walker is about to give up when the voice mail message begins.

"You've reached Alan and Monica," the man on the line says. "We're not around to take your call, so leave your name and digits at the beep." It beeps. Walker hangs up quickly. The tall grass beneath the transformers swishes back and forth. He gets back in the car and starts the engine.

The address in the phone book leads him to a part of town he rarely visits. It isn't dangerous or run-down; it's just out of the way. The houses on the street are adjoining, with small grass yards in front. At one corner there is a video store. Walker doesn't recognize any of the movies in the front window. On the opposite corner, two women smoke cigarettes outside a Piggly Wiggly.

Alan Gass lives in the middle of the block in a three-story house painted light blue, so light that it's almost white. To the right of the front door there are three buttons, a label taped above each. The third doorbell says GASS 3B.

He pushes it and stands back. After what feels like an eternity, a small speaker in the wall crackles and a man who sounds like he might have been asleep answers with a cough.

"Bobby? That you? You're early."

"I'm not Bobby," Walker says.

The line crackles. "Okay, who are you, then?"

"Sorry for just showing up like this," he says, "but there's a chance we know each other through a friend. Do you have a moment to talk? I promise I won't keep you long."

The man doesn't answer. A buzzer sounds, and the door clicks open. The stairway inside is narrow and long, with a dirty blue carpet runner, smudged with old black gum, shredded at the edges. The door at the top of the stairs is half open.

"Mr. Gass?" he calls, and steps into the apartment. "Hello?"

The room is almost as narrow as the staircase. Walker feels like he's looking down the barrel of a shotgun. The half of the room nearest the door serves as a living area, with a small television against one wall and a futon-couch against the other. At the far end of the hall a single window provides light. The parts of a dismantled computer are scattered across a flimsy table beneath the window. Alan Gass emerges from a room to the right of the desk. As he steps into the light of the window, his tall Art Garfunkel hair is illuminated a wispy golden brown. He looks nothing like the man Claire has described.

He cannot be the real Alan Gass.

Walker feels idiotic for coming and tries to think of the best way to extricate himself from the situation as quickly as possible. The man wears a starched red shirt with pearl buttons tucked tightly into a pair of gray corduroys despite the summer heat. He is a small man, shorter than Walker. His eyes are gray, almost translucent.

"I think I've got the wrong Alan Gass," Walker says. "But just in case, do you know a Claire?"

Alan licks his bottom lip. He says that he knew a Claire once, way back in middle school, but he hasn't heard from her in decades. So, no, currently he does not know any Claires.

"That's all right. Like I said, wrong Alan Gass. I'll let you get back to whatever you were doing." Walker turns to leave.

"Before you go," Alan says, "now that you're up here, could I get your help with something right quick? I got a kid coming later who's supposed to help me, but he's not the most reliable."

Walker nods and asks what Alan needs from him. They go into the kitchen. The refrigerator has been pulled away from the wall and unplugged, the door ajar. A towel dropped across the floor absorbs the water as it drips from the defrosting freezer.

"I'm selling it," Alan says. "Got a good price for it. Only catch is that I gotta have it downstairs by noon."

Walker has never moved a fridge, but he knows the job will not be easy. Looking at the refrigerator, he's not even certain that it will fit through the front door. And then there's the matter of the staircase. But Alan says he has a dolly for that. He promises that it won't take long. He'll even throw in a few home-brewed beers as a thank-you. Walker says that won't be necessary. He rolls up his sleeves. He's ready to do this. Alan goes into a back room and returns wearing a back brace.

"Old injury," he explains. "You don't need to worry."

They tip the fridge backward so that Alan can wedge the dolly underneath. Slowly, they wheel it out of the kitchen. The doorway is tight. The entire wall shakes as the refrigerator passes through the frame.

"So you're looking for some other Alan Gass, huh?" he asks. "Never really think about there being other Alan Gasses out there."

Walker nods. The funny part, he says, is that the Alan he's looking for might not exist.

"Might not exist?" Alan asks.

To his own surprise, Walker tells him everything—about Claire, about the other Alan Gass, about the dreams.

"Huh," Alan says. "That's wild."

They wheel the fridge out the front door of the apartment and then take a break on the landing at the top of the stairs.

"So what if I'd been him? What would you have done?"

"I have no idea. I didn't plan that far ahead."

"Pretend I'm him."

Walker remembers the ghostly man in the Lexus. The white shirt. The blurry face. "I suppose I'd tell him to stay away?"

"But she's my wife," Alan says. "I've been with her longer than you have. I should be telling you to stay away. I love her and I'm never letting her go."

"Okay, I get it."

"You think she loves you like she loves me? She *married* me. That's a sacred vow." Alan smiles. "Whoa, you should see yourself right now. You look like you want to hit me. Is this really bothering you?"

"You're making me feel a little like he's the real one and I'm the dream," Walker says, trying to make himself laugh.

"Don't flatter yourself. You're no dream. Look, you want to know my honest opinion? You got nothing to worry about. We all got an Alan Gass," Alan Gass says. "We all got our fantasies. In high school, my Alan Gass looked a little bit like my Spanish teacher, only she was so . . . How do you say *sexy* in Spanish? I forget. She had this shiny dark hair and a little vine tattoo on her back and this amazing accent. I can't tell you how many times I thought about her late at night alone in bed, if you know what I mean. But she had no blood in her veins, you follow? There was nothing to her. Her skin was made of the same thing they use for movie screens. You can project whatever you want onto someone like that."

They lean the fridge back toward the stairs on the dolly and slowly lower the wheels down onto the next step. Alan has the dolly handles; Walker is below it, keeping it balanced. They lower it another step, and then another. Walker is sweating. On the next landing, they take another break.

"I wouldn't care about a fantasy," Walker says. "Fantasies I understand. But Alan Gass isn't a fantasy. Fantasies don't have faults. But he does, and she still loves him. That's what's so un-nerving."

They rock the fridge back on the dolly and drop it down an-other step. Walker counts off the steps as they approach the bot-tom. Three, two, one. They are in a very small space.

Walker opens the front door with his backside. They try to roll the fridge through, but it's too wide for the door by almost five inches. Alan can't believe it. He says he measured the frame. Walker glances at his watch. He has to go soon, he says. He's al-ready almost an hour late for work. They're in the middle of a new production, a play that takes place on a cruise ship lost at sea. He needs to be there soon to meet with the costume designer. Alan looks exhausted. He says he understands. Even if he has to take the whole goddamn fridge apart later, they'll get it through that door one way or another. He tells Walker to wait right there on the stoop. He's got something for him.

Walker fixes his sleeves and wipes the sweat off his forehead. When Alan returns, he's holding a small boxy tape deck. He pushes the Eject button and extracts a gray cassette with a thin white sticker across the front. It says I ♥ MONICA KILL DEVIL HILLS SPRING BREAK SISTER GODDESS, but that is scratched out. Below that, it says ZZZZZZZZZ.

"This is going to save you," Alan says.

"An old mixtape?"

"Ever heard of sleep suggestion? I audited a class at the university a few years back and made a tape to listen to while I slept at night. Don't laugh. It really did the trick. You can have this. I think it needs D batteries. Press this button, and you can record. Create your own tape. Tell her she's married to you, not Alan. Tell her whatever you want. Once she's asleep, press Play. Few weeks of this, you'll never hear another word about this marriage thing."

The machine is heavy for its size. Walker holds it like a handgun in a paper bag. He tries to give it back, but Alan refuses to take it from him.

Claire gets some bad news. A lab somewhere in Europe has constructed a black sphere and plans to flood it with something called K-matter. She emails Walker about it at work with a frowny-faced emoticon. If the experiment in Europe works like they think it will, she says, then particles cannot half exist. The researchers will have effectively disproved Daisy Theory.

That night he gets home late and finds Claire already in bed under the covers with her grandmother's rosary beads. She isn't religious. He's never known her to even set foot in a church, but she loved her grandmother. The beads are wrapped so tight around her white palm that they leave small indentations when Walker pries them loose.

"Say they disprove it," he says. "Where does something go when it stops existing?"

"Where does it go?" she asks. "Nowhere. It doesn't exist."

"But nowhere is somewhere."

"This isn't *where* versus *somewhere else*. This is being versus nonbeing."

He strips down and gets into bed, cuddling up behind her. Once she is asleep, he waits for something to happen. He's not sure what. Claire's dream marriage makes a certain kind of awful sense: a theoretical husband for the woman who spends her days in a theoretical haze. Her advisor was never the threat; it was always Alan. He watches her sleep as if the drama is unfolding just behind those eyelids. Maybe she will say something in her sleep. It would be like eavesdropping on a conversation taking place in a universe that Walker cannot reach, one where Walker does not even exist. He tries to imagine not existing. He imagines darkness, the absence of thought, but then his thoughts invade, and he exists again. *Claire*, he wants to call out. *Claire*.

"Claire." She doesn't budge. He places his palm flat between her shoulder blades, her skin warm through the T-shirt. He shakes her gently and feels her body tense.

"What's wrong?" she asks.

"Where were you?"

"What?"

"Were you with him?"

"You've got to be kidding. Go back to sleep."

"If you ever stopped dreaming about him, for whatever reason, would you be upset?"

She rolls over to face him. Her loose state championship volleyball T-shirt twists tight under her stomach.

"I'm beginning to regret I ever told you about Alan."

And why did she? Guilt, he assumes, or as a provocation. A part of Walker fears this is her way of pushing him away. She turns back over to sleep. Walker climbs out of bed and goes downstairs. He digs some D batteries out of a cluttered drawer and plops down on the sofa with the tape deck. The old batteries are corroded, crusty and white. He inserts the new ones, rewinds the tape to the beginning, and presses Record.

"You are . . . very sleepy."

He presses Stop, Rewind, and then Record again, his lips within kissing distance of the microphone. "You will not dream about Alan Gass. You will not dream about Alan Gass. Alan Gass does not exist. Alan Gass is not a man. Alan Gass is not made of daisies. He is made of nothing."

He rewinds the tape and presses Record again. A new and less sinister idea: he could make a tape for himself.

"You *will* dream about Alan Gass. You will tell him to stay away. You will dream about Alan Gass. You will dream about Alan Gass."

He presses Stop. This is going to take too long. He needs to think out a strategy. Is there a button that makes the recording loop?

"What are you doing?" Claire is at the top of the stairs.

"Nothing," he says, and goes to the hall closet. He shoves the tape deck up on the high shelf and joins her in bed. That night he doesn't dream about Alan. His dreams are uninteresting and unhelpful, a slurry mess of anxieties and fears from his waking life. He is lost and swimming in a giant ocean with small gray waves. In the distance metal transformer towers jut up into the sky crackling with electricity, and far away a boat crests each wave, a boat that he cannot reach no matter how much he swims.

In the morning he wakes up to steam slipping under the bathroom door in misty curling puffs. He can hear Claire humming in the shower. In her dreams she is able to visit an alternative universe. It's hard not to feel a little jealous.

Everywhere he goes he sees a Lexus. Lexi. They are a species, classifiable but indistinct. He sees one in the fire lane in front of the liquor store, then another in the parking lot at the gym. The cars are empty. He feels ridiculous each time he glares into a car. The tinted windows reflect only his own face, grim and warped.

Before Claire, he once dragged a date to a five-year high school reunion and made the mistake of telling her that he'd slept with one of the girls in the room. The date wouldn't let it go. She had to know which girl. She wanted him to point her out. She said she wouldn't be comfortable until she knew. But why? Walker asked her. "So I can avoid her," the date said. "Or maybe introduce myself. I don't know. Something." At the time, Walker found it amusing. God, he even made her guess the girl.

He makes a full tape of his Alan Gass mantras and tells Claire it's music for the play. When he wakes up, his ears are hot and sweaty from the foam headphones and, even more frustratingly, he remembers almost nothing of where he's been for the last seven hours, an amnesiac tourist whose film rolls have come back from the lab damaged and half developed—ocean waves, broken escalators, his mother's scowling face, a pack of vicious blue-eyed dogs. It's all meaningless dribble.

Walker's Alan Gass calls with what he can only describe as amazing news—news that he won't share over the phone. Walker agrees to meet him at a pizza buffet called Slice of Heaven.

They sit across from each other in a red vinyl booth that squelches under their butts. Aside from two dumpy women at a table on the other side of the restaurant, they are alone. Walker has already eaten lunch and doesn't plan to stay long.

Alan is distracted. He wants pizza. A certain kind of pizza. He's waiting for the waitress to bring it out on a tin tray. When she does, at last, dropping it on the buffet at the center of the room, Alan is up in a hurry. His body pressed hard to the sneeze guard, he loads his plate with one slice after another. He comes back to the table and takes a large bite. The pizza is yellowish and drizzled with a translucent pink sauce.

"What is that?" Walker asks.

"Strawberry cheesecake. Try a piece." He slides the plate across the table, still sticky from the waitress's rag. Walker declines and asks about the news that couldn't be shared over the phone.

"Be patient. You'll find out in"—he checks his wristwatch, digital with an orange Velcro strap—"about ten minutes."

Walker takes the tape recorder out of his bag, slides it across the table to Alan.

"Did it work?" Alan asks.

"I'm letting it go. Like you said, some dumb fantasy."

Alan smacks on pizza and dabs the strawberry sauce from the corners of his thin pink lips. Though a wiry man, he has the look of physical inactivity. He has a curved back, flaccid arms, and probably a poor heart. Something about this pizza buffet—the quality of the light or the greasy floor tiles, perhaps—makes Walker feel exhausted.

"Until you came to see me," Alan says, "I'd never really thought about there being other Alan Gasses in the world. But that got me thinking. Somewhere out there is the best possible Alan Gass."

"And somewhere else is the worst." Walker motions to the waitress.

"I'd like to think I'm somewhere in the middle. Most Alans are. Statistically speaking."

The waitress waddles to the table, her stockings tan as crust, her eyes green as bell peppers. Walker asks for a coffee.

"Over the last few days I've been digging around online and making some phone calls," Alan says. "To other Alans."

"And?"

"There's an Alan Gass in Utah who runs a ranch. There's an Alan Gass in New York who travels the country selling baseball cards."

The waitress brings over a mug and a hot pot of coffee, its steam thick with the smell of burnt peanuts. Walker dumps three creamers into the cup, turning the liquid a cardboard brown.

"Oh, good, you're here," Alan says to someone behind Walker.

Walker turns. A heavy man in a blue polo shirt with eyebrows so dark and thick they look like two black holes in his flat face smiles at them. His short hair is parted neatly down the middle.

"Walker," Alan says, "I'd like to introduce you to *Doctor* Alan Gass."

The man shakes Walker's hand firmly. His knuckles are hairy. Alan makes room for the other Alan on his side of the booth and explains that the second Alan lives only an hour north of here and when he discovered he was a doctor, well, he thought Walker might be interested in that.

"Doctor of what?" Walker says.

"Of religion," the man says, and grabs the menu from behind the napkin holder. "Mainly Eastern philosophy."

"You gotta try a piece of this," the first Alan says. The second Alan says no, thanks, he doesn't have a sweet tooth. He's going to have a calzone.

"There's another Alan Gass two hours from here," the first Alan Gass says. "He's invited me to see his collection of North American beetles. He studies them. Amazing, right?"

"I wonder how many of us there are in the world?" Dr. Gass asks.

"At least a thousand," says the first one. "We should organize a party. Wouldn't that be something?"

Walker imagines an army of Alan Gasses. They are the building blocks of something larger and more monumental. He sips on coffee, listening to the two men compare their lives, both of them amazed that two people with the same name can have had such different experiences and opinions of the world. How did Walker end up here, in this booth, with these men? He drops a few dollars on the table and says he must be going. Both Alans reach out to shake his hand.

The experiments in Europe—with the black sphere and the K-matter—have failed horribly. Claire comes home so excited she almost tackles Walker. The failure doesn't exactly prove Daisy Theory, but the theory does emerge relatively unscathed. Particles, for the time being, can still half exist. Walker joins when her advisor takes the entire team out for celebratory drinks. In a suit jacket, jeans, and sneakers, his boyish face glowing, her advisor steadies himself on an assistant's shoulder and steps up on a booth, raising his dark whiskey glass high. Claire lets out a whoop.

The music in the bar is disco music: Donna Summer, maybe, but with a newer backbeat. Claire's advisor lures a research assistant onto the dance floor. Claire lures Walker too. They dance in the middle of the group. She spins under the flashing lights. She moves away from him. The dance floor is crowded. Bodies merge and move like extensions of the same creature. Claire orbits around Walker, but when he turns she's disappeared. He stops dancing, the only stationary body in that sea, until she reappears again, moving away from the group and toward Walker with hands raised. She's looking right at him. Their waists meet first.

"I want to take you home tonight," he says.

"What?"

She can't hear him over the music. He kisses her. Kisses are a kind of vocabulary, he thinks. This one, both lips parted, tongues touching with the most delicate of flicks, has a particular message.

The message is, *Let's be happy*, and that feels like the wise deci-sion, a conscious decision to be happy.

They have to leave their car at the bar that night and take a taxi home.

"Fun time?" he asks, but she's already passed out against his shoulder. The last round put her over the edge.

The taxi pulls up in front of the house, and Walker, too tired to do the math, tosses the driver a twenty before going around to the other side and helping Claire stand. He throws her arm over his neck, and they cross the dew-wet lawn together. She mumbles into his shoulder as he fumbles with the door key. Upstairs she crawls across the bed and then collapses, hair flowering out in all directions across the pillows. He unzips and tugs off her boots and lays a blanket across her back. He's sitting on his side of the bed, untying his own shoes, when Claire says she loves him.

"You too," he says, and shimmies out of his pants. He slides across the bed to her. Her eyes are closed, her face long and re-laxed against the pillow. She may already be asleep—or on the verge of it. He considers testing her, giving her shoulder a light shake, but she looks so tired and content. Waking her wouldn't be right.

Grasshopper Kings

The boy scrapes the stick across the grass a few times and flings it behind the hedge before Flynn can even get his car into the driveway. Flynn is home late from work, and driving up he saw it in the darkness, the small flame eating the end of the stick. The boy is alone on the front lawn in a red T-shirt with the sleeves cut off. He stands very still, pale arms crossed behind his back. The smoke hovers around his head like an apparition. "Ryan," Flynn says, rising from the car with a huff, "I thought we'd put this fire business behind us."

His son's eyes are like his wife's eyes, which are like an owl's eyes, hardly blinking and gigantic. Nothing else about his wife is very owl-like. She is skinny as a ferret and not at all nocturnal. She's in bed by eight, or seven-thirty if *Jeopardy!*'s a repeat.

"Whatever you used, give it here," Flynn says, and Ryan forfeits a small yellow matchbook. Flynn shoves the matches deep into his pocket and grabs the stick out of the hedge. The dark ash smears his hand, and with his index finger he smudges his son's nose. When he opens the front door, the boy darts under his arm and runs ahead down the carpeted hall to his room.

By the time Flynn gets there Ryan is already under the covers with the stuffed blue bear, Mookie. His wife used to call her older sister Mookie, but that was years ago, before cancer killed Mookie at the nearly young age of fifty-one. His wife doesn't like to talk about her sister's death. "Why Mookie?" his wife is always asking. Meaning, why, of all names in the world for a bear, why *that* one? Ryan and Mookie (the bear) share many common interests: kites, Erector Sets, matches, magnifying glasses, flaming sticks, aerosol sprays. Ryan and Mookie (the aunt) never met unless you count the birth, and Flynn doesn't, as his son was not then a real, thinking human animal.

Watching his son sleep—or rather, pretend to sleep—he swishes a toothpick back and forth across his lower lip. The toothpick is a sorry substitute for a cigarette. He rations out his pack across the week as a means of quitting, and he smoked the last of the day's allowance at work.

Flynn is the activity director at an upscale drug and alcohol treatment center in the mountains, and as such, he arranges outings and adventures for patients—nature walks, movie screenings, theater performances, and so on. Today he drove a van full of recovering addicts to a chain bookstore, which would have been a pleasant excursion if not for the fact that one of the patients hadn't shown up at the appointed time. The missing man—Small Paul with the needle marks between his toes, "Small" because you really could just about fold him into a shoebox—had checked himself in to the center voluntarily, but Flynn had still feared the worst. Along with a nurse he'd spent the rest of the afternoon going from store to store before finding Paul in a Sharper Image at the mall, testing out back massagers. "Already time to go back?" he asked when he saw them.

Flynn sits down on the end of the bed, and the boy's eyes flicker open, then close again. His brown hair is wild and messy, the small snub nose just above the covers. He's short for his age, just over four feet, but then again so was Flynn at nine.

"I don't need to tell you I'm disappointed," Flynn says. "Because you already know that."

The closet door is decorated with Ryan's old school paintings, and on the other side of that door, Flynn knows, there's a black ring burned into the beige carpet, hidden by a doormat. Ryan is not a pyromaniac, or not yet, anyway. The doctor calls him a "fire-starter." He's more curious than compulsive.

"I'm sorry," the boy says.

He wonders if it is because of his smoking. If the boy has seen him light too many matches. Does Flynn work too much? Does he not pay the boy enough attention? Should they be playing more catch? Does the boy need hobbies? Flynn's father used to take him fishing and made him gut the fish in the sink behind the house, and at the time he'd hated it but looking back on it makes Flynn smile. Should he take Ryan fishing? Would he like to learn how to weight the line and wipe the gummy knife across his shirt? Is the boy bored? Is it a feeling of boredom? Is it a feeling of not belonging? When he looks inside his heart, does he see clouds or sunshine? Isn't that how the doctor put it?

"This isn't over," Flynn says, giving his son's foot a gentle squeeze, before going next door, to his wife's room. The boxy television on the edge of her dresser flickers blue across her bedroom.

They sleep separately because of the snoring. His snoring, not hers. She is asleep, or was, nestled in her mechanized queen bed with the hospital controls. She isn't sick but kept the bed after Mookie died because, supposedly, it helps her back. He flips on her bedroom light, and she moans. She gives him a look like, *Please, not tonight.*

"He's doing it again," he says. "I don't think he ever stopped. I think he's been hiding it from us."

She rummages for the control, and the bed vibrates into a sitting position. "We should call the doctor first thing," she says.

"What, so he can squeeze another three hundred dollars from us?"

"The doctor said to call him."

"He can't fix the problem."

"And the problem is—what?"

"The problem is a feeling. A feeling of not belonging."

"What does that mean?"

"It means the boy needs friends. He needs to be included. You know, to really *belong* to something."

Her bed vibrates backward into a reclining position.

"I'm going to sign us up," he says. "For the Grasshoppers."

"To be continued," she says.

Grasshoppers aren't allowed at the father-son Grasshopper Camp until they've been in the program for a full year and earned enough beads. Flynn learns this in one of their brochures. Unfortunately, he's never even taken Ryan to a Grasshoppers meeting.

Flynn goes to see Bill Tierney, a malpractice attorney in town with an ad on the back of the phone book. Tierney's son, Grayson, is older than Ryan, president of the student body at the elementary school—and a Grasshopper. Tierney is the Head Guide.

The attorney wears a tan suit and offers Flynn a seat on the other side of his desk. Bill Tierney wonders if maybe Flynn would like some pistachio nuts. Bill Tierney is crazy about them. Was Flynn aware that the nuts have been part of the human diet since the Paleolithic? That they're one of only two nuts in the Bible?

"What's the other one?"

"The other what?"

"The other nut in the Bible," Flynn says.

"Hell, I don't know. Noah? Sorry, bad joke. Let's get down to business. Tell me about yourself."

"I'm a father," Flynn says. "And I love my son very much."

"Yes, of course. Family's got to be number one."

"Right. And I want my son to feel like he's a part of something bigger than himself."

Flynn uncrosses his legs and reaches for a pistachio. The shell doesn't want to pry. He admits that he should have signed his son up earlier and that he knows about the requirements for the father-son camp, but he'd be very grateful if the organization could make an exception in the case of his son, Ryan, who's nine years old and who, Flynn thinks, would make a natural Grasshopper. His son is a good boy and loves the outdoors, and the camp would do him so much good. It would be a great fit. Flynn spins the chalky nut between his fingers.

Tierney squints, his mouth hanging open. "I'm sorry," he says finally. "I was under the impression you were here looking for representation."

"No," Flynn says. "I was hoping you could help me. As the Head Guide."

"Ah," Tierney says.

"Right."

Neither of them says anything for a few moments. Not many people know this, but Tierney has a brother named Herbie who's an addict. Flynn has tried to help Herbie at the center, but Herbie doesn't want to be helped. That's how it is with some people. Flynn considers mentioning this now, as a way of creating a bond, but decides against it.

"It would mean so much to my son," Flynn says.

"Sure, okay."

"Okay?" Flynn didn't expect it to be so easy.

"Done," he says, and pretends to sign an invisible piece of paper suspended in the air between them. "The Grasshopper district office is in Charlotte. You can go there and fill out the paperwork, pay up for camp. I'll take care of the rest." He stands and smoothes the wrinkles from his suit pants.

"Thank you," Flynn says.

"Glad I could help. Now I'm afraid I need to . . ." His voice trails off as he motions vaguely at his empty desk.

Father and son rise early to depart on a Saturday morning, shafts of sunlight through a rising fog, the birds tweeting in the syca-more tree on the front lawn, its bark hanging like strips of beef jerky. You couldn't ask for a more suitable morning, Flynn thinks.

His wife comes outside in her bathrobe. "Couldn't we just go to the beach?" she asks Flynn, a little upset because after three years without even using a sick day, Flynn is taking an entire week off from work, and he's not using it to take his whole family on vacation. Instead he's only taking his son to some mysterious camp in the woods. "Are you sure this is what he needs? He won't know any of those kids."

"This will be good for him," Flynn assures her. "Kids make friends fast."

When Ryan comes outside with a bowl of cereal, milk dripping down his chin, she gives him a cell phone. "Pay as you go," she explains to Flynn. "I'll feel better." To Ryan, she says, "So you can call me if you want."

The car is packed with sleeping bags, a tent, an electric lantern with the price-tag sticker still on it, and all the other equipment necessary for two human animals to live comfortably in the woods for five nights. Once they're on the road, the boy is the navigator and is responsible for tracking their progress, his index finger across the atlas, and for calling out each step from the printed directions.

"Grasshopper Pledge," Flynn quizzes him. "Go."

"There's a way," the boy says glumly, "around every wall."

"The beads you can earn and their colors."

"Beads of Truth are the red ones. Beads of Mercy are the white ones."

"And the third?"

The boy shrugs.

"They're black . . ."

"Oh," Ryan says. "Beads of Skill."

"And how many beads does it take to move up a level?"

"Six beads."

"Exactly," Flynn says. "And you'll have them in no time at all. Last question. The salute."

Ryan points to his heart with his index finger, and then Flynn does the same.

"Aren't you excited?"

The boy says he's not sure if he's excited. His brown shaggy mop—he hates haircuts—makes his small, narrow face seem even smaller. "What if it, like, rains?"

"That's what the tent is for. We're sharing a tent. That will be fun, right?"

The boy gives him an uncertain look. They drive into the mountains and then down a long road with thick woods the color of katydids and khaki: muted greens and browns. Ryan directs Flynn onto a paved road that turns to gravel, the rocks popping under the tires. Then the gravel road becomes a dirt one, a volcanic cloud of dust behind them in the rearview mirror.

Up ahead, rough beams form an arch over the road. The camp's entrance.

"You should probably put on your uniform now," Flynn says.

The shirt is yellow cotton with a white rugby collar and the Grasshopper patch sewn over the heart. It hangs loose on Ryan's small, pale body.

Flynn pulls up in front of the director's cabin, and a man in a green T-shirt much too tight for his potbelly comes out with a clipboard. He wants their names. He wants their district number. He's got the pen top in his mouth, a small red ink stain on his bottom lip. What was that last name again? The man's sweat drips down onto the pages. How do you spell that last name? He's shuffling through the pages. That was with a *C*? No, he doesn't see that one on here. Wait, here it is, on the back. There's a problem. Ryan hasn't met all the requirements for camp. He still needs eighteen beads. That's three levels up from where Ryan is now, which is nowhere, according to the information on the clipboard. Can Flynn show documentation that Ryan has earned even one bead? Flynn can't, of course, but he explains that he's cleared this with Ryan's Head Guide, Bill Tierney, who can sort all this out for them. Special arrangements have been made for Ryan.

The man puffs out his upper lip with his tongue, sniffing at his blond mustache hairs. All right, he says, wait over there. The walkie-talkie, crackling all along, comes off his belt, and he asks for someone named Bryant. Father and son sit together on a bench outside the cabin, slapping mosquitoes off their legs and arms and necks. Flynn didn't bring any bug spray.

Tierney arrives on a golf cart. He's wearing a linen shirt with pink stripes and an Atlanta Braves baseball cap. He doesn't smile or wave.

"What can I do you for?" Tierney asks the man with the clipboard.

"This gentleman says you told him he could bring his kid, even though he doesn't have his beads."

Tierney lean-sits on the front of the golf cart, his arms crossed. "Right," he says. "I'm sorry. I meant to call the district office about that. This going to be a problem?"

"Maybe," the man says. "The rules are pretty clear."

The two men are talking low now, their lips quiet and slow like butterfly wings. Flynn can't hear what they're saying. Tierney laughs a little and pats the man on the back. The man nods and motions to the lake. Tierney nods then. Maybe Flynn should go over and join them. He can help make this okay. He stands too late. The conference that will determine his son's fate has ended. Bill Tierney strides over to the bench.

"Here's the deal," he says to Flynn. "Ryan can stay. Only he won't be able to do some of the activities since he doesn't have his beads. Like the canoe trip to the island on the lake. That's for kids who've got their Swimming Skill Bead and their CPR Bead of Mercy. You understand, right, why we can't let him go on that trip?"

Flynn says he understands, of course. He gives his son's shoulder a squeeze.

The tent is old and once belonged to Flynn's father. The canvas is military green; the paraffin wax that kept its corners sealed from the rain has long since lost its shine. Father and son tie the canvas strips to the metal poles they've erected in the wide-open field with all the other tents. In all directions are tents: red, yellow, orange, and green nylon rain-flies spilling out around the domes like fruit candies melting in the afternoon sun. Beside every tent is a parked car. The field buzzes with bugs and the sound of a dozen car-powered air pumps blowing up mattresses, palatial beds two and three feet thick. Flynn has brought a number of thin foam pads and stacks them under their sleeping bags.

"Do you want the left or right?"

The boy picks the left.

"Where's your pillow?"

He forgot his pillow, but here's Mookie the blue bear, smuggled inside a pillowcase.

"I thought we agreed not to bring the bear."

His son prepares a throne of T-shirts for the bear at the end of his sleeping bag. Its cold dark eyes are fixed on the two of them.

"Just for the first night," Flynn says.

A bell echoes across the lake, and fathers and sons, a hundred of them, begin the boisterous migration to the dining hall. Like a herd of buffalo, Flynn imagines, and they're part of it. The boys, ages six to fourteen, run circles around the fathers, some as old as sixty.

One small boy with a round and ruddy face stops to examine an overturned kayak. "Snake," he announces, and they all gather around him to admire the discovery, their first significant encounter with wildlife for the week. A dark, fat snake is coiled in the sand by the water.

Water moccasin, one of the fathers determines, and then they're all moving away at once, the fathers dragging the boys backward by their arms and shirttails. Someone should tell the camp director! Snakes in the lake again! Hadn't they hired someone to take care of this after last summer? Remember that kid last year who somehow trapped a water moccasin in a shopping bag and hung it from the rafters in the shower house?

"Clearly that kid didn't have any Beads of Mercy," someone up ahead jokes.

"He wasn't allowed back this summer," yells someone farther back.

They converge on the flagpole outside the dining hall. The man with the clipboard has traded his paperwork for a megaphone. The boys are organized into single-file lines radiating out from the flagpole like spokes from a hub. Flynn helps Ryan find his place, the line for his group, Bill Tierney at the head. Two Grasshoppers take the flag down and fold it military-style into careful triangles. Time for the Grasshopper salute. Time for the Grasshopper Pledge. *There's a way around every wall,* hundreds of shrill voices yell out in near-unison. Time for dinner.

"Go ahead," Flynn tells Ryan. "Find us a couple of seats."

Flynn lingers on the porch, where a handful of men furtively smoke their cigarettes. They huddle near the steps, a conspiracy of tobacco. Flynn asks for a light. The man who gives him one introduces himself as John Price. "You a newbie?" he asks.

Flynn says he is. John Price sports a chinstrap beard that doesn't much help disguise his marshmallow chin. He owns a dealership. Toyotas and Hyundais, he adds. Ever need a new car, give him a call. Come on by. That's how this works. Grasshoppers isn't just for the kids. The dads stick together, you know? Help each other out.

Flynn nods his head enthusiastically. He couldn't agree more. That's how this should work.

One father says, "Marty, your kid ever tell you about his Truth Bead?"

"Never," says Marty.

"My kid never told me neither," another man says. "I guess that shouldn't bother me, but it does."

"Only two Beads of Truth," John Price explains to Flynn, "and the dads never get to know what they mean. The Head Guides decide when the kid is ready. I think it's just like a single sentence that gets whispered in their ear. But the kids aren't supposed to repeat it. Ever. I've heard that the first one is about the nature of time. My kid's got that one, but he's just as tight-lipped as the rest of them. When I press him about it, he smiles at me like

I'm an idiot who wouldn't understand. Just wait, it'll drive you crazy when your kid gets his."

Bowls of mashed potatoes, platters of chicken fingers, and pitchers of lemonade are on all the tables when they go inside the dining hall, a flurry of hand-waving, lip-smacking, and spilled drinks.

"Wouldn't mind a little vodka in that lemonade," John Price says with a forced laugh before wandering off to find his son.

Flynn navigates the maze of tables and children. He watches one kid drown a chicken finger—perfectly fried on one side but mushy and gray on the other—in a gush of ketchup from a sticky red squirt bottle. Another boy, with a blue bandanna wrapped around his tiny head, drums on his plate with metal silverware until a father leans across the table with a stern look. All the kids are wearing their yellow uniforms. From the right pockets, on leather strings, their white, red, and black beads dangle.

Ryan, in his unadorned uniform, is sitting at the end of a table at the far end of the hall, three seats away from the next person. He's barely touched his food. Flynn asks if he'd like to move over a couple of seats, but the boy says no, he's fine where he is. So they sit together, apart from the others, poking tunnels into their mashed potatoes, drinking more and more lemonade, until the man with the megaphone, the camp director, stands at the front of the room with some announcements: tomorrow's activities are posted on the back wall; the bonfire ceremony will be three nights from tonight; a special visitor is coming to help construct a genuine Native American sweat lodge; oh, and the water moccasins are back in the lake, so watch where you step.

That night it rains, but only a little.

. . .

The nature hike the next morning is a success. Flynn is waiting at the tent when Ryan returns; his legs are bramble-scraped but he's happy. Did he see any wildlife? No, no wildlife. Did he see any plants? Yes, they saw a few plants. Flynn has trouble understanding what exactly Ryan enjoyed about the expedition, but he doesn't want to spoil the effect with questions, so he lets it go. That afternoon, after lunch, Ryan isn't able to go on the canoe trip, as expected, so Flynn finds a tub of toys in the shed behind the director's cabin. He takes out the soccer ball and tries to get Ryan to kick that back and forth across the field. But Ryan isn't interested.

"Basketball, then?"

"Nope," he says. The boy is satisfied to sit in the rocking chairs on the dining hall porch.

"What are you thinking about?" Flynn asks.

"I don't know," the boy says.

He's inscrutable, his large eyes blinking and looking but not conveying any secret meaning. Flynn wonders if some fathers instinctively know what their sons are thinking, if there exists between them some kind of private language, little symbols and gestures that only the two of them can decode. Who are you? Flynn is tempted to ask.

One of the cooks comes outside on the porch and says Ryan can ring the dinner bell if he wants. Ryan takes the cord like it might shock him, then gives it a gentle tug. "Needs more than that," the cook says gruffly; Ryan pulls harder. The sound is immense, a physical presence, a peal felt in the bones. The boy is smiling, and Flynn is hopeful.

John Price finds Flynn at dinner. Does he want to smoke a cigarette? They go out on the porch with the other fathers. They struggle to keep the matches lit in the breeze.

"So you never told me what you do for a living," John Price says.

Flynn tells him about the treatment center. How you can't understand addiction until you've seen someone fight one.

"I got a sister-in-law who used to do cocaine," John says. "Even at Thanksgiving."

"Did she get help?"

"Maybe, I don't know. My brother never talks about it anymore, so I guess she did."

Flynn opens a new pack and offers up cigarettes. Almost everybody accepts. They use the first butt to light the second because of the breeze.

"My kid's up for his Second Truth Bead this week," a father says.

"Mine too," John Price adds.

The others perk up at that.

"The Second Truth is about what happens when you die."

"That's not what I've heard."

"What'd you hear?"

"My son told me it's about how the universe got started."

"Was it with a bang or a whimper?"

"The Big Banger. That's what my oldest daughter calls God. I think she does it to get under my skin. She's a Unitarian now."

"Does that make Satan the Little Whimperer?"

"You guys don't know shit. The Second Truth is about the end of the universe, not the beginning."

"So enlighten us. How does it end?"

"The earth goes up in flames. God already tried drowning us once, so the next time he'll smoke us out."

"Bring it on," says a father with smoke sneaking out his nostrils.

"If it wasn't for these Truth Beads, my kid would have dropped out years ago. He's obsessed. If I ever found out what they are, I'd just tell him so we could be done with it."

"Anyone else think it's bullshit we don't get to know these Truths? We do half the work."

"If you ask me, I think the whole process is bullshit. Why is it the Head Guides get to decide who's ready for those beads? Grasshoppers didn't use to be this way."

"It can be a little clubby," John Price admits.

"A little?"

"We're just in it for the camping trips."

"Us too. I wanted my son to stop playing his stupid computer games."

"Has it worked?"

"Not really. He's got some kind of portable thing. Miracle he never trips."

"I wanted my son to feel like he's a part of something," Flynn says.

"Even if what he's a part of is a little cultish? I'm sorry, guys, but it is, right?"

"It is, yeah."

"A little bit."

"My boy's alone most afternoons," Flynn continues, "and that gets him into all sorts of trouble."

"What kind of trouble? Because there's trouble and then there's *trouble.*"

"I don't know," Flynn mutters. "Typical kid stuff, I guess."

"My boy used to trap squirrels so he could drown them in the pool."

"My kid used to shoot a crossbow into the neighbor's yard, and one time he put an arrow in her leg. She's almost eighty! God, that was awful."

"Alex, he's my stepson. Years ago we caught him with a hammer standing over his little sister's crib."

"My son likes fire," Flynn says. "But I think he does it for the attention."

"My kid Gene had a fire thing for a while. He almost burned down the garage."

The camp director pokes his head out the door and asks them to come inside for announcements, and they look at each other like, *Is this guy for real?* Flynn smiles at his new friends.

That night in the tent, Flynn lets his son fall asleep first. He takes Mookie the bear out to the car and hides him under a piece of luggage. He's stripping down for bed when he sees his son's eyes on him.

"Just try it without the bear," Flynn says.

The boy closes his eyes.

But Flynn has not won this battle, not yet. In the morning, the bear is back on its T-shirt throne. Flynn is undaunted. The dew sparkles with sunshine and, Flynn imagines, with promise. Ryan goes off to the art shack for leather making. The camp isn't really designed for earning beads—that's what the weekly meetings are for—but he might be able to earn a bead of skill this morning.

Flynn crosses the field, and by the time he reaches the edge of the woods, his boots are soaked. He has offered to help build the sweat lodge. John Price is there with a cup of coffee and a cigarette. The camp director, a giant ring of keys jangling from his belt, introduces a special visitor, a man with a long brown-and-gray ponytail down his back. His name is Henri, pronounced the French way, though he has a distinctly southern accent. He says he's one-sixteenth Cherokee. He has a certificate in Native American studies. Sweat lodges are used as a means of purification, he says, of the body and the spirit. Sitting in a sweat lodge can help you reach a deeper level of consciousness. Sometimes the spirit travels.

Henri asks for volunteers to gather the firewood and rocks. He asks for more volunteers to cut down and strip small saplings. He distributes hatchets. He uses string and a stick to sketch out a circle with a ten-foot diameter. He instructs everyone to be as silent as possible. He's tapping on a drum. John Price rolls his eyes at Flynn. They jam the saplings into the ground and bend them toward the center. Henri sends John Price and Flynn to collect grasses for the floor of the lodge, and if they find any sage, even better.

They move through the trees, hunched like hunter-gatherers.

"Where did they find this guy anyway?" John Price asks. "Do you think they just Googled *hippie* and *bullshit* and this guy was number one on the list?"

Flynn's not sure. Will John Price try it out, though?

"Sure, why not?"

Their arms are full of green grass and dead leaves. "So," John Price says, smiling, "I finally got it out of my son last night. The First Truth."

72

"Oh."

"Yeah. He was on the verge of falling asleep. I feel a little guilty about it. To be honest, I thought it was kind of anticlimactic. But I suppose that's the way it is with these things. There's a reason the Catholic Church only wanted priests reading the Bible, you know? You want me to tell you what it is?"

"Okay," Flynn says.

"You sure you want to know?"

"Yes."

"Okay, here it goes. *Let the mind enter itself. Let the dark burn bright.*"

They're walking back to the sweat lodge. Flynn is quiet.

"It's okay," John Price says. "I have no idea what it means either. My kid definitely doesn't. Probably doesn't mean anything. You know the guy who founded the Grasshoppers did time in prison, right? He also wrote fantasy books. That's how he made all his money."

"What was he in jail for?"

"Tax evasion, maybe. I can't remember. Something very white-collar. This was way back. In the fifties. Before he came up with this Grasshoppers idea. You probably know this already, but in the beginning the group had a strong flower-power element. Very antiestablishment. Very get-in-touch-with-your-inner-self. You can tell from the pledge. That bit about finding your way around walls? All the beads and the rules and the levels, that got added later, along with all the membership fees."

They emerge from the woods, and the fathers have stretched a black tarp over the skeletal sapling frame. Henri is still tapping on his drum. They spread the grasses across the interior and then stand back to admire their construction. The camp director takes a photograph for the Grasshopper newsletter.

The sweat lodge sign-up sheet is posted now in the dining hall and at lunch Flynn schedules time for him and his son. Ryan returns from the leather-working class with a bead and a new friend. The boy's name is Trevor. His face is freckled, his hair red and wild. They find seats together in the dining hall. Both boys are sporting the moccasins they made in class, the thin leather tight around their feet. They don't talk to each other, only sit and slurp up spaghetti casserole. Flynn asks Trevor about his father, if he'll be joining them for the meal. Trevor shrugs.

Does Trevor like being a Grasshopper?

"Sometimes," he says.

What does Trevor's father do for a living?

"He flies airplanes. He's a pilot."

"I'll bet you get to fly all the time, then, huh?"

"Definitely."

The camp director concludes the meal with his usual announcements: thank you to all the fathers who helped build the sweat lodge; the snake problem has been resolved, and the lake is open for swimming again; and would the fathers who smoke kindly stop dropping the butts off the edge of the porch?

Trevor's father, a skinny man with blue jeans sagging, finds them after lunch.

"There you are," he says to his son.

"I hear you're a pilot," Flynn says, and introduces himself.

The man gazes down at Flynn's feet for what feels like a long time. "You've got me confused," he says, and then walks ahead toward the tents with his son.

. . .

The sweat lodge fits ten father-son pairs at a time. Thick steam rises from the rocks at its center. The hot coals beneath glow orange in the darkness. As instructed, Flynn sits cross-legged next to his son, both of them shirtless, dressed in swim trunks. If anyone feels faint, Henri warns them from the door, they should come outside and drink some water. Flynn can feel the trickles of sweat traveling down his back and his arms. He's swaying a little. His son stares wide-eyed at the rocks, then at the door, shifting restlessly.

Flynn wonders what his son might be thinking. About fire again? Does the steam remind him of smoke? He's made a friend and earned a bead. Is it belonging he feels? If he painted a picture, what colors would he choose? If he wrote a song, would the key be major or minor? Flynn worries he's failed the boy. Could Ryan be ashamed of him? Does he wish Flynn had more money? That he flew airplanes? Flynn feels like he is in an airplane now, the air rumbling all around him, a bumpy takeoff. He can feel himself rising—or, maybe, falling.

Flynn opens his eyes. He's outside again, in the sunlight. Three faces hover above him. They put the water to his lips, and he drinks. Flynn passed out in the sweat lodge, but he's okay. He just needed some air. He should have had more water.

Henri is there. "Go someplace interesting?"

As Flynn guzzles down an entire canteen of water, Ryan sits nearby on a stump, drawing shapes in the dirt with his finger.

"You should probably lay down for a while," someone says.

Flynn nods and stands to go, his legs like two iron bars hinged at his hips, but somehow he gets them swinging. He's moving down the trail, and thankfully so is Ryan, though he lags a few feet behind until they reach the tent. The air inside the tent is hot and sticky, so hot that Flynn throws the door up over the rain-fly to let in the breeze. He slides across his sleeping bag on his belly, not bothering to take off his shoes, his toes in the grass just outside the door. In the distance he can hear a stereo and laughter, and closer by, just outside the tent, his son's voice, his words like stones skipped across the water, such little soft bursts. He's talking to someone.

"No, he's not dead," Ryan says. "Just tired."

"Someone said he was dead." It's Trevor.

"Nope."

"You still got that cell phone? Let's call something."

"Like what?"

"I don't know. I'm starving. Nothing good to eat here."

"There's no one to call," Ryan says. "This is all there is. Besides, just a few more days left."

"I'm never coming back," Trevor says, his voice mousy and distant. They're walking away from the tent together.

Exhausted, Flynn closes his eyes and lets his body sink. He sleeps.

When he comes to, it's morning. He unzips the tent door. Pale sunlight slips into the tent. Flynn is still in his swim trunks, though his shoes have been removed and placed under the rain-fly. The entire camp is quiet, and he flips to find Ryan's owlish eyes on him, hardly blinking. In his arms is Mookie the bear.

"You missed dinner," the boy reports.

"Who'd you eat with?"

"Trevor."

"Sorry I missed it," he says.

Flynn spends the day in a daze. He digs his emergency smokes out of the glove compartment. The lighter is dead, but in his pocket he discovers the yellow matchbook, the one he took from Ryan on the front lawn. In plain black letters on the cover it says *Big Fixin's*, which is a diner they used to go to when Ryan was little. Flynn blows through half a pack on the dining hall porch while Ryan is off at archery and then smokes a few more while Ryan's at the low-ropes course.

Aimlessly, Flynn walks the perimeter of camp, exploring its boundaries. He finds a tennis court, cracked and full of puddles. Somewhere high up in the trees he hears bees. A thin path through the woods takes him to the back of the director's cabin. Flynn smells the cigar smoke before he sees the men on the back deck.

"Who's out there?" the camp director yells.

Flynn emerges from behind the trees with a wave. "It's me," he says, "I was just exploring."

Bill Tierney is there, along with a few other men. They're holding glasses with a light brown liquid. Scotch. Flynn can almost taste it.

"Come on up here," Bill Tierney says.

Flynn climbs the steps. He feels like a kid called to the principal's office.

Tierney offers him a drink, and Flynn says no, thanks.

"Come on, just one drink."

"I can't," Flynn says. "What I mean is, I don't anymore."

"I see, I see," Tierney says, and brushes a pine needle from his puffy hair. "We were just talking about Vince's son"—he pats one of the other men on the back—"who's up for his Second Truth Bead tonight. At the bonfire."

"My boy has no idea," the man says, grinning.

"This is the last stage," Tierney says. "Once you get both Truth Beads, you're a Grasshopper King. A very high honor. How's your boy doing, Flynn? He enjoying himself?"

Flynn says that Ryan has made some good friends. That he's loving it here.

"They always do," the camp director says. "My son's too old to come back now, but I remember the night he got his Second Truth Bead. We were so proud."

"Flynn, your son's starting a little later than most," Tierney says, "but if he works hard, he might be able to finish."

"How old's your kid?" the director asks.

"Nine," Flynn says.

"Oh," Tierney says. "For some reason I had it in my head he was seven or eight. Statistically speaking, he may not have enough time to be a King. Not that he should give up. It's not all about becoming a Grasshopper King."

"I'd love to see Ryan get there."

"Of course," Tierney says, grinning. "Anything is possible, I guess."

They swirl the ice in their liquor drinks.

"Hey, now," the director says to Flynn. "You the one who passed out in the sweat lodge yesterday?"

Flynn turns red. "That was me."

They all take long sips, smiling into their ice cubes. An old Willie Nelson record plays from a speaker propped up in the screen window. Then Bill Tierney turns to the others and says, "All right, fellas, should we get started? You'll have to forgive us, Flynn, but we have some planning to do for tonight. Logistics and whatnot. We'll see you there, right?"

"You will." He leaves them on the deck and sets off for the dining hall. Inside every group, he decides, there are more groups. Circles within circles, and inside of those, more circles still, all of them infinitely divisible. You could spend your whole life wondering which ones you're in and which ones you're not and which ones really want you and which ones are holes that have no bottom.

The bonfire is built in the outdoor amphitheater at the edge of the lake. The logs are stacked two across two, up and up, the kindling stuffed inside the column and doused with kerosene. The fathers cross their legs and swat mosquitoes. The boys fidget and squirm. John Price is there with his son. The camp director stands to the side with Henri, who's wearing overalls now, his drum put away. The sun sinks behind the pine trees on the opposite bank.

The ceremony begins with a procession of boys, most of them probably twelve or thirteen years old, gawky and pimpled, moving down the center row, some goofy and others somber. The one in front carries a long torch, rolls of toilet paper jammed on the end of a stick. Another torchbearer approaches in a canoe on the lake, a starlike light and its rippled reflection moving through the darkness toward the assembled. Flynn is reminded of the First Truth. *Let the dark burn bright.* The boys are forming a semicircle around the unlit bonfire, waiting for the second torchbearer to reach the shore. They all have one Truth Bead on their uniform. Are they thinking about the First Truth too? Is this ceremony designed to invoke it?

The torches meet at the logs, and the entire structure, almost ten feet tall, bursts into flames, red and blue and yellow. Flynn is five rows back and can feel the blaze. Next to him, his son's face shines too. But he's not looking at the flames. He's looking up at Flynn.

"Can you see okay? What do you think?"

The boy says it's interesting.

The camp director opens a notebook. He tosses some grass into the fire, and the smoke curls around him. His voice is hoarse and thin.

"Grasshoppers feast on the grass," he reads, "and so do the flames. Grasshoppers are virtuous and vibrant, resourceful and resilient, patient and peaceful, creative and kind. These are the qualities we, this community, value most. When the first grasshopper molted and shook the morning dew from his new wings, the world marveled at this development. The world took notice. Tonight, some of you have sprouted wings, and we are here to marvel at your achievements, to take notice, to bask in your light. Tonight, we are awarding ten boys with their Second Truth Bead."

One by one, the director names the boys in the semicircle around the bonfire, and, one by one, those boys step forward with unusually good posture. A red bead is placed in ten sweaty palms.

The boys are all smiles as they're led to the other side of the fire, away from the audience, and the director whispers something in each of their ears, one by one.

"They're learning the Second Truth," Flynn tells Ryan.

"What's the Second Truth?"

"Only Grasshopper Kings are supposed to know," Flynn says. He puts his arm around his son, who will never be a Grasshopper King. One day he'll have to explain to his son how most games are rigged, and how sometimes it's best not to play at all.

After the ceremony, Trevor comes over with a Ziploc bag full of marshmallows and a coat hanger for Ryan. Flynn overhears Trevor telling Ryan how his uncle once branded himself with a red-hot hanger.

"Then your uncle's an idiot," Flynn interrupts.

"My uncle is a military general," Trevor says.

Flynn grabs their coat hangers and then rummages in the brush for two sticks. He gives those to the boys, and they run off to the fire. Flynn walks over to John Price, who stands next to his son. The son has a chin like his father's, one that slopes down to his chest in a gentle, fleshy curve.

"He did it," John Price reports. "He got that Second Truth."

"Congratulations," Flynn says. "You must be proud."

"Oh, of course. And maybe now I can get that next Truth out of him. I'll let you know what I find out. Say, you feeling better after the sweat lodge? I heard you passed out? That true?"

"Didn't drink enough beforehand," Flynn says.

"Yep, number-one hippie rule. Hydrate before going on your vision quest. Listen, you'll have to excuse me, Flynn. Apparently, all the Grasshopper Kings and their dads are supposed to go to some kind of function now at the director's cabin. Probably a cake-and-punch thing."

Circles within circles, Flynn thinks. He finds his son by the fire.

"You ready to call it a night?"

"Okay," he says, and tosses his marshmallow stick into the bonfire.

They leave the light of the ceremony. Their eyes slowly adjust to the darkness of the field. Ryan is swinging his arms and looking up to the stars. Flynn wants his boy to be happy.

"What are you thinking about?" Flynn asks.

"Nothing."

"What else are you thinking about?"

"I don't like this uniform," he says.

"That's okay."

"I hate it. It makes my armpits itch."

"You don't have to wear it again," Flynn says. "If you don't want."

They're following the edge of the lake now. A cool breeze twists the leaves in the trees. Flynn is still thinking about circles within circles. Also, he's thinking about snakes curled into circles by the water.

They reach the tent and climb inside. They stretch out on the sleeping bags and lie awake, side by side. The cell phone dings, its screen glowing blue inside his son's sleeping bag.

"She wants to know if I'm ready to come home," Ryan says. "I can talk to her tomorrow."

Flynn burrows into his bag and takes off his socks, trying to get comfortable. They're still not asleep when the thunderstorm starts an hour later. The thought of all those Grasshopper Kings caught in the downpour brings a smile to Flynn's face. The tent shakes in the wind, the rain loud as bullets on the canvas. Everything is dark, but they can feel water dripping from the seams. The water bubbles up from below too. Tonight they will get very wet. Tonight they may get washed away. Even Mookie the bear on his T-shirt throne will not be spared. The water will cover all. Soon, nothing will ever burn again.

Flynn rolls over onto his side with the yellow matchbook. When he lights the match, his son's face is there, just beyond the flame, the light reflected in his eyes. They watch the tiny fire move down the paper stick toward Flynn's fingers. Before it hits the bottom and goes out, he leans toward his son. "Do you want to hear a truth?"

Why We Ate Mud

How will we know when the biscuits are ready?" Ellie is staring into the oven window. The tray is on the second rack from the bottom. The dough, still wet, isn't doing much. Harry sits on the countertop, the back of his tennis shoes thumping the cabinet door. His black hair hangs sheetlike over his forehead, and he flicks his head quickly. It's a tic he's got.

"My mother's making me go to church in the morning," he says.

"When I was little, we went to church maybe once a month," she says. "But I prayed every night, and I had this magazine cutout on my wall, and I thought it was a picture of God but later I realized it was just Allen Ginsberg."

"You should just see my mother at church," he says. "It's obscene. She waves her arms like this during the songs." He has his hands up over his head.

Ellie can't help but laugh. Harry is living at home again and that means he has to do certain things. Take out the trash. Keep his nails clean. Believe in a higher power.

The biscuits glisten in the oven.

"Sometimes I wonder if my mother is on something," Harry says. "I wish there were more drugs. Different ones. I wish there was a drug that made everything look two-dimensional. Like we were living on a sheet of paper."

"I wish there was a drug that made everything taste like fried chicken," Ellie says.

"I wish there was one that let you see every kind of light there is and all the colors we can't see now."

She looks back in the oven, and the biscuits are golden, maybe even a little brown.

"Let's take them to the park," she says. She wants to hang upside down from the jungle gym. The way they used to.

They go to the park with their biscuits protected in paper towels. Ellie has blueberry jam on her biscuit. Harry has butter on his. A little girl is already on the jungle gym so they sit down on a bench like the parents do. Ellie tugs loose a strand of her long brown hair and slips it into her mouth to suck on the loose ends. Her mother doesn't like this habit, says it's something little girls do and not women. "You could be so much prettier if you acted like it," she sometimes says, which makes Ellie laugh because *pretty*, to her mother, means plucked and proper with a big pink Easter hat. Aside from her chin, which Ellie fears is maybe a tad doughy, she is satisfied with her body, the large blue eyes, the waist thin as a wine bottle. Her boyfriend, Bryan, says she's got a "classic" look, plus amazing lips.

"I'm not a big fan of Bryan's," Harry says when Ellie brings him up. "He's okay, I guess, but I don't get you two together. As a couple, I mean."

Ellie has been dating Bryan for not quite a year, but she doesn't object when Harry puts his hand on her bare knee on the bench. It's like old times. They finish their biscuits, and Ellie leads him into the women's bathroom in the public park and locks the door. He lifts Ellie onto the edge of the sink, and the sink is wet. She feels herself sliding back into the basin.

"It's kind of gross in here," Harry says. "Sorry."

He's right, but that doesn't stop them. They keep their tops on, and Harry is fast. He goes outside to wait on her. She needs a moment in the stall. On one of the walls, someone has written, HALLELUJAH BATHTUB. Ellie wouldn't mind a hallelujah bath, whatever that is.

She joins Harry on the bench outside again. The little girl is gone from the jungle gym, but they don't feel like hanging upside down anymore.

"I know I was a little fast," Harry says.

"Next time will be better," she says.

Next time is a little better. They are in her bedroom on top of the covers. Her mother is out to lunch. When it's over they agree a nap seems like a nice idea, but neither of them can fall asleep. She tries to extrapolate an entire life from this moment, the two of them spooning together in her bed, time marked by the spray of the sprinkler slapping the window glass, by the whir of the overhead fan. She shuts her eyes and sees Allen Ginsberg's shining bearded face. Harry, arm draped over her side, pretends to snore, then asks if she wants to make something in the kitchen. Biscuits— or maybe éclairs? His mother recently taught him how to make an amazing cream from scratch.

"Do you ever want to be somewhere other than here?" she asks.

He sits up, his back against the cloth headboard, silent.

"I used to say I was going to study dolphins when I grew up," she says. "Bottlenose, Long-Beaked, Short-Beaked, Spinner. I had all the species memorized."

"I do remember you having dolphin stickers on all your notebooks."

She slides out of bed and stretches with her hands on the back of her head, spinning back and forth like a weather vane before a storm. "I've got plans with Mary now," she says. "But call me later, okay?"

Ellie doesn't really have plans with Mary because Mary is working today. Instead she drives over to her boyfriend Bryan's house because he's been out of town for the last few days to see his aunt and uncle. They watch some television and eat fruit Popsicles. During a commercial break, Bryan mutes the volume and announces that he may be moving to Charlotte.

"Why?"

"My uncle got me a job at his bank."

"But you're a drummer."

"I'm still a drummer," he says. "And now I'm banker too."

But she suspects that it is not really possible to be both things. Bryan asks if she'd like to move to Charlotte too. It would be a big step, he knows—their names on the same mailbox, on the electricity bills, on a one-year lease. Ellie says she wants some time to think about it, and then they kiss for a little while.

During a commercial, she asks, "Did you know millions of years ago dolphins lived on the land and they looked like rat-wolves?"

He mutes the volume again. "Wait, what are we talking about now?"

"Dolphins. They had legs. So, basically they evolved from being water animals to land animals and then went back to being water animals again."

There is an analogy here, somewhere, she's sure of it, one in which she is the dolphin and Charlotte is either dry land or the ocean.

When she leaves Bryan's house, Harry is parked across the street in his mother's car. He has followed her here. His window is down but he doesn't say anything until she's all the way at the car, one hand on the roof. The paint between the ski rack and the top of the door is bubbled and cracked, the windshield splattered with dark berry bird shit.

"I thought you'd broken it off with Bryan," he says.

She never said that. Not exactly.

"Get in," he says. "Please."

They drive to the top of a small mountain and park at the overlook. He sits on the guardrail with his legs over the side. With his phone he takes a picture of Ellie on the hood of the car.

"I'm ready to go home," she says. "Let's go."

They stop for soft serve first. In the car his paper cup springs a leak. He's got vanilla ice cream dribbled across his jeans. She rubs her hand up and down his knee a few times and points at the milk.

"That was fast," she says, a bad joke. "Sorry."

He crushes his empty cup and drops it on the floorboard with all the other trash—receipts, old printed Google Maps directions stomped with dirty bootprints, napkins, fast-food bags, straws with crushed and chewed-up tips. She worries the state of his car is a manifestation of some inner turmoil. Your car is a temple, a twenty-first-century Bible might say.

By the time they pull up in front of her house, she's made a decision.

"I'm moving to Charlotte," she says.

Harry says that's awful news. The worst kind of news. Just what's so bad about where they are now? he wants to know. He might be crying. Or maybe it's the car's dry heat. She can't tell. "It's not definite," she says, and he perks up a bit.

"Good," he says. "Then we can talk about it more later."

She moves to Charlotte and works in an art gallery. Her favorite painting is on the back wall. Two red squares intersected by a blue. If someone asked why she likes it most, she'd have nothing to say. Every afternoon she drinks a small iced mocha with whipped cream on top. Bryan goes to work in a suit and within the year has gained twenty pounds. But their apartment is well decorated. The furniture comes from various online catalogues. She craves biscuits on the weekends but never makes them. She wants to stop taking birth control but Bryan says he's not ready for that. He has a friend named Kara who also works at the bank. Kara wears thick mascara and speaks German, and she invites them to go tubing on a river outside Charlotte. "I could live my whole life floating down this river," Kara says. Ellie thinks Kara is possible friend material. But one evening Bryan comes home and says, actually, he wants to be with Kara now. "I'm sorry," he says. "I didn't plan it this way." Ellie wishes she were more surprised. When he moves out of the apartment, she can't afford to stay for more than a few months. She has to move back home again.

She calls Harry on her mother's phone but hangs up when he says hello. It has been two full years since the day in the park. If only there were a way to ensure a phone call went straight to voice mail. Voice mail was invented for rehearsed apologies. She could leave one for him, like a little gift on a doorstep he could unwrap again and again, without having to worry about what he'd say next.

Her old restaurant, despite new management, gives her a job again but now she's required to wear black pants and a black shirt.

The bartender is new. Everyone calls him Big D for some reason, but he's not very big. He drives a blue truck with a faded Dole–Kemp bumper sticker that he says came with the truck when he bought it.

"Where are you from?" she asks.

"From Georgia."

"What do you like to do? For fun?"

"Sudoku," he says, then adds, not at all sheepish, "if you want to know the truth, and probably you don't, I spend a lot of time reading about aliens because I don't think that we're alone in the universe. I think we made contact a long time ago. Did you know that Eisenhower was on vacation in Palm Springs in 1954 and that he disappeared for a whole night? Later they said he was getting a cap put on his tooth, but there's evidence he met aliens for the first time that night at Edwards Air Force Base. It's possible aliens are already living among us. You don't believe me, I can tell, but go to this website."

He writes down the address on a bar napkin and slides it to her.

"What if God is an alien?" she asks. "Like, a really advanced one. So advanced that we wouldn't know the difference."

"Wouldn't that be nice," Big D says.

Ellie isn't so sure.

Big D takes her to a restaurant with a thirty-page menu and every item seems to include cheese—macaroni and cheese, cheese strudels, cheese salads, cheese sticks, cheeseburgers, cheese chips, cheese on cheese. Then he takes her to a dinosaur museum, where they buy *T. rex* T-shirts. Then he takes her to a theme park with roller coasters named after movie franchises. One night, a little tipsy, they wind up in a tattoo parlor that smells like cigarettes and bleach. They flip through the floppy binders and laugh at the skulls, roses, the confused Chinese symbols for courage and harmony and whatever else.

"You could get a flying saucer over your heart," she says.

"I know bartenders are supposed to, sort of, love tattoos," he says. "But I can't stand the idea of something being on my body forever."

"Forever, in your case, being anywhere from thirty to fifty years," she says.

"I've got more than that in me. I'm healthy as a—"

"—as a thirty-two-year old man, I know." She peels the binder's laminated pages apart, their stickiness making wet static sounds. "One day they'll probably come up with extremely permanent tattoos. They'll be genetic or something. You'll get a dolphin on your ankle and your baby will come out with a dolphin on *her* ankle and her baby too and on and on until the end of time. Dolphins, all the way down the line. Then, *real* accountability."

He smiles. They come to a picture of a gray cartoonish alien holding a bong. She draws a line in the air between the picture and his right shoulder. "There," she says. "Perfect. It'll look so great on your son too." Immediately she regrets saying it. He gives her an odd look. *Our son*, he might be thinking. She's been sleeping over at his house a few nights a week, and he's already asked her to move in with him. She's been evasive on this issue.

"Don't rush into it." Her mother's advice. She's not thrilled that Ellie is dating a bartender, of all things. What Ellie really needs to do, her mother says, is get her life in order. And that starts with a new and proper job. Her mother has been making phone calls, and a friend of a friend has arranged an interview at her company, if Ellie's interested, and of course Ellie is, right? Ellie doesn't want to wait tables for the rest of her life, does she?

. . .

The entrance to the building is lined with prickly bushes. Ellie is there early. Not because she wants the job. It's just that parking was easier to find than she expected. She couldn't care less about this job. When people ask her what kind of job she wants, she usually says, a job studying dolphins, or at least a job where she can use her hands. "Your hands?" her mother often says. "But we all use our hands." Her mother sells insurance policies and uses her hands every day. How else would she dial out?

But Ellie wants to use her hands to fix something. Bones, maybe—or pocket watches. A hundred years ago, you probably could have made an entire career out of repairing pocket watches.

Inside the building, she gives her purse and keys to the guard and walks through an X-ray detector. She watches the guard watch the screen. Maybe he can see her bones. She hopes her bones are beautiful, or at least average. At the front desk, she gets a sticker that says TEMPORARY. In the elevator, she peels the sticker off her chest.

She has to wait for her interview. She sits down beside a man in a rough-looking suit. He seems nervous. When he scratches his mustache, little flakes of dandruff fall out of the hairs. His wristwatch is two minutes off the digital clock on the wall. He fiddles with the silver knob on the side until the times are perfectly synchronized.

Later, the secretary calls Ellie's name and leads her down the hall to an office with glass walls. The man on the other side of the glass motions for her to come in and sit down. He is on the phone but smiles at her.

"Let's talk about it over dumplings," he says to the person on the phone. "You ever eat them? Good Lord, you gotta try the dumplings at this place I know around the corner. Yeah, they got chicken in them. You don't eat chicken? Did I know that? Shit, sorry. I'm pretty sure they got fish ones too."

The phone call ends. He stares at Ellie with bright green eyes, his hair combed forward and cut straight across his forehead, his blue shirt almost shimmering under the lights. He introduces himself as Burton. He takes some papers and a pen out of a desk drawer. He taps the pen against his chin.

"You might find our method unusual," he says. "But we've found that the typical questions don't tell us anything useful. We like to start with hypotheticals."

"Okay," Ellie says.

"Excellent," he says. "Here we go. You're given a shoebox. In the shoebox are three mice. All the mice are going to die, but if you smash one with a hammer, the other two can live. What do you do?"

Ellie has never killed a mouse before, not even in a trap. When she was growing up, her family had a cat that took care of things like that. She tries to imagine smashing a mouse with a hammer. She imagines the mouse as a very still fluffy thing on a cold cement floor. She imagines the hammer in her hand. She swings the hammer down, but instead of a crunch, she imagines wind chimes.

"Don't think about these questions too long," Burton says.

"I guess I'd kill the mouse," she says.

Burton makes a mark. She asks if she answered correctly.

"No right or wrong," he says. "These are hypotheticals. Next.

You're on a spaceship. You're set to become the first person to leave the galaxy by traveling at the speed of light. But then you realize that, because of relativity, a hundred years will have passed when you return to earth, and everyone you know will have expired."

"Expired?" she asks, and thinks of milk.

"Yes," he says. "They'll all be dead, but you will be the same age. Do you complete your mission?"

"So," Ellie says, "I only realize this once I'm all the way out there in space?"

Burton makes another mark. Then, without waiting for her answer to the space question, he says, "You're a devout member of a religious group. You discover that your Spiritual Leader, henceforth referred to as SL, is a charlatan. He's stealing money from all the other followers. This one's multiple choice. Do you: *A*. Call the authorities. *B*. Interrupt a religious service and present evidence of the SL's wrongdoing to the followers. *C*. Alert both the authorities and the followers with a strongly worded letter. *D*. Confront the SL in private. *E*. Claim to be a new prophet and banish the SL from the existing group for reasons unrelated to the financial crime. *F*. Leave the religious group and write a tell-all book. *G*. Blackmail the SL for a cut of the stolen funds—"

"How many choices are there?" Ellie asks. "I think I'm losing track."

"I'm almost done," Burton says. "*H*. Start a new religious group and declare spiritual war. *I*. Go on a pilgrimage to a religious shrine and ask for God's guidance. *J*. Wear a recording device and try to get the SL to admit the financial crimes on tape. *K*. Become an atheist."

Ellie doesn't know what to say. She grew up Methodist and

nothing like that ever happened in her church. Their wine was grape juice. The minister played an acoustic guitar.

"I guess I'd do the thing where you confront the SL in private," she says. "I mean, how much money are we talking about here?"

He doesn't answer but makes another mark. Then he says, "You find out you're pregnant and—"

He stops talking and looks up at her.

"Just so you know," he says, "we ask the men this one too. Okay, you find out you're pregnant, and it is revealed that your baby will very likely save the entire world one day. But giving birth to this baby might result in your own death. Would you terminate the pregnancy?"

"God," Ellie says. "I guess I'd have to keep it, right?"

"And if that child only has a fifty percent chance of saving the world?"

"I guess I'd still keep it."

"Twenty-five percent chance?"

"Maybe not," Ellie says. "No, in that case, I probably wouldn't go through with it."

Burton makes a mark.

"I like you," he says. "You seem to have your head on straight. You'd be surprised how many people don't. By the way, do you know how to make a spreadsheet?"

Ellie says she does. Burton makes another mark and then presents her with a booklet and a pen for the essay portion. Ellie had no idea there would be an essay portion. He says it's nothing major, just a few quick paragraphs. She'll have fifteen minutes.

"Here we go," he says. "The question is: How will the world end, and what will happen when we die?"

He leaves the room. Ellie didn't get much sleep last night. She was out late for her friend Mary's thirtieth birthday party, and her mind feels like Swiss cheese. She starts writing:

The end of the world will be like when the candles get blown out on a cake. Everything will end very fast but with a final little flicker so that we at least know it's happening. Then the earth will just stop existing. And we won't know why. We won't even care why. Our souls will still exist but in a different way and they won't care about why it ended because we won't need the earth anymore. When we talk about the earth, we'll laugh about how silly it was to be here. Earth will be like some dream we all had together. It will be like one of those dreams where you eat mud because in the dream eating mud seems like a perfectly natural thing to do. After the earth ends, it will be like waking up from a dream like that. We'll all stand around wondering why we ate all that mud. Also, we won't have private parts.

After Burton collects her essay, he shakes Ellie's hand and says he'll be in touch. She doesn't feel confident. She probably shouldn't have mentioned the bit about the mud. She probably shouldn't have said she'd abort the baby with a twenty-five percent chance of saving the world.

Outside the snow is falling into the prickly bushes along the building entrance, collecting in the green groove of every leaf. She can tell the leaves are prickly but sticks her hand into a bush anyway. It pricks her in a few spots. She can't tell where it hurts most. When she squeezes her palm, a few small drops of blood rise to the surface of her skin.

Ellie walks to the parking garage. She should call her mother. Her mother will want a full report. That can wait. She feels something in her pocket. She pulls it out. It's the sticker that says TEM-PORARY. She sticks it on the dashboard above the heater and drives to Pop-Yop, the soft-serve place where Mary works.

"But if they offer you the job, you'll take it, though," Mary says, wiping down a tabletop. Her friend, who used to say she was going to travel around the country in a Volkswagen Beetle selling homemade jewelry, has recently developed such a practical streak. She says she's even been thinking about asking her brother for a loan so she can make an offer on this Pop-Yop. Ellie pulls the silver handle on the wall and fills her cup. Mary gives it to her for free so long as she doesn't overdo it with the toppings. Ellie tries to never overdo it with the toppings but sometimes she can't help herself.

Two weeks later, Burton calls to offer her the job.

"You're our top choice," he says. "And that essay. Loved it. So funny. I showed a few people. Hope that's okay?"

Ellie doesn't ask him what exactly he found so funny. She's not sure she wants to know. She tells him she'd like a day to think about the offer, as if she has ten others to consider, but Ellie knows, eventually, she will accept. Otherwise her mother would kill her.

Big D organizes a small going-away party on her last day at the restaurant. He brings in chocolate cupcakes from the grocery store since the kitchen restaurant isn't open yet. All the waiters and cooks stand around with dark chocolate in their teeth, asking Ellie questions about what's next. *This job,* she wants to say, *and after that, probably, some other job.* Big D pours everyone a shot. He's ready to pour another round but the manager says that's enough.

She's shopping for Christmas gifts at the mall when she sees Harry for the first time since moving back to town. He's in the parking lot, loading giant boxes into the back of his car. He can't believe it's really her. Yes, she changed her hair. It's shorter. He looks different too. He has a patchy beard and tired eyes.

"My oh my," he says.

"Let's get coffee," she says.

They leave in his car. It's snowing.

At a café, they order holiday coffee drinks and waters and a figure-eight pastry with some kind of cream filling in the holes like little yellow swimming pools.

Harry runs a food bank now. His jeans are too big for him. They sag low on his hips.

Ellie tells him she's sorry, about everything, and he nods.

"So, you changed much?" he asks.

Yes, maybe, she says. But then again, probably not. She's back home, after all.

Harry has big news to share. He's engaged.

"Who's the lucky lady?" she asks.

He whips out his cell phone and shows her a photo. The woman in it has brown hair, and she is very aware of the camera.

That is, she's smiling broadly, her teeth twinkling, brilliantly white and possibly a little sharp.

"Her name's Caroline," he says. "We met at the church."

"As in, your mother's church?" she asks.

"Technically it's *my* church now too," he says. "Caroline's a teacher. We live on the other side of town."

Ellie considers asking Harry if his fiancée waves her arms during the songs at church. But she decides that she shouldn't. That would not be kind. Then she asks it anyway.

Harry smiles and blows a dent into the foam of his pumpkin spice latte.

They haven't touched the pastry. Harry insists she take it with her, but the look of it makes her feel sick. She isn't ready to go home yet, and so he drives them to the park, which is empty and a little cold. She wraps her jacket tight and leans into Harry. Through the metal bars of the jungle gym, she watches two gray squirrels chase each other around a tree. Around and around and around. So gratuitous. Harry puts his hand on her knee, and she doesn't object. It's like old times. She asks him if he thinks they are alone in the universe, and he smiles and says he reckons not. They climb onto the jungle gym and hang upside down. His hair touches the ground. Her face turns pink. She hopes they'll make biscuits later.

Saint Possy

O ur house was more than a hundred and fifty years old
and full of mysteries and we loved it. We'd bought it
for the original hardwood floors and the ornate plas-
terwork and the stone fireplace. Soon after we arrived, the man
across the street, the unofficial neighborhood historian, dropped
off his self-published pamphlet. It included a lengthy essay that
said our place had been, at various points, a boardinghouse (1840s/
50s), a convalescent home (1890s), the boyhood home of a famous
neuroscientist (1920s/30s), a lawyer's suite (1960s), and a drug
house (1990s). Now it was ours: its history, its shoddy plumbing,
lead paint, crumbling foundation, all of it.

Reorganizing our boxes in the attic one afternoon, my wife
discovered a silvered daguerreotype hidden in the eaves. The
woman in the photograph had a pinched, severe-looking face, and
she was dressed in some sort of black frock. On the back, the script
slanted and faded, was a single word: *Lang.* This made sense.

According to the brochure, the area had been settled mostly by German immigrants.

Not long after that, I was fixing the basement stairs and discovered two red candles and what I guessed was a possum skull concealed beneath the boards. It looked like it had been there a long time. The skull was gray and thin, two small pencil-prick nostril holes below the eyes, the front teeth fanglike and awful and covered in dried drips of red wax. My wife, who grew up Catholic and who can be pretty grim, dubbed the relic Saint Possy and stuck it on our dresser, which meant we had to fall asleep looking at it.

The first night it was there, I dreamed I needed surgery and had to watch a doctor pull what looked like dirty linguini from a hole in my side. The second night I dreamed I was pregnant.

"You can't blame that stupid skull," my wife said, and patted its crusty crown.

"Don't even try to tell me that thing isn't evil," I said.

"It's just bone," she said. "Just carbon atoms, same as you and me."

Still, I didn't want it on the dresser. The skull absorbed light, and after dark it was the brightest object in our bedroom. I threw my shirt over it whenever we had sex because surely any child conceived in its sight was going to come out a monster. I tolerated it for as long as I could—a month, maybe—before packaging it in a shoebox and shoving that toward the back of the closet.

We went out for dinner one night, and I ordered mussels and french fries, and we talked about money because we'd spent most of our savings on the house and we still had more repairs to make. We were thinking about taking in a roommate to make ends meet. When we came home, I polished off a bottle of wine and fell asleep fast, but around midnight I woke up with a full bladder. When I got back from the bathroom, the skull was on the dresser again, the sockets empty and dark.

I shook my wife. She didn't even open her eyes. She patted my arm. A slow smile crept across her face.

"You're a jerk," I said. "Don't you know you married a man with a gentle heart? Can't you see what you're doing to me? And you know that may not even be a possum—the truth is, we don't know what it is. It could be anything. It could be a deformed baby skull. Remember the photograph from the attic? Maybe it was her deformed stillborn baby, and she built a shrine for it under the stairs."

I thought my wife had already fallen back asleep, that she wasn't paying me any attention, but two days later, she came home from work with a strange look on her face, a nervous half smile. I asked her what was wrong, and she pulled a mess of paper towels out of her purse. She unraveled the ball, and there was the skull.

She said she'd taken it to her friend Barry, who taught biology at the university in town.

"And?"

"It's not a possum skull," she said. "It's not a baby skull either. But don't freak out. He doesn't really know what it is. He's never seen anything quite like it."

We were at the kitchen table. I got up to doctor the soup I was making and then sat back down. I asked her if she thought we should just bury it in the backyard instead. To be done with it.

"Maybe we should put it back under the stairs where we found it," she said. "It was probably there for a reason."

The skull was on the table between us. It seemed to breathe. I was losing my appetite. She scraped some of the red wax off the bone, studying it. My wife hadn't been to church since she was a little girl. She was a Buddhist now, and one of the wonderful things about our house was that she had a room entirely for her meditation, which she did every morning.

"You don't really think it's evil, do you?" she asked. "Because I don't believe in evil. I don't see things black-and-white."

"It's at least a very dark gray," I said. "If what we're talking about is a spectrum of goodness."

"Why were there candles?" she asked. "That is eerie, right?"

We didn't say anything for a while. The skull grinned at us. Maybe we were waiting for it to talk.

"This is silly," she said. "I mean, really, what are we so afraid of?"

She snatched the skull off the table and threw it at the floor. The skull didn't break. It ricocheted toward the door and slid to a stop at the doormat.

My wife went into the hall closet and took out our bucket of tools. I asked her what she was doing. She rummaged around and pulled out a socket wrench.

"Wait," I said, but it was too late. She was down on all fours, bashing the skull as hard as she could. She hit and she hit and she hit, and when she was done, there were fragments of bone everywhere. She looked at me with wild eyes.

"Quick," she said. "Help."

I was brushing the pieces into a pile, trying to collect all of them together. If we weren't diligent now, we'd never be rid of this thing. Months from now we'd still be finding tiny shards. What if we got a bone splinter? What if there were bone particles in the air and we breathed them in? She got out the broom and swept as thoroughly as she could and then told me to do the same. Then we wiped the floors with wet paper towels.

"I feel funny," she said. "Something's not right."

She looked like she was bracing for a sneeze but the sneeze wouldn't come. I gave her a Kleenex and advised her to blow her nose. Then I blew mine. We weren't hungry anymore. I threw out the soup. We went to bed early. The next morning neither of us mentioned what had happened, but I saw her scanning the floor while we ate breakfast, and also later at lunch. That night I had another dream. I was pregnant again, but in this one whatever was growing in my belly could talk. It had a smooth voice, baritone, vaguely southern, muffled by my flesh, and it called me a coward. It called me a wretch. It spoke with the power of all the saints in heaven. It called me names I don't even remember but still feel.

I told my wife about it in the shower.

"No skull to blame for it now," she said. "That's just your own inner weirdness."

I worried that the voice in the dream had been my own.

After that we rarely talked about the skull, except as an anecdote at dinners and parties. Oh, yes, I'd say, she was wild-eyed when she destroyed it. Well, you should have seen *him*, my wife would say, he was such a baby. We'd make ourselves sound silly. We made ourselves sound temporarily insane. That always got big laughs. The more we told the story, the stranger we seemed. We told it until the people in the story were barely recognizable versions of ourselves.

Years later we sold the house and bought a newer one on the other side of town, in a better school district. We were unloading all our mixing bowls in the new kitchen when I saw it at the bottom of the box: the tooth, gray and small. Nothing had changed. We hadn't changed.

"You know what we have to do," my wife said. "So we might as well get it over with."

We drove over to the old house. We hadn't yet handed over the keys. Standing there one last time under those beautiful high ceilings, the floorboards creaking under our feet, I thought about how soon we'd be just another footnote in our neighbor's pamphlet. My wife moved to toss the tooth into the fireplace ash but I stopped her. What if what was required was a little pageantry?

"Such as?"

I led us up to the attic, where we had, perhaps unkindly, left behind a few boxes of our junk and trash. We didn't have any candles, so I jabbed the tooth into an ugly old teddy bear's mouth, which made the bear look country-poor and sad and creepy. I placed it in the attic eaves alongside the daguerreotype. It felt right to unite them. I don't mind admitting now that I performed a little farewell dance as I backed toward the door, where my wife waited with her arms crossed.

"You think that's necessary?" she asked.

I shrugged: What was the harm? Just after pulling the light cord and leaving the attic forever I even whispered a few quick words into the darkness. When I turned, my wife had her eyes closed and hands clasped. A little prayer, she called it later, in the car, joking, though we both knew that's exactly what it had been.

Felix Not Arriving

In his aisle seat near the front of the plane, Felix concentrates unsuccessfully on a crossword in the airline magazine, half finished by a previous flier. All the easy clues have already been answered and now he needs a six-letter word for a muzzle-loading tool. The third letter is *m*. He stares at that *m*, a bit dazed, doing his best not to think about what happens when they land in Atlanta. Rattling the ice in her cup, Laura leans over his magazine and peers down at the puzzle. "Ergo," she says, and points at 27 Down. "Ramrod," she says, and points at his *m*, and then, pointing somewhere else, "Pandora."

He looks at that particular clue. *First woman.* "You think it's Pandora? I was thinking it might be Evelynn. Eve was just a nickname, right?"

"Adam and Evelynn, a lovely couple, we really need to have them over for dinner some night soon. I hear Adam's a terrific gardener. I hear Evelynn likes apple pie."

Felix closes the inflight magazine and tucks it into the seat pocket. He looks around for a new distraction. On the television show Felix works for, *Pets!*, Gonuts the CGI Hamster has this thing he is always saying before climbing onto his metal wheel and running mindlessly. "Don't get so stressed. You got to wheel it out." Felix provides the voice for Gonuts. He doesn't love recording different iterations of the same phrase week after week, but he has to admit the little furball is onto something in this case: life is not easy and without distractions you can make yourself crazy.

He munches on some dried apricots and asks Laura to close the blinds since the sun is so bright and hot across their laps. Her jean shorts are wedged high and her pale knees glow like two beautiful snowy peaks, the crease of her legs a tight valley. If he wanted, with the aid and cover of a blanket, he could walk his hand right up that valley. Would she resist? Probably. Not that she always insists on decency. There was the time in the changing room at Nordstrom's. There was the night in the chair on the roof of their apartment building. But he won't slide his hand between her legs. A Neanderthalic impulse, his mother would have called it. The fasten-your-seat-belt light blinks. The overhead bins rattle.

"I'm not going to finish this drink," he announces, his whiskey and soda hovering near his lips. He has Laura's attention. That's all he wanted anyway. She watches him, amused, as he tips back the cup, the ice crashing into his teeth, the liquid draining out. "I'm *not* going to push this," he says, and pushes the overhead button for the stewardess. "I'm not going to order another drink and fall down drunk on the tarmac like an idiot."

"Tell me more about these red tights," she says, and crosses her arms. "Does Hank wear them to bed too? I don't get it. When does Bet wash them?"

Felix shrugs. "I don't think he lets her wash them. That's part of the problem. They're stinky, I'm sure." Hank, Felix's four-year-old son, is obsessed with a pair of red tights from last year's Halloween costume when he dressed up as a strawberry. In a few weeks he will start kindergarten, and Bet, his mother, is concerned about what the other kids might say. "Did you ever do weird stuff like this when you were a kid?" Bet has asked Felix on the phone. "I'll bet you did. Hank is funny—just like you. The other day I found gravel in his juice cup. I asked him why and he said he likes his juice on the rocks. Can you believe that? Where do you think he got that from? When you get here, be sure to ask him about the sprinkler and the frog. It's his best bit. You won't regret it." Bet is always doing this, insisting that Hank is funny, as if otherwise Felix would stop believing the boy was his.

Felix is a comedian, though he hasn't told a joke onstage in almost a year, not since he started lending his voice to Gonuts on *Pets!* A huge hit with kids, the hamster has his own lunchboxes and T-shirts. It is despicably commercial, but the paychecks sure are nice. Felix is not especially proud of the show. The jokes are too easy; the laugh track irks him. When people ask him what he's up to, he often doesn't mention the show and says only that he's developing some new material, something he hasn't done since his *Keep Your Hands to Myself* tour that took him to Atlanta, where he met Bet. She was at a table near the front of the show. She was a barista in a coffee shop near the university, a student there, in fact, though Felix only learned that later when she called to tell him about Hank—or about the bundle of cells that would eventually become Hank.

There was never any expectation that Felix would relocate

his life to Atlanta (and he certainly didn't ask her to join him out West). But without any lawyers having to get involved, he started mailing her monthly checks, checks that sometimes Bet didn't even bother to cash. She didn't need the money. The checks were purely symbolic. Her father worked for a certain soda company—that's what her father was always calling it, *a certain soda company*—and she moved back in with her parents once Hank was born. With their help, Bet was able to finish school and get a job in a gallery. Ever since Hank's birth, Felix has been flying into town three or four times a year for long visits.

But now, after not dating anyone seriously since the birth, Bet is getting married—to someone named JT, the heir to a carpet-cleaning business, a "good man," according to Bet. Felix is prepared not to like him. Though he usually makes these trips alone, Laura volunteered to come along for the weekend to provide moral support, to help him get through the engagement party.

Laura is emphatic that she never wants any children of her own, but the fact that Felix has a son does not faze her. "How many women did you sleep with while you were on the road?" she asked him when he first showed her a photo of Hank on his phone, as if she were calculating the probability of other babies in other cities. This was on their second date, at a Mexican restaurant, fajitas sizzling on a metal platter between them. Felix wasn't sure how to answer her question. Too many women and he was a sleaze, but too few and he was inadequate. He settled on six and flashed three fingers on each hand. Laura nodded and announced, matter-of-factly, that six was a number she could live with. Ten months later, and they are on the verge of a more encompassing merger—of door keys, of bedsheets, of utensils, of wireless Internet accounts. Strangely, none of this scares Felix at all. He doesn't know if he has Laura or his upcoming thirty-ninth birthday to thank for this sudden blip of maturity, but he is ready to embrace the change.

When the stewardess brings him his second whiskey and soda, he takes a long sip. Two gigantic hands descend from above. They latch on to the top of Felix's headrest and pull it back like the arm of a catapult. Ready, set—when the man stands and releases the chair, Felix is rocked forward, some of the whiskey splashing over the plastic rim of his cup.

"Watch it," Felix says to the man, who's crouching beneath the bins. The man clears his throat and says nothing. Where is Felix's apology? He glares up at the guy through the gap between the headrests. "Buddy, you made me spill my drink."

"Your what?" The man has a face like tapioca pudding.

"My drink," Felix says. "When you stood up, you made me spill it."

"Oh," the man says. "Sorry, didn't hear you. My ears are no good with the pressure. These headphones are pointless. I turn the volume up all the way, and it's just noise. All these movies to choose from and I can't hear a word of dialogue. Plus I have to stretch every twenty minutes. Ever heard of DVT? If I don't move around enough I might get an embolism."

"By all means, then," Felix says, "run a few laps."

"You'll have to excuse him," Laura says to the man. "He's been a little edgy this morning."

"Flying will do that to you," the man says. "They don't make it easy, do they?"

"They don't," she says, reaching for the inflight magazine,

and then she starts back on the crossword puzzle without further comment.

Has Felix been edgy this morning? Even if he has been, this man doesn't need to hear about it. Quietly he says to Laura, "He bumps my seat and you ask him to excuse *me*? What's that all about?"

She pats his arm. "Here's something good: you don't know how to feel about the mother of your child getting married to another man, and you've brought me along because you want me to be a part of your life, and I love you for that. Here's something bad: part of you doesn't want me on this trip." This technique of hers, the something-good-something-bad, is from a book she read years ago. She swears it is the key to strong communication, but Felix doesn't care for it. Hearing something good doesn't mitigate the bad. The bad is still just as bad.

"I do want you on this trip," he says. "*All* parts of me want you here."

"Okay," she says. "I'm glad to hear it. And here I am. I'm here."

A miracle: the plane lands three minutes earlier than expected. They don't have any checked bags. Unlike his usual visits, when he rents a car and stays for the entire week, they can be here only for the weekend. Both Felix and Laura have to be back on Monday for work on *Pets!* She does makeup for the show and two others on the network.

Down the long sunlit terminal, floor-to-ceiling windows above and on all sides, he drags their shared green roller suitcase across the hard white floor. Felix can imagine the distance between heaven and earth like this, bright and spare and seemingly endless. Laura strolls a few feet behind him, giant white sunglasses on her small face, pink oxford shirt knotted over one hip. At the bottom of an escalator, they pass between two sliding doors, and Felix scans the crowd for Bet's dad, Mr. Ash, who was enlisted to pick them up and chauffeur them to the hotel, the Commodore, Felix's usual haunt on these trips.

Mr. Ash is in his sixties, but hasn't retired yet. Maybe he never will. In his work for a certain soda company, he often jets off to New Delhi and Shanghai, defending the company brand in places where trademark laws aren't always enforced very stringently. Save for the wire-frame glasses always at the end of his nose, Mr. Ash has the look of an elderly football brute. The first time Felix met the man was right here in the baggage claim, the screens flashing arrivals, the swishing of so many suitcase wheels across the carpet. Bet was there too, of course, her belly round under a T-shirt, black hair cut shorter than Felix remembered it. Mr. Ash towered behind her like an Easter Island statue. It was the moment Felix had dreaded most ever since Bet's first phone call about the Hank-in-progress.

"So you're the comedian I have to thank for all this," Mr. Ash had said, unsmiling, and then stuck out his dry freckled hand.

"So you're the dad who probably wishes my plane had crashed," Felix answered. Felix has a knack for saying the exact wrong thing. He says things defensively and without thought. Partly it's what initially drew him to the stage.

"Is that him?" Laura asks now, and points toward a sharp-chinned man with fine brown hair. He is holding a piece of paper that says FELIX PENN in Magic Marker. It isn't Mr. Ash.

"Felix?" the man calls out. "It's got to be you. Bet told me to look for the middle-aged pirate."

An old line of Bet's; she used to say Felix's gray-flecked beard and earring made him look like a character off Captain Hook's ship.

"I'm JT," the man says, and crumples up the paper. "Mr. Ash got held up at work, and Bet asked if I could come get you. So, here I am."

"Nice to meet you," Laura says. "And congratulations."

"Yes, congrats," Felix says.

"Thank you. Thanks. I'm out in short-term," he says.

JT leads the way through the double doors and into the sunlight, his red polo shirt tucked tightly into his neatly pressed khaki pants. The white van at the end of the lot is his. Across the side: JONES & SONS CARPET CLEANERS. "Your chariot," he says. "The back is full, so we'll have to all sit up front in the cab." He opens the passenger door. On the dashboard is a coiled brown and gold snake and, in the driver's seat, a yellow one with an open mouth and vicious red fangs. "Rubber," he says, and tosses them on the floorboard.

"Why do you have those?" Laura asks, climbing up first and sliding toward the floorboard transmission.

"Oh," he says. "Kind of a joke. I work in some rough neighborhoods. We like to say it scares off the criminals. Are you hungry? You need a snack before tonight?"

"We ate some on the plane," she says. "So, are you excited about the wedding?"

"I can't wait. I'd do it tomorrow if I could." He walks around to the driver's side as Felix joins Laura in the cab. When he's behind the wheel, "Bet wants the real deal, though—flowers, big white tent, all of it. Can you imagine me in a tux?"

Felix doesn't take the bait. The van rumbles to life. JT grips the vibrating stick shift and reverses out of the space. Felix has his window down, and once they are on the highway the warm air blows pleasantly across his face.

"It feel good to be back South?" JT asks him. "You're from around here, aren't you? Originally, I mean."

"Not from Atlanta," Felix says. He grew up in North Carolina but hasn't lived there since college and no longer considers himself much of a southerner. He has aunts and uncles he doesn't visit and who would probably dislike him. His parents live in other cities now, Pittsburgh (his mother) and Phoenix (his father), each with different partners. They've started entirely new lives for themselves. "A second chapter," his father called it once. "A page-turner, I'm sure," Felix said to that. Growing up, Felix had never thought of his parents as particularly unhappy. His father had always opened doors for his mother, and she'd rubbed his neck when it was sore. Sure, his mother would look away disgusted whenever his father belched into his hand, or complain about his habit of never filling a gas tank more than three-quarters; and yes, Felix had once overheard his father call his mother "sexless" to a group of his cigar-smoking buddies, a word his father would pretend to not recognize when a nine-year-old Felix asked for its meaning.

That his parents had so rarely argued with each other would later make Felix wonder if the marriage had all been a charade for his sake, an idea that made them seem less like parents and more like actors in a bad play about parenting.

The brown and gold snake is under his foot on the floorboard. He grabs it by the tail and makes it slither up Laura's bare leg. She slaps it away playfully.

"You know," Felix says, "I used to have an uncle who kept a rubber snake in his truck."

"That right?" JT asks.

"Yeah, he said it scared off black people."

JT is quiet, both hands on the wheel. Laura shoots Felix a quick but discernible look: *Please don't.*

"Why are you looking at me like—" Felix begins. "Oh, come on, I'm not saying that's why *JT* has a rubber snake in his van."

"It's definitely not why," JT says.

"Right, exactly, and that's not what I meant. The snake just made me remember about my uncle. That's all."

"Your uncle sounds like a lunatic," Laura says.

"He wasn't all bad. He taught Bible class to the sixth-graders. He used to take me deer hunting."

"I can't imagine you hunting deer," Laura said. "I can't imagine you hunting anything. You get queasy at the grocery store looking at the meat behind the glass. You get this funny face—" Her eyes go wide and her lips part a little, like she's watching a spaceship land. "I always think you're going to pass out right there in front of the butcher."

"Ha. Ha," Felix says. "We both know that's not true."

"You're funny," JT says, and Felix has to peer across Laura to see that JT means her and not him. He is accustomed to this. People always seem let down to discover that he—a comedian!—is not particularly funny in most situations. His clever one-liners and retorts arrive days too late. He considers himself more of a story-teller than anything else. Tell us a joke, people sometimes request, and his mind goes empty, not even a single knock-knock joke to be found (not that he's ever told a single knock-knock joke). "It doesn't work that way," he usually tells these people, and that it does work that way, for some comedians, is a source of not a little anguish.

JT drops them off at the hotel and says Mr. Ash will be by in an hour to get them. The engagement party is the next day and tonight the family will eat together at the Ashes' house. Upstairs in the hotel room—sand-colored wallpaper, white fluffy bedspread, a remote control at the end of the bed—Laura strips down for a quick shower. Felix flips through the channels on the flatscreen and then joins her in the bathroom to examine himself as she towels her hair dry.

"You're a real piece of work," she says. "What possessed you to say that about your uncle?"

"About the snakes?" He pastes his toothbrush, then hers. "It's a true story."

"Who cares if it's true? Truth has nothing to do with it. It's not a great way to start any sort of relationship with the guy."

"Don't you wonder, just a little bit, why he had the snake on the dash? It wouldn't surprise me if—"

"Felix." Her hair is a damp frizzy explosion of blond. "You don't mean that."

"I might."

"If you feel that way, then I suggest you keep your mouth shut about it. Give the guy a chance. You shouldn't always assume the worst about people. The last thing you want is to make an enemy of the man who will be raising your son."

They are talking to each other's reflections. Felix glances at his own. *Geez,* Gonuts sometimes says, *you look like you just swallowed a furball.* The furball: that JT will eventually be closer to Hank than Felix ever could, that Hank will come to think of JT like a father. It is inevitable. The kid is only four, and JT will be the man in his underwear at the breakfast table on Saturday mornings. With proximity, intimacy. Felix will be just some ghost on a phone line.

"Shit, my moisturizer," Laura says, digging in her orange toiletries bag. "I must have left it."

Felix unzips his own bag and produces the small plastic travel bottle that he spotted by the sink just before they left the apartment. He stands behind her and rubs some of the lotion into her shoulders. "See, we're good for each other. I keep you moisturized, and you call me on my bullshit."

"Well, it's just that sometimes you're your own worst enemy."

"And that's exactly why I need you here. My enemy's enemy is my friend."

She bumps him away with her butt and smiles. "Go change."

He slides into a fresh pair of dark jeans and puts on a gray blazer. "I'm not going downstairs to sit at the bar," he says. "I'm not going to drink as many whiskey drinks as I can before Bet's dad gets here."

"Be down in a minute," Laura calls from the bathroom.

The bar, Felix discovers, is empty. None of the little glass bowls have any nuts in them. Rod Stewart rains down from the overhead speakers. Felix sits down on a stool and drums on the bar's wooden lip. "Helloooo," he calls, but no one emerges through the door between the liquor shelves. He considers hopping the bar and grabbing a bottle of whiskey and a glass. He doesn't require any ice.

"Felix," Mr. Ash says. He is standing at the entrance to the bar in a dark blue suit, his red tie loose. "I thought I might find you in here."

Felix isn't sure if he should be offended or not. He settles on *not*.

"I'd offer to buy you a drink but"—Felix gestures at the bar—"it's like *The Shining* in here. Do you get that vibe? Redrum."

"I was told you were bringing someone."

"She's upstairs. Down in a sec." Felix taps on the bar. Then scratches his face. Then lets his arms hang. He can't seem to find the right thing to do with his hands. "Excited about the wedding?" The easy question.

"Of course I am. So long as Bet is happy, I'm happy." He sits down at a table and kicks out one of the chairs for Felix. "I won't lie. JT isn't exactly who I had in mind for her. But then again, neither were you."

"Please, tell me how you *really* feel, Nick." Felix rarely uses Mr. Ash's first name. Even now, after all these years, it feels indecent. He sits down across from the man. "But it did happen kind of fast, didn't it?"

"Eight months."

"Has it been that long? I feel like I only heard his name yesterday."

"Selective hearing, I guess," Mr. Ash says.

Neither of them says anything for what feels like minutes. "But the thing about Hank is," Mr. Ash says, as if continuing some conversation that has been playing out in his head, "he's really a sweet kid. And smart. I've already got him reading. It's incredible. And he's taking piano lessons, did Bet tell you?"

"He played 'Baa, Baa, Black Sheep' for me over the phone the other night. Not too shabby." Felix knows all about the reading and the piano breakthroughs and about Hank's recent gummy worm addiction. Bet—dependable, lovely Bet—keeps him informed. Her name for these updates: *Another installment in the Adventures of Hank.* Mr. Ash is a recurring and popular character in Hank's adventures, the one who makes Hank the three-layered grilled cheese sandwiches for dinner, the one who brings home new sodas from all over the world. Though Mr. Ash had naturally been upset to discover that his daughter was pregnant by a foul-mouthed comedian, one who had no intention of "doing the right thing" (not that he would have been much happier if she'd done the "right thing" with Felix), Mr. Ash fully embraced his role as a grandfather. He loves Hank, and for that Felix is of course grateful.

"How's Susan doing?" Felix asks. Bet's mother has rheumatoid arthritis and recently had her knee replaced. "She back on her feet yet?"

"She's still on a cane," he says. "You should have seen what they replaced her knee with. She's a real bionic woman now. They're doing the other one after the wedding. You know, I think once this wedding hoopla is over with, Susan won't know what hit her. I don't even think she realizes yet how different things will be once Hank and Bet are out of the house."

Felix nods. Out of the house. Part of his anxiety about the wedding stems not from the fact that Bet and Hank are moving *into* JT's house but that they are moving *out of* Nick and Susan Ash's. He can't help but wonder if this change will somehow put the boy at a disadvantage.

"How far away does JT live?"

"Little less than an hour. Just outside of town. It's not going to be easy." He seems more wistful than Felix has ever seen him. He uncrosses his legs. His eyes narrow. "So, Bet tells me that show of yours is really taking off. I confess, I haven't seen it yet and I don't claim to understand half of what they put on television. But that must feel good? Some validation after all these years?"

"Sure," Felix says, "I suppose so." Though he in no way considers his success on *Pets!* a validation of all his hard work, he doesn't want to squelch that idea for Bet's father, who until this moment has never offered Felix a single encouraging word regarding his career. Early on in their relationship, after too many drinks, Mr. Ash once let it slip that he thought Felix was a silly man, not at all serious, one of those types who complained about everything but never *did* anything. "Well," Felix said to that, "I've actually considered jumping into the soda industry. I have an idea for a soda that comes in a baby bottle. Get 'em started early, right? First, though, we might have to wipe out the milk lobby."

"Do people really think you're funny?" Mr. Ash asked. "Because I don't see it."

"Honestly, I don't either," Felix said, which like all good jokes was grounded in truth. Throughout all of it—the club circuit, the bit parts here and there on bad television shows, the one-hour comedy special that almost happened but didn't—Felix's career had bumped and bounced, but it had certainly never soared. The closest he might ever come to mainstream success is as Gonuts the CGI Hamster whose most popular catchphrases are increasingly difficult to voice without feeling a little sick.

When Laura comes downstairs, finally, they leave the hotel in Mr. Ash's car. Laura sits in the front passenger seat. With the air-conditioning on full blast, Felix can't hear their conversation, but Laura is smiling and nodding quite a bit, her hands prim in her lap. *Prim* is not an adjective Felix frequently associates with Laura. *Vivacious*, maybe. *Vital. Voluptuous.* Felix is stuck on *v*'s. For the dinner she has changed into a conservative blue dress that falls just below the knee, but she still has on her giant white sunglasses.

The Ashes live in a three-story house with dark colonial shutters on all the windows and squat dome lights planted in the mulched beds on either side of a brick sidewalk that connects the circle driveway to the front door. Susan comes out first on her metal cane and gives Felix a frail hug, then hugs Laura. Bet comes outside next, a new pixie haircut, eyes bright and blue. Felix has been slightly uneasy about this moment, about introducing these two women, Bet and Laura, past and present, and he watches them examine each other surreptitiously while they make small talk, moving toward the house. Hanging behind the group for a brief moment just outside the door, Laura squeezes Felix's arm and mouths the words, *She's very young,* before moving ahead of him into the foyer.

.   .   .

Describing his relationship with Bet to others—particularly to women his own age—Felix has learned over the last few years to omit certain details. For instance, that Bet was a sophomore art history major when he impregnated her. Why mention such a thing? There is no need to vilify himself unnecessarily. She looked young then too, yes, but not *that* young, and he certainly didn't need to convince her of anything. She was a more-than-willing participant.

But there are other details he omits. For instance: He has not told Laura about what happened the winter after Hank was born—when he flew down to Atlanta for a two-week visit with his new son. He was staying in a room at the Commodore but after the first two nights, since he was already spending so much time at the house, Mrs. Ash insisted that he stay in one of their guest rooms. That way Felix could find out what it was like to rock a six-month-old back to sleep at three a.m.—a gift, she said, that no new parent should be denied. Mr. Ash, in particular, seemed giddy setting up the baby monitor in Felix's room.

"Don't worry. You'll get the hang of it," Bet said before bed. "Besides, babies are mostly math. Ounces eaten. Hours slept. You'll see."

The crying began sometime just after midnight. Felix did his duty, creeping down the hall and peering in on the little red-faced crank, who shook his tiny arms like they were meant for flight. Felix hoisted him out of the crib and nestled down in the rocking chair across the room, humming a little Van Morrison. The Van

Morrison worked nicely. Hank calmed down, his eyes heavy again, but when Felix tried to deliver him back down into the crib, Hank went off like a car alarm.

"There's a trick to it," Bet said, small face in the door. Felix wasn't sure how long she'd been watching him. "Do what you were doing before."

He sat back down in the rocking chair and started humming the horn section of "Into the Mystic." Bet, in a loose and ghostly nightgown, hovered near the crib. When Hank quieted down again, she motioned for Felix to bring him over. At the crib, she told him to blow gently on Hank's face while lowering him down.

"Really?"

She nodded and smiled. He blew gently, and Hank's nose scrunched up like he might sneeze. But when his butt hit the blanket, he actually stayed quiet. In the hallway, Felix asked her what that was all about.

"I have no idea why it works, but it does. I figured it out by mistake." She blew gently in Felix's face. "Feels nice, right?"

He kissed her. Later he wouldn't remember what exactly had prompted him to do it. Maybe it was her blowing in his face. Maybe it was a quick but powerful feeling that all of this was theirs—this baby, this life, this house, this night-light shining around their bare feet. She pulled him into her bedroom, next door to the baby's. She lifted her gown and stretched back on the bed. He kept his feet on the floor and leaned toward her, arms on either side of her shoulders. It was different from their first time at the hotel, almost a year earlier—less hurried, less boozy—and as he finished, he said it, or something like it, *like* or *love* or, the old Annie Hall joke, *luff*. But then again, maybe he hadn't. He might have only sighed pleasantly. No, he'd certainly said *something*. He kissed her on the shoulder and said he should probably get back to his room. "Okay," she said.

The next morning, at breakfast, he avoided eye contact with all of them. The Ash family whirled around the kitchen, dishes clattering as they unloaded the washer, discussing plans for the day, a Saturday, and Bet breast-fed Hank at the table. Watching the three of them, Felix felt like an intruder. He had an impulse to run, but he finished his cereal and then showered, whistling in the steam.

They spent the day Christmas shopping. In the car, Mr. Ash asked Felix if he even believed in Jesus, and Felix said, "Jesus . . . Jesus . . . didn't he drum for the Beatles before Ringo?" Mrs. Ash looked back at Felix scandalized. "Sorry," Felix said. At the mall, he wandered through a toy store alone with Hank, who seemed to like the lights and colors and not much else. Then they went to find Bet and discovered her in the neighboring department store, checking the tag on a mannequin's jacket.

"You like it?" she asked. "I think I could wear it in the spring."

"Let's see it on you." With Hank gurgling in his arms and Bet wrestling the jacket off the mannequin, Felix forgot, just for a moment, that this wasn't his everyday existence. She bought the jacket, and they strolled through the mall together, like any other couple, hands on the stroller.

That night she snuck into his room after her parents were asleep and climbed into bed. On the monitor they could hear Hank breathing through the fuzz of static. She was on top of him, and he certainly wasn't resisting. "You okay?" she asked. He wasn't sure what to make of that and shrugged up at her: yes, he was okay. When they finished, she fell asleep on his arm and didn't wake up again until Hank started crying in the early hours, milky light in strips across the bedspread.

In all, this happened three more times before Felix flew home. She would sneak into his room and stay until Hank's first morning fit. She did this without ever asking what it meant or where it was leading. Each time, afterward, Felix felt more agitated, as if the stakes were that much higher, though he tried not to show it. What was he doing? Possibly he cared for her more than he'd realized. He began to doubt his initial decision to stay on the West Coast. He even entertained notions of bringing her back West with him. His apartment would be too small for both Hank and Bet, but he could find something more suitable. If he really wanted to, he could make this work, couldn't he? When Bet drove him to the airport, she gave him a short kiss and asked him to text when his plane landed.

"Maybe you and Hank could come and visit me sometime," he said, and when she nodded, he added, "To see how you like it out there."

Had he been too subtle? Not subtle enough? He couldn't tell. Her cheeks were pink and she smiled uncertainly. "Okay," she said.

On the flight home, he tried watching a movie but couldn't concentrate. He folded the vomit bag into tinier and tinier squares. He drank three whiskey-and-sodas. The woman sitting beside him asked if he was feeling all right. Felix wasn't sure. "I used to be the same way," the woman said. "Have you ever listened to the black box recording from a plane crash? Don't. They're all on the Internet. It's addictive. It always ends one of three ways. It's either *Oh, God* or *Oh, shit* or *Oh, no, the flaps!* Religion, panic, or blame.

Every time I fly now, I think, *Well, that's it. So long, farewell. There's no possible way I'm going to survive this.*"

"There are worse ways," he said. But really, every flight felt like a little death. What died was the place you were leaving and the person you'd been there. The more distance between him and Atlanta, the less real it all seemed to him—the Ashes, Hank, Bet, all of it. The only inescapable constant was himself: miserable, unfunny Felix.

Waiting for his suitcase at the baggage claim back in Los Angeles, he called Bet's cell despite the time difference.

"Hey," she said, surprisingly not groggy.

"I'm here and—" His bag approached. "And that's it, I guess. I'm here now."

"Good," she said. "I'm glad. Hank already misses you." She cleared her throat, and he could hear a door close. "Listen, Felix, I've been thinking. About what happened this week. Going forward, I don't think we should complicate things, you know?"

Felix grabbed his bag and wheeled it back and forth across the baggage claim floor as Bet explained all the reasons why it didn't make sense for them to be together. She had no intention of leaving Atlanta, and though she'd always care for Felix, she wouldn't love him, not like that. When she asked him what he thought, he said that, yes, well, she was absolutely right, it would never work. Only later—weeks later, trying to recall Bet's exact tone during this conversation—would he wonder if it had been some sort of test. Regardless, they didn't discuss it again. Whether Bet had told her parents about what had happened between them, Felix couldn't be sure, but they never offered him a guest room again. After that, he began staying exclusively at the hotel.

· · ·

Hank comes stomping down the stairs after an especially long afternoon nap, looking a little bit like a high Shakespearean actor: red tights, wild brown hair, eyes a tad droopy. Felix holds out his arms for a hug, a little worried that he is about to be rebuffed in front of Laura and Bet and the Ashes. JT, who is apparently a master chef, is in the kitchen preparing a "gourmet" dinner. Hank launches off the bottom step and lands in Felix's arms. Felix spins his son's legs out like a helicopter. They all file into the living room for an early round of cocktails—vodka tonic for Laura, screwdriver for Bet, whiskey for Felix and Mr. Ash, and a seltzer for Mrs. Ash, who rarely drinks any alcohol aside from white Zinfandel. They sit in a rough circle, encamped on various pieces of antique furniture: a green leather sofa, the two wingback chairs, the ottoman under the flatscreen on the wall.

"Lovely house," Laura says, taking it all in. "Bet, won't you be sad to leave in a few months?"

"I will," she says, and squeezes her father's arm thoughtfully. "But I've been imposing long enough. It's not fair to my parents."

"We've loved every minute of it," Mr. Ash says.

Felix wonders if it is guilt—for living off her parents, for delivering chaos into their otherwise peaceful golden years—that is pushing Bet toward a man like JT. Her fiancé seems nice enough and is even mildly handsome in a second-place-homecoming-king sort of way, but he is certainly no genius; his face doesn't suggest much depth. Felix begins inventing a quiz: What book is on JT's nightstand? Can he name the last ten presidents in order? Who was responsible for 9/11? Though Felix won't be able to explicitly call it a test, that's what it will be. Over the course of the evening, he will have to sneak in his questions and keep track.

"So," Felix says to Bet, "how long has JT been your rug man?"

Laura gives Felix's hand two quick squeezes.

"His dad started the business," Bet says. "It's pretty big. They've got three offices now across the state, and contracts with most of the school districts. He's been doing it ever since he graduated."

"Ph.D. in red wine and bloodstain removal?"

(Another squeeze.)

"Come see my treehouse," Hank says, eyes on Felix.

"I'd love to, buddy," he says.

"I'd like to see it too, Hank," Laura says. She stands with her drink and holds out her hand. Hank eyes it suspiciously, so Felix takes it and then offers Hank his other hand. Through the white French doors, they walk out across a brick patio and down the steps into a neatly manicured lush backyard. Hank breaks free and runs down the hill to a grove of slim oak trees, between which, about five feet up, Mr. Ash has constructed a platform. A rope ladder dangles from a hole at its center. Red tights a jostling blur, Hank ascends the swinging ladder and emerges gopherlike on the other side of the hole triumphantly.

"He's very cute," she says. "Are we going up?"

"I'm fine down here. You look great, buddy. What do you do up there?"

The boy scrunches his eyebrows. "Different stuff."

They watch him kick some brush off the edge of the platform.

"So," Laura says quietly. "Bet."

"Bet."

"I can see what attracted you to her. She's beautiful. And young."

"You're not going to get weird on me, are you?"

"How exactly would I get *weird* on you?"

"I don't know, but the way you just said *weird* felt a little weird to me."

Laura adjusts her sunglasses and crosses her arms. "I'm curious if sometimes when you say things you ever hear a little alarm bell in the back of your head? Whoop whoop whoop. Do you ever think, *Am I saying what I think I'm saying?*"

"Alarm bells? I don't follow. What I say is what I mean. Or what I mean is what—"

"I think you need to take a deep breath and process what's happening this weekend. Here's something good. Actually, you know, I'll just skip to the bad, if that's all right. Don't take this the wrong way, but not everything is about you. Not everything is about Felix. There are seven billion people in the world, and sure, you're funnier than most of them—you're in the top three thousand, probably, but—"

"Three thousand?"

"Two thousand, whatever. It doesn't matter. My point is that you need to pull your head out of your ass. You get me?"

Felix does not get her. Is she calling him selfish? Self-involved? Delusional? He is ready to argue, but here comes Hank, singing and swinging back down the ladder, his business concluded, whatever it was, the rope swishing circles in the dirt at the bottom.

"Before we go back inside," Laura says, "is there anything else I should know?"

"Maybe," Felix says, irritable. "Probably, yes, there is, but I can't for the life of me figure out what it might be. How far back should I go?"

"This isn't funny," Laura says.

What else is new? They are almost to the brick patio when the entire family emerges through the double doors.

"All of us are going for a walk before dinner," Bet announces. "It's been decided."

The first person to bring up Gonuts the Hamster is JT. He's not only seen the show but is in fact a humongous fan and tunes in every Thursday night. They are on a wide and mulchy trail that follows the conservation easement behind all the houses in the neighborhood. JT and Laura stroll alongside Felix. Bet and the Ashes are a few steps ahead. Hank is between both packs dragging a stick he found in the brush.

JT wants more details about *Pets!*, he wants behind-the-scenes dirt. Some of the people at his work, JT says, are in love with the Rhesus Monkey on the show, the one that's always stealing and swallowing important things like zip drives and legal papers and car keys. Does Felix ever get to hang out with the monkey? Is it funny in real life too? Who is the voice of the monkey, because that dude deserves a frickin Oscar—

"Emmy," Felix says. "And the guy's name is Joel. He's been in a few things over the years but not much. You're right, he's great."

JT nods enthusiastically. He asks if Felix could do the hamster voice for everyone, just once, and then he'll never ask again. He promises.

Through his pocket Felix pinches the hamster (his leg) until it throbs: "Somebody better let me outta this cage," he says, forming a little bubble in the back of his throat. "'Cause I'm about to get wheel on these motherfuckers."

Everyone, except JT, turns to shoot Felix the same look: *Hank*.

"Amazing," JT says. "Amazing. It's so surreal to hear that voice coming out of you. Now, you couldn't say that on television, could you? You couldn't say *mother-f*?"

"What book is on your nightstand right now, JT?" Felix asks him. "I'm curious."

"People recognize Felix's voice everywhere we go," Laura says. "We were out to eat the other night, and the waiter figured it out. But he didn't say anything to us. He just drew a little hamster wheel on our check. It was so cute."

"That's really funny," Bet says. "You're famous, Felix!"

"Or at least your voice is," Mr. Ash says.

"What's the difference?" Felix asks. "I am my voice, aren't I?"

"I don't know," Mr. Ash says, without turning around. "Are you your anus?"

Their footsteps are quiet on the mulch. It's like all the sound has been sucked out of the universe. Where are all the birds? There should be birds whistling up in the trees. Felix is on the verge of saying something, can feel words inching up his tongue. What he will say, exactly, he can't be sure, but most definitely it will be the wrong thing.

"In my experience some people are more anal than others," Laura says then, eyebrows arched.

A short burst of laughter, like gunfire, escapes Mr. Ash's tight gray mouth. Felix has never seen him laugh that way. Not once.

"What's *anal*?" Hank asks.

"It has to do with your bum-bum," Bet explains, a nervous smile. "Hank, that reminds me, do you want to tell your daddy about what happened with the frog and the sprinkler? Remember that?"

Hank nods yes, that he remembers, but then he mutters, no, he doesn't really want to tell that story.

"Oh, come on, Hanky," JT calls up to him. "It's such a funny one."

Hank doesn't look up from his feet.

"Honey, don't ignore people when they're talking to you," Bet says. "It's rude. Tell your dad the frog and sprinkler story."

"Don't be afraid," Mrs. Ash says, head turned back. "You can do it, Hank. Remember how it starts? With us turning on the sprinkler?"

The boy throws his stick into the woods, eyes still on his feet.

"Hank," Mr. Ash says, clearly irritated. "Hank, your mother and Grammy are *talking* to you."

"It's okay," Felix says, suddenly aware of all those eyes sharply focused on his little boy. He imagines Hank, half asleep, being led downstairs night after night to a room full of strange squawking dinner guests, all of them demanding he tell the one about the frog and the sprinkler. He imagines these people laughing, and Hank not knowing what it was he said, *exactly* said, that made them laugh so much. Even if it was the funniest frog story since Mark Twain's jumping frog, Felix does not want Hank to have to tell it against his will. "Leave him be."

"But I want you to hear it," Bet says. They've stopped walking now. Through the trees other backyards are visible—trampolines and garden beds, a swimming pool.

"Hank, no one is forcing you to tell the story," Felix says, leaning toward his son, whose eyes are still trained downward. "It's totally up to you. Maybe later you'll want to tell me, or maybe you won't. Either way is fine. Okay, buddy?"

"Remember what happened when the frog landed on the sprinkler?" JT asks. "What happened when we—"

"Drop it," Felix says, looking hard at JT. "Didn't you hear me? Lay off him. Can't you see he doesn't want to tell it?"

"All right, calm down, no need to be an ass about it, Felix," Mr. Ash says.

Felix digs the heel of his shoe into the dirt. Here it comes: the wrong thing, welling up in him. "Nick, if I want your opinion, I'll ask for it."

"Enough," Mr. Ash says.

"Enough what?"

"Enough everything."

"Does anyone know the story about the old man's asshole and the sprinkler?" Felix asks. "'Cause that's a really good one."

"Not appropriate," Bet says.

"You don't have to be here, Felix," Mr. Ash says. "No one said you had to come this weekend. You chose to come."

"Daddy, that's not going to help anything," Bet says.

"Yes, Daddy, you're not helping," Felix says.

"Felix," Laura whispers. "Stop."

Hank looks at all of them, confused. Felix pivots and starts back for the house. They aren't far from the house, maybe three hundred yards. He can feel their eyes on his back. Along the trail, at the top of long metal poles, are wooden bird boxes. If he shook one, would a bird fly out? Only now does he remember that he has no rental car back at the house in which to make his retreat. He'll have to wait for someone to give him a lift back to the hotel. More than anything he does not want to turn back around and ask to borrow a car. The ability to run away: it's part of what makes one an adult. Laura catches up with him, her eyes wide.

"I apologized for you," she says.

"I didn't want to apologize."

"Never hurts to apologize."

They walk fast over the trail and then turn left into the Ashes' backyard. If he continued walking, maybe Laura would agree to wait and ask to borrow a car. She could pick him up down the road.

But Hank. Shit, he never said goodbye to Hank. He could leave something for the boy, a gift of some kind, something that would communicate how sorry he is for bailing like this. He fishes around in his pockets and finds his keys. On the ring he has a small metal hamster trinket, a gift from the network when the show started its second season. Felix spots the treehouse. He could hide it for him up there, as a surprise. The rope ladder stretches when he steps onto the bottom rung, bringing it all the way to the ground. It bucks as he climbs, his feet swinging ahead of him.

"What are you doing?" Laura asks.

"Just give me a minute," he says, head and shoulders through the opening now. He barely fits. When his butt clears the jagged and splintery circle, he sits back and admires the new view of the yard. Laura looks up at him, her arms crossed like a none-too-satisfied audience member. Spread across the platform are the corpses of mangled action figures. A small white bucket near one of the tree ballasts contains a dozen rotten crab apples. Felix doesn't have any paper for a note. He takes out a pen and looks for a suitable place to write a message.

"You don't have to go." It's Bet, calling up to him. She's standing beside Laura on the ground. "If you really want to, I'll take you. But I think for Hank's sake you should both stay. But Felix, please, take a walk or something. Get yourself together. You've been acting strange ever since you got here. And what's this about the rubber snakes?"

So JT told her. That makes sense. They are together now, a real couple, and naturally they will share such information. They will talk about people, judge them. Felix is one of those people. He is someone for them to discuss, to judge.

"I don't think Felix meant anything by the snakes," Laura says to Bet.

"JT was pretty sure Felix was calling him"—her voice drops to a whisper—"a racist."

"It wasn't like that," Laura says. "Not exactly. Don't get me wrong, I'm not excusing Felix. You're right. It was very poorly put."

Felix watches them talk.

"I'm sorry about the snake thing," he says. "I am. And yes, you're right, we should probably stay. For Hank. I can hang up here for a while and cool off. Go eat dinner. I'll eat mine up here. I'll come in for dessert. What's for dessert? It's not your mother's pecan pie, is it?"

He begins etching Hank's name into the wood beside his knee. He has to drag the pen back and forth, against the grain, to make the ink visible. The others emerge from the woods, and Bet tells them all to go inside and wait there.

"You should send him packing," Mr. Ash says quietly, though not inaudibly, to his daughter before Mrs. Ash drags him off toward the house.

"Sorry about the snake thing," Felix says as JT passes.

"All right," JT says, and keeps walking.

The rope ladder shakes. A small head emerges. It's Hank—small, wonderful Hank up in the treehouse—the red tights stretched thin and transparent at the knees and toes, a somber expression on his face.

"What's up, buddy?" Felix asks. "I'm not leaving. Don't worry. The adults were just having . . . an adult moment."

Hank gazes down at the half-finished *H* in the wood beside Felix's knee.

"The frog," Hank says, and sighs deeply. "It died."

Felix smiles. He can't help it.

"Honey, that's not the best way to tell the story," Bet says, from below, and then appeals to Felix. "I mean, the frog *did* die, he's right, but it's not as bad as all that. The other way he tells it is actually funny."

But it is funny. Can't they see that? That no one is laughing is proof of that. It is beyond laughter. The frog died. Bah-dah-dum. End of frog. Oh, shit. Oh, God. Oh, flaps: Which was it for the frog? The boy looks up at him thoughtfully, with what Felix wants to interpret as an expression of mutual understanding. He stands and lifts his son off the platform into a high, soaring hug. "You told it perfect," Felix says. "I'll bet that frog never saw it coming."

Hank's little arms give Felix a squeeze. The boy's red legs dangle loose at first but then begin bicycling wildly, ready to touch back down on the platform. "Let go," Hank says, squirming, but Felix resists. He's not ready to let go just yet. If he does, those little red feet might carry the boy away at a tremendous speed. Laura and Bet watch from below. Bet has her hands out like she thinks Hank and Felix might both come tumbling down off the platform. "Careful," she says. "Please."

"You told a good one," Felix says, and sets his son down gently. The boy smooths out his shirt. "Let's talk about these tights. What's going on? And where can I get myself a pair?"

Hank walks to the platform's edge and steps off. Shit. God. But no, the fall is barely five feet, and Hank is fine. It seems that he does this all the time. He lands on all fours, cat-like, then sprints across the yard. Bet follows him up to the house. Felix approaches the brink, gazes down at the patchy grass. "I guess I'll jump down too," he says to Laura.

"Your choice," she says, "but don't ask me to take you to the emergency room when you break your ankle. I won't do it." She turns for the house without him and climbs the grassy hill to the patio door. Felix takes out his pen and finishes the *H* and then lays the metal hamster there beside it, a terrible gift. But he's still here, in Atlanta, and he has more time to make it up to the boy. He considers the distance to the ground, which really isn't so far, just a few measly feet. The yard is quiet and empty now. A bright glare across all the windows on the first floor of the house makes it impossible to tell if there's anyone left to watch him drop.

Videos of People
Falling Down

How NOT to Ride Down Stairs HUGE FALL

A boy with floppy brown hair and freckled arms pedals his mountain bike toward some concrete steps outside of a high school. There are twenty-five steps, and they lead down to the teacher's lot. The boy's friends are waiting at the bottom to see what happens. When he reaches the first step, he leans back in his seat to keep from toppling over the handlebars. His name is Davy, and he can draw a hand perfectly. Nobody draws a hand like Davy. His art teacher wants him to apply to art schools next year. She believes one day Davy will draw not only a perfect hand but also a perfect wrist and a perfect arm and, if he is diligent, a perfect shoulder too. Beyond that she dares not hope. Necks are the most beautiful part of the female body, and no one has ever captured one as it really is.

The art teacher possesses a neck more elegant than most. If it wasn't indecent, she'd pose for Davy. At the moment of his stunt, she is locking up her room, a box of school-bought art supplies under her arm. She doesn't see Davy fall, but she's the first adult on the scene. Davy is conscious, on his back across the bottom three steps. She orders him not to move an inch. The bone has punctured the pale skin of his left arm. She calls the ambulance and follows it all the way to the hospital in her beat-up Acura. In the emergency room, she finds a seat beside a big man whose leg is wrapped in a bloody towel. The teenager to her right doesn't cover his mouth when he coughs. She flips through a *Golf Digest*. The old woman across from her is reading a novel with bees on the cover. "What happens in it?" she asks the woman, and the woman says, "Two beekeepers fall in love but it's impossible for them to be together."

Old Woman FALLS into Polar Bear Habitat

The book about beekeepers is *Now a Major Motion Picture* starring Julia Roberts. "Swimming," one of the songs on its sound track, has become very popular on the radio. The song was written and performed by Simon Punch, a whisper-voiced guitarist with a hip Rasputin beard and a long thumbnail painted black, and the lyrics are based on something that happened to him as a boy at the zoo with his grandmother.

They were watching two polar bears paddle around in a clear blue pool when she leaned too far over the concrete wall for a photograph and fell eight feet down into the water. Simon was too young to do anything but watch as she splashed and screamed, scraping at the wall like a lunatic. A crowd formed. A man dangled his jacket down to her and she grabbed hold of it. Because she wasn't strong enough to hold on for very long she kept plunking back down into the water. A lady who worked for the zoo ran over with a bucket and tossed fish parts into the pit to keep the polar bears distracted, but one of the bears lunged and bit his grandmother's leg. When she finally emerged over the concrete wall—dripping wet, bleeding, embarrassed—they ripped away her pants and discovered that the bite wound, thank God, wasn't life-threatening. Still, all these years later, Simon sometimes dreams about polar bears. They come after him with impossibly large teeth and suffocative fur. They chase him down streets and up stairs—to the perimeter of his dreams. When he wakes he can feel their chilly wet breath on his neck.

Stupid People Falling Ouch Try Not to Laugh

A man is on his way to meet a friend for a late drink and stops at an ATM for some cash. His wallet is ridiculously fat—not with cash but with movie stubs, wads of receipts that he will never actually sort, a photo of his wife, a photo of his long-dead basset hound, and all his cards: the Anthem insurance card, the library card, the one-year pass to the contemporary art museum, and of course his many credit cards. The bank is closed for the night. The lights are off in the main lobby. The ATM is not directly on the street but in a small glass anteroom. Accessing it after hours requires that you slide your bank card into the slot by the door.

The man inserts his card, and a tiny light above it flashes red three times. He inserts his card again and pulls it back out more deliberately. The light blinks red again.

His name is Marshall, and he manages a nearby stationery shop. He is also an accomplished cellist. He is third chair in the city symphony. His favorite composer is Brahms. Sometimes when he hears Hungarian Dance No. 5 he has a funny feeling that is difficult to explain to others. He's told only one or two people about it. The feeling involves the possibility of a past life.

Through the thick bulletproof glass, faintly, Marshall can hear music playing—not Brahms but something else. It's that Simon Punch song, he realizes, the one from the Julia Roberts movie about beekeepers. He consults the pictogram on the card reader to make sure his card was properly oriented. He rubs the magnetic strip back and forth across his pleated khakis to make sure it wasn't dirty and then he inserts it again. The red light flashes. Maybe something is wrong with the reader or with the ATM behind the glass. Maybe it's out of order and the bank forgot to hang up a sign. A woman with jangly gold earrings approaches with clacking cowboy boots.

"Let me guess," she says. "Broken?"

"Might be," he says, and steps aside so she can try her own card.

Her card is silver. She slides it in the slot and pulls it back out hard and fast, and when it flashes red, she does it again, hard and fast. Marshall can't help drawing certain conclusions about this woman. He pictures the woman naked and on top. The light flashes red, red, red.

"What a piece of shit," she says. The woman looks to be in her forties. She taps the bottom of the door with her stiff boot toe. She has on way too much mascara. It's like her eyes are at the back of a dark cave. "There's another machine around the corner outside a liquor store," she says, "but it'll charge you a hundred dollars practically."

"If it's broken, they should have put out a sign," he says.

"I only need like ten dollars."

If he had ten dollars, Marshall would give it to her. They stand there, peering through the glass for a few more moments, the traffic moving lazily behind them on the street. Marshall imagines throwing something at the glass, shattering it, the two of them stepping through together triumphantly.

The woman pushes at the door without sliding in her card at all. It opens, magically. The red light was meaningless; the room was unlocked all along. They roll their eyes at each other: *Of course it was open!* She goes in first, and he waves her toward the machine. He says, "Be my guest."

"I'll be quick," she says. He waits a few feet behind her. This isn't a large space, and he could see her screen if he wanted. When the ATM spits out the woman's money, she turns to him and holds up her receipt, victorious.

She leaves, and Marshall inserts his card, punches in his number, and selects the fast cash option. The machine buzzes and the money pops out and the receipt curls toward him. He checks it quickly, then looks again. His account balance, it's very low. Thousands of dollars are missing.

Susan. This has to be Susan's doing. She recently moved out. "Temporarily," she said. It was a total shock. Sure, they argued—about the way he drags his feet when he walks, about who it was that forgot to recork the red wine before bed—but this made them no different from any other couple.

Susan said she was going to stay at her sister's place, but he suspects his wife has a lover. That's the only way to explain it.

When Marshall called Susan's sister, she said Susan was in the bathroom, but when his wife returned his call later that night it was from her cell phone and there was strange dance music in the background. She was at some kind of party, obviously drunk, and all she wanted to talk about were tiny chairs. She could barely hear him. She wasn't answering his questions. It was infuriating.

"Enough with the Brahms," his wife used to say.

Many years ago he told his wife how he feels hearing Hungarian Dance No. 5, about that hazy cloud that descends, about the cascade of images both familiar and unfamiliar, a long dusty street, a distant flat mountain, ships on a waterfront, white horses and carriages, a ten-story hotel with ornate columns and a large gold clock in the lobby, a bag over his shoulder, a beautiful woman in a maid's outfit, a bustling kitchen, a pantry with white shelves full of food, the light sneaking under the door, the woman's dress raised high, her legs spreading to receive him, the flour spilling onto their shoulders, her breath hot in his ear. "That's not a past life," his wife told him, "that's historical porno."

Marshall examines the receipt as he turns away from the ATM. His wife, who hasn't even collected all her clothes from their closet yet, has basically robbed him. He can think of no other word for it. She's stolen his money; she's going to strange tiny chair parties; she's sleeping in another man's bed.

Marshall has forgotten that he is enclosed by glass. When he runs into the glass wall, it doesn't shatter or crack—but wobbles. He falls back onto the floor. One palm lands on the greasy white tile, the other on the dark rubber mat with the bank's insignia. The receipt is on the ground in front of him. There's a tiny camera in the ATM and another security camera looking down on him from the top right corner of the room.

Edison Kinetoscopic Record of a Man Falling Down

Among Thomas Edison's earliest films you will find footage of zooming trains, electrocuted elephants, boxing cats, and a snuff-induced sneeze. Surely an early documentation of a falling man comes as no surprise. There had to be a first. The footage is grainy, and the frames skip. The man is one of Edison's assistants. Until they tripped him with a wire, he was under the impression they were making a film called *Edison Kinetoscopic Record of a Man Jumping Up and Down*. Falling down has never been the same. Now we can watch the same fall a hundred times. We can laugh at it. We can study it. We can slow it down. We can speed it up. We can linger on a single frame. We can see the birth of fear and panic in a human face. We can identify that moment when a person suddenly realizes that he is no longer in control of what happens next. But the simple truth is that we are never in control of what happens next.

Falling down is the universe being honest with you, finally. It's life as it really is.

This occurs to Marshall as he walks home from the bank, his plans canceled, an ugly bump already bulging on his forehead. His wife is out for the night, no doubt, probably having the time of her life with all their money, and he will spend the rest of his evening with a bag of frozen peas pressed to his head, like an idiot. He feels like throwing a rock at the canoodling couple across the street. He wants to kick the cat that darts across his feet on the stoop. That airplane overhead, the little flashing dot of light, he wishes it would come crashing down out of the sky and just put him out of his misery, kaboom.

People Falling on Snow/Ice Funny!!!

Twenty-two thousand feet overhead, Beth is on her way out West. When her seatmate leans toward her and says his name is Randolph, she laughs.

"What's so funny?" he wants to know.

"Nothing," she says, embarrassed, hand rising to her mouth. She's never been the giggly sort. Her father used to call her his Gloomy Little Mac-Beth. She wonders if it's possible her seatmate is having this effect on her. "I'm just excited," she says. "That's all. I drank too much water or something. Maybe it's the air pressure."

The man has a white linen pocket square in his sports coat and some kind of gel product in his brown hair that makes it shine. He's in the window seat and he has his shoes off, one socked tumescence rubbing the other. She tries not to examine his feet. Through the porthole the darkness is interrupted every few seconds by the flashing bulbs on the wing. Sometimes the wings appear to wobble, a fact she finds very disconcerting.

"Let me guess," Randolph says. "A ski trip."

"Snowboarding, actually," she says. The trip is an early graduation gift from her mother. Beth is meeting a friend at the airport. In a few months Beth will have her B.A. in sociology. Her thesis is a case study of frequent-flier programs. According to her laptop's Find function, the term *sociotechnical* appears in her paper seventy-three times. Though she has studied frequent-flier programs, Beth does not belong to any herself. She doesn't find this fact ironic, as she has flown maybe three times in her entire life, present flight included.

"I do development," the man says. "For a children's hospital."

She nods politely, too politely, and the man unloads about the latest capital campaign, how they're trying to raise $5.2 million, and how he's close to getting it—so, so close. Fingers crossed he's lined up a very famous actor to help raise the last few million. She asks him what actor, and he says he shouldn't reveal that yet, but then nuzzles close and whispers, *Skeet Ulrich*. "I'm sorry," she says, "who?" He gives her a wounded look.

When the plane lands, they stand up too early, together, and have to hunch beneath the bins. "Well, it was nice to meet you," she says when they start to move, but then there's another delay, and he says, "We're never going to get out of here, are we?"

"There must be some kind of way out of—" she says but doesn't finish the lyric because the line is moving again.

They part ways in the terminal, but she sees him again at baggage claim. Before wheeling away his roller suitcase, he tips an imaginary top hat to her. When her bag shows up, Beth takes a bus to the rental car office. Amy, her friend since grade school, is already there with the keys. The drive to the resort is almost two hours. They talk about the end of school and the drugs they've never tried but might still and all their friends who are already engaged and how statistically at least three of those friends will be divorced within five years. They eat gross fast food on the way into town, and by the time they check in to their condo, it's after ten but feels more like one a.m.

The next morning, amazingly, she spots Randolph at the bottom of a slope. She taps him on the shoulder and says, "Good morning, seatmate."

"What are the chances?" he says. "I'm surprised you recognized me in this getup."

His sunglasses are up high on his forehead. He wants to catch the next lift with her: then, he says, they can be *liftmates* too. The joke seems to embarrass him. Beth doesn't know where Amy is, but they don't have plans to meet up, until later at the lodge for lunch. "Sure," she says, "why not? I can do another run."

They ride the lift together to the top of the mountain, the metal parts creaking, their legs dangling over the white. "See you at the bottom," he says at the top and shoves off with his poles. He skis very fast. He might be showing off for her. She has trouble keeping up with him on the snowboard, cutting back and forth through the powdery snow, but she tries her best. She's moving faster than she ever has before. *I'm a gazelle,* she thinks. *I'm a gazelle gazelle gazelle . . .* She's moving so fast she can hardly hold on to that one simple thought. She almost collides with another snowboarder but she doesn't fall on the slope.

Her fall comes later in the evening as she and Randolph—still together—are descending a short wooden staircase outside one of his favorite restaurants in town. The steps are icy. She comes down on her right knee and right side. Her jeans are wet and grimy now. Possibly her foot is broken. As Randolph helps her stand, his arm under her arm, she sees a kid across the street in a lime green parka, his cell phone's camera eye aimed directly at her.

"Try walking on it," Randolph says. "Just walk a little."

She hobbles around in a circle. It's not as bad as she thought it was. It might just be a sprain. She has her arm draped over his shoulder now. They go inside together. He's made a reservation for two. After sharing a dessert, both of them a little tipsy from the wine, he confesses that Randolph is actually his *middle* name, and if she'd rather, she can call him Arnie.

"Hello, Arnie," she says, and giggles again. "I'm sorry. I don't know why I'm laughing. I'm not usually like this. I'm not. I think it's possible that I've been overserved. Is that possible? I've lost track."

Funniest Thing You Ever Seen—Drunk Guy in Convenience Store

Lots of people fall down drunk.

Marshall, the cellist, is in the 7-Eleven next door to the stationery shop that he manages. It's a little after midnight. The bump on his forehead healed a few days ago, but his wife, Susan, hasn't been home in all that time. She won't even return his calls about the missing money. He roams the aisles in search of snacks and cheap wine, dragging his feet, in a daze. He slips in front of the fridges.

"You all right?" the cashier asks, worried he might have left a puddle with the mop, worried about a lawsuit.

The cellist grabs the fridge door and pulls himself off the sticky floor.

"Where's the Big League Chew?" he asks.

The cashier points to the next aisle. Marshall hasn't chewed any Big League chewing gum since he was in grade school. He buys two pouches of it and takes it home. He sits at the kitchen table alone, tucking grape strands between his gums and bottom lip. He puts on a record.

The gum doesn't taste at all like he remembers it, and Susan is never coming back home. He drags all her clothes out of their closet, wire hangers bouncing across the carpet, and dumps them on the bed with the intention of bagging them for donation. Near midnight he wakes up, sprawled across a mountain of her dresses and sweaters, his lower back throbbing. He swallows a few chalky white ibuprofens in front of the bathroom mirror and calls Susan's sister again.

"Stop leaving messages here," she says. "I refuse to be a part of this. I refuse to be the go-between."

"Just put her on the phone," he says. "Please."

"I'm not going in there. No way."

"Going in where? Is she with someone?"

She takes a deep breath. "Marshall, let's not do this. Besides, it was more hers than yours anyway, wasn't it?"

"What was more hers?" he asks—the money or the marriage? But she's hung up. Marshall, groggy, digs for his pants under all Susan's clothes. He grabs his fat wallet off the dresser. He's halfway down the block when he realizes he's forgotten his keys and locked himself out.

Funny Blooper TV News

A reporter for CNA29 News stands in front of the camera with her microphone, preparing for a live stand-up. Her bangs are like cartoon puffs of blond smoke, and she's wearing a teal jacket with brass buttons and monstrous shoulder pads. Behind her, across the street, is a blue two-story house. All around it a maze of yellow police tape wraps through the lean pine trees.

A man was murdered in the house last night. Jealous lover situation, one officer said earlier. At this point there is very little to report about the murder but because it occurred in a nice part of town the reporter's producer thought they should probably cover the story anyway. Why she needs to introduce her story live in front of the house, the reporter isn't quite sure. It feels indecent somehow.

She never used to flub her lines but lately she's been having issues—skipping words, mixing up clauses. Once upon a time her producer called her One-Take Tammy, but she's been so distracted recently. She shouldn't even be here, she realizes, but at the hospital with her mother. "I'll haunt you forever if I die in this hospital alone," her mother said yesterday. Why would any mother say such a thing to her daughter?

When she was growing up, her mother was always bringing around different boyfriends. When Tammy was sixteen, one of the boyfriends lumbered into her room around midnight. He climbed into her bed and grabbed hold of her, and when Tammy squirmed loose and flipped on the lights, the boyfriend pretended to have been confused about which door was which. If Tammy's mother dies, so much will have gone unsaid between them. Tammy should be the one haunting *her*.

Last night Tammy slept in the hideous recliner beside her mother's hospital bed. Around two a.m. her mother turned on the television.

"What are you doing?" Tammy asked. "You need to be sleeping."

"I would if I could," her mother said. She flipped through the channels and stopped on a home shopping network. Tammy swiveled her chair toward the television. They watched a woman model some clip-on earrings. The woman looked a little bit like Tammy in the face, her mother pointed out, "Just around the nose. Don't you think?" Tammy didn't answer that. The woman on the television had an ugly little snub nose.

Tammy couldn't get back to sleep after that. They watched prices for more clip-on earrings flash onto the screen, and then they watched a bald man with a thin mustache show off a vacuum that could suck up wet stains.

"That could come in use around here," Tammy said, and patted the end of the bed.

"Ha. Ha. Ha," her mother said.

When the nurse came into the room, around four a.m., her mother asked Tammy to leave the room for a minute.

"What for?"

"Because I need to ask the nurse something in private."

"Mom, don't be silly."

"You can come back in a few minutes."

"Fine," Tammy said, "I need to get going anyway." She grabbed her overnight bag out of the closet and left the hospital. On the drive home she stopped by a coffee shop for lattes to go. Billy was just waking up when she came into the bedroom and stepped out of her shoes and shimmied out of her underwear in front of the closet. She went into the bathroom for a shower. He followed her in to sit on the toilet lid and drink the latte she'd brought him.

"You want to talk about it?" he asked.

She said she didn't. The steam curled over the shower curtain rod. The vanilla bar soap, from a farmers' market, turned to goop in her hands. Billy stripped down and stepped into the shower with a hard-on.

"Not now," she said. "Tonight maybe."

"Just because I have an erection, doesn't mean I'm asking for sex."

She laughed and left him in the shower. She got to work early but then fell asleep with her head on her desk. The supervising producer came in to nudge her awake. She'd missed the morning editorial meeting. He gave her the assignment.

"But listen," he said. "You don't have to go. Take a few more days. Go be with your mother."

Tammy didn't want to take any more time off from work. She would do the story.

Standing in front of the crime scene, she collects her thoughts and waits for the cue from her cameraman. The air is muggy and her hair frizzy. Their van is parked down the street.

"Details are sparse, Gary, but it's here that—" As she says this, she twists, ever so slightly, to reveal more of the house, and her heel sinks deep into a bed of soft pine needles. She falls, not at all gracefully, her legs opening wide, skirt sliding up toward her waist, her black underwear and panty hose and who knows what else exposed to the camera. The microphone rolls.

The network, thankfully, cuts away to her prerecorded story.

"Are you all right?" the cameraman asks Tammy, extending a hand. He's relatively new to the station. His name is Mike or Mel or Matt maybe. He helps her off the ground and swats away the dirt from her skirt and jacket.

"I'm fine, thank you," she says, her face flushed red.

On the ride back to the station, he sticks out his pinkie. "I pinkie-swear that I'll delete that footage as soon as I get back." She hooks her pinkie in his, amused by the gesture despite the fact that thousands of viewers already saw her fall.

"Could you see my underwear?" she asks, doing her best to smile.

"Yeah," he says. "But just a little. Not much. Nothing X-rated."

Fatty Kids Falling Watch N Laff

A slightly pudgy boy in his white underwear slides across a blue tarp on his belly. Dish soap keeps the tarp slippery. There's a garden hose positioned at the top, the chilly water gurgling out of it and streaming around his small body. The boy, Adam Fitzgerald, has tight curly hair, wet-dark, and he's sliding headfirst. He didn't bring a bathing suit to the party. Nobody told him there would be a Slip 'N Slide! Why didn't anybody tell him? If they had, he would have brought his suit. Back home he's got a blue one with a pocket that has another pocket inside of it. He keeps coins in there, and shells, and sharks' teeth, and his house key.

He's still sliding. The girls at the party in their pink and purple swimsuits, the red coolers with the white tops, the green blanket over the card table, the tall creamy brown birthday cake and the white plastic forks—everything is a colorful blur as he slides downhill. Time falls away. Space too when he squishes his eyes shut. He imagines himself like a bolt of lightning. Bodiless. An electrical current, sharp and fast. This is his third slide of the day, but it's as glorious as the first. The sunlight warms his back. When it goes cool, he knows he has moved into the second half of his journey, the half under the shadowy cover of the oak trees. Is his heart even beating? Is he breathing?

But then his slide comes to an end. Half of his body goes over the edge of the tarp. His chest and arms land in the scratchy green grass. He stands and wipes his palms across his bare legs. Grass blades stick to his skin like a disease. He picks off each one and flicks it away with his pruned thumb and index finger.

Adam sees Madeline too late. She was next in line, and she's sliding fast. She knocks out his legs. He falls forward and face-plants on the sudsy tarp. Madeline is pinned beneath him. She's kicking and shoving. She's crying. Mr. Bell comes running. Adam rolls over onto his side. Mr. Bell helps up Madeline, his hands under her soapy armpits. Adam can hear other kids laughing behind him. He runs his tongue along the bottom of his teeth. One of his front teeth is chipped, its edge so sharp it slices his tongue.

If you were watching *America's Funniest Home Videos* on October 9, 1993, then you saw Adam Fitzgerald's fall on the Slip 'N Slide at his friend's birthday party. His video was seven seconds long and appeared in a montage of children getting mildly hurt in a variety of ways—on bicycles, on jungle gyms, with hammers, with sprinklers. His friend's father submitted the home video, though Adam's mother had to sign a release form before it could air. She signed the form without really thinking much about it.

She assumed it would be cute. She's always been impulsive that way, and she regrets it.

All grown up now and living in another city, her son doesn't always answer her calls. It rings and rings, and she has to leave two and three messages before he ever calls her back. It's not the worst arrangement. In truth she has an easier time saying I love you to a person's answering machine than she does to the actual person.

SCARY—*Elevator FAIL*

Adam Fitzgerald shed his baby weight in grade school, and now he runs one of the most influential right-wing Listservs in the country. What he writes in the morning often winds up in the mouths of certain cable news anchors that evening. He keeps an office in an ancient building with ancient elevators.

The elevator doors ding open in the lobby, and a group of people rush inside together, a confluence of hot breath, bad breath, mouthwash breath, wool suits, cotton tops, warm flesh, sweaty flesh, perfumes, and colognes. One of the passengers bundles mortgage-backed securities. Another one believes the Bible should be read literally, that Jonah really did get swallowed by the whale, that there really will be four horsemen with steaming nasty breath at the end of days. A man and woman near the back, both of them married to other people, are in love with each other and sometimes sneak into the out-of-order men's bathroom on the twenty-first floor.

Together, this group weighs 1,922 pounds. "Too many of us," someone says, but the doors shut, and they are moving. The elevator rises arthritically up the shaft, and they are very quiet until, just before the sixteenth floor, something overhead pops. They scream, and the elevator plummets, down and down and down, all of them surely about to die, about to collapse into a dense mangled heap of body parts.

They fall for six floors before the brakes engage. They are breathing hard, their hot breath, bad breath, and mouthwash breath mingling. Somehow, miraculously, they have survived.

If you looped the video, the elevator would fall forever.

SCARY—*Elevator FAIL Looped Forever* MAKES YOU THINK

Randolph is on that elevator. As it fell, he thought about . . . well, he can no longer remember what he thought about. Quite possibly he was thinking of nothing at all. After the elevator stops falling, the woman to his left sobs into a Kleenex. The mood is somber, but then a man behind him says, "Well, that was unexpected," and a few people manage to laugh. But the laughter is uneasy. The elevator is frozen between floors, and they aren't free yet. This could still go wrong.

They have to wait another twenty minutes for a group of firemen to drag them up and out by the arms. Once lifted out, Randolph checks the plaque next to the elevator. He is on the eleventh floor. The passengers mill around until everyone is entirely free and safe. The woman who was crying says someone should really complain, someone should sue the building, someone should write the mayor. Nobody responds to her. Some people press the button for another elevator. Other people go looking for the stairwell. Randolph wonders if this choice between stairs and elevator is significant. His immediate impulse is to take the stairs—but it's not as though he's never going to take an elevator again. What happened was a fluke, rare as being struck by lightning, and it would be foolish to spend the rest of his life climbing stairs or avoiding tall buildings altogether.

He takes the stairs.

He's in the building to visit Adam Fitzgerald, his racquetball partner. Sometimes, between games, they discuss their work, but Randolph can never quite make sense of Adam's job, of how a Listserv can generate an income. "So who's paying you, exactly?" he's asked his friend.

"You are," he says.

"What do you mean, *I* am?"

"I mean, all of it, everything, what people say, the entire system. It feeds itself."

These conversations are always elliptical and frustrating, and so mostly they just play racquetball in the gym on the second floor of this building, where they are both members.

Randolph climbs twelve flights of stairs. He's breathing heavy when he knocks on Adam's suite door.

"You're way late," Adam says.

"I had to take the stairs from the eleventh floor. Your elevator almost killed me."

"Did it drop again? We're supposed to be getting a new one," Adam says, and then turns his computer slightly sideways so that Randolph can see the screen too. He clicks through his in-box. "Come and look at this. Someone sent it to me."

They watch about two minutes of a video montage. A chubby man rides a motorbike over a dirt mound and gets tossed. A woman with a birthday cake gets knocked by a small child into a swimming pool. In front of a crowd of people at Kennedy's Eternal Flame, an older woman trips and stumbles forward forward forward and down onto her chest. A man, Marshall, turns away from a bank ATM and slams into a wall of glass before falling back onto the floor. A small pudgy boy gets knocked down on a Slip 'N Slide.

"Look at that fat little fucker," Adam says, and replays the Slip 'N Slide accident. He doesn't tell Randolph that it's him, that he's the little fucker. The first time he clicked on this video link, he was mortified to find himself among its victims. But then he started playing it for people and forwarding it. He started posting cruel comments on the video's thread, subjecting the fat little fucker to all sorts of online abuse. "Take it easy," another commenter said once in response to Adam. "He's just a poor kid."

Adam watches his friend react to the Slip 'N Slide fall, smirking, then lets the video play forward. The falls are repetitive and hypnotic. It's hard to believe these are the same mammals that sent one of their own to the moon. When the video ends, it suggests ten more just like it. Adam clicks on one. Beyond each video are ten more. It could go on forever, a video fractal.

"Who has the time to compile all this?" Randolph asks. "Who makes them?"

"We all do."

"I don't."

"Not you specifically. But all of us, what we watch, what we want, everything, the entire system. It's all of us." Adam has his sleeves rolled up to his elbows. His hair is tight and curly. They're watching reporters now. One reporter falls after getting kicked in the nuts by a giant bird. Another one, Tammy, falls backward and flashes her panties.

"God, I love local news," Adam says. "Isn't it the best? This morning they did a story on defective treadmills. Oh, man, you should have seen it. Funniest thing ever. The reporter actually interviewed a guy while they were both walking on treadmills."

"You ready to play? I've got to be back at work in an hour."

They leave the suite, and Adam locks the door. Downstairs at the gym, they play two games of racquetball. They are evenly matched, but Randolph wins both games today.

"Everything all right?" Adam asks. They are in the changing room, in towels after their showers, arranging themselves in the steamy mirror. "You seem a little out of it."

Randolph combs his hair and tells his friend about the elevator, how his mind emptied out while he was falling.

"Sounds like you went Zen, brother. It means you're an enlightened dude."

Enlightened. Randolph tries on the word like a pair of pants that won't ever fit right. He doesn't know a lotus from a lama. The only time he ever meditated—"Your thoughts are balloons," the instructor kept saying—he fell asleep and started snoring in front of the entire class.

"I never believed in heaven," Randolph says. "Not as an actual place. But I always kind of hoped that at the moment we die, time no longer works the same and your final three seconds of brain activity might feel infinite. Like a dream that doesn't end. And your last conscious thought would determine the dream."

"The average male thinks about sex every eight-point-five seconds, so—"

"But I wasn't thinking about anything. It just would have been over. Just like that."

That night Randolph gets home very late. Beth, now his wife, is already in bed, reading the novel about beekeepers. He brushes his teeth and then lies awake in the dark beside her. Their five-year-old daughter is asleep in the next room.

"How was your day?" she asks.

Sometimes when they sleep with their backs to each other, her voice sounds impossibly distant, like the bed is twenty feet across and they're on either edge. He pretends, for a moment, that the bed really is twenty feet across and that he is the sort of husband who tells his wife nothing, who holds on to stupid little stories simply for the satisfaction of possessing something she knows nothing about. Pushing her away could start here, now. But he tells her about the elevator, about the nothingness, even about his fear that this life is all there is. She takes his hand and asks him for more. He tells her everything.

Funniest Treadmill & Stairs Falls Ever

Carol Spivey—whose beekeeper novel was on the *Times* bestseller list for forty-two weeks—runs on a treadmill in a wide and bright gym. Her speed is 6.2 miles per hour. Affixed to the treadmill is a small television screen. She has the news on but forgot her headphones, so she has to read the captions. The anchor is interviewing the defense attorney representing the cellist who murdered his wife's lover. The case has been all over the news because the wife's lover was a semi-famous musician. *Musician-on-musician violence,* the banner at the bottom of the screen says. The anchor asks how the cellist will plead, and the lawyer says that hasn't been determined yet.

"We just don't know all the facts yet," the lawyer says.

"But I think it's fairly open-and-shut, isn't it?" the anchor asks. "They have a witness, the sister. They have a motive."

"We just don't know all the facts yet," the lawyer says again.

Carol changes the channel. She doesn't like to watch that kind of filth. It pollutes the mind. She runs to clear her head and think of new book ideas. But then again, the cellist's story *is* an intriguing one, full of interesting contradictions. In his picture he looks like such a mild-mannered man. They say he worked in a stationery store, of all places. He was capable of producing such beautiful music, and yet he committed this horrible crime. Carol has never explicitly written about murder. She's never inhabited a killer's head (a type of head she has always assumed to be very different from her own). Already she is constructing a plot, an intricate one, with so many characters and story lines that she'll hardly have to focus on the murder at all. She'll be able to write all the way around it without touching the dark sticky thing itself.

The treadmill makes a disconcerting whipping noise, the belt kicks sideways, and it spits Carol off the back end. She rolls into a stationary bike, and its gray plastic pedal nicks her neck. She is the 342nd person injured by this type of treadmill. It leaves a small, light scar.

Later that year she joins the class-action lawsuit against the manufacturer, which coincides with the cellist's trial. In spite of herself, Carol finds herself tuning in for the highlights every evening. They say the cellist is guilty; the cellist is not guilty; the cellist lost his mind; the cellist was depressed; the cellist was lonely;

the cellist was a good man in a bad situation; the cellist was a bad man who had always acted like a good man; the cellist was jealous; the cellist had been treated poorly; the cellist had so much to be grateful for; the cellist is deeply sorry; the cellist should be put to death; the cellist should be put in a hospital; the cellist should get locked up with his cello but without a bow and rosin ha ha ha; honestly, who cares about the cellist?

Eventually Carol loses interest in the cellist like everyone else. She doesn't write a novel about him. Instead she does what everyone wants her to do, which is write a sequel about the stupid beekeepers.

Babies Falling Down SUPERCUT

"Are you liking it?" Amy asks, and flicks the cover of the beekeeper sequel.

"Not really," Beth says, dog-earing her page. "It's not as good as her first book. The main character just got back together with her husband because he promised to give up his violin for her. It all feels a bit contrived."

They are in the park down the street from Beth's house. Beth hasn't been snowboarding in years, but she does have a credit card now that earns her frequent-flier miles. She and her husband, Randolph, try to go on at least one adventure a year.

Her friend Amy is visiting from Georgia with her five-year-old daughter. Beth's own daughter is only a few months older. The girls are on the seesaw: up and down, up and down. The playground equipment is shiny and new, the mulch beneath it still humid and smelly. There are rope ladders and tunnels and shaky bridges and towers and bubble-windows and slides and poles and swings. Play*ground* isn't the right word for this place. It's a play-*kingdom*.

"They should make playgrounds for adults," Beth says.

"I think they're called bars."

"No," Beth says, "I mean it. If this place was twice as big, we would be out there playing too. Admit it."

"Why don't you just go ride a roller coaster?"

Beth and Amy lived on the same street as girls, and their mothers were best friends. That life can repeat itself so neatly is a fact that Beth, depending on her mood, finds either comforting or unsettling. But having her friend here for the week has illuminated certain differences between them. For instance: Amy's suggestion that they just pick up some fast-food biscuits for the girls on their way to the library yesterday morning. Beth tried her best not to sound like a judgmental yuppie, but really—fatty lard biscuits? And later, when Beth broached the idea of dropping the girls off at a yoga class for kids, Amy looked at her like it was the funniest thing she'd ever heard: "For five-year-olds?" she asked. "Next you're going to tell me you're raising a little whirling dervish."

So what if she was? Beth wanted to ask. Amy never left Georgia, and while it would be easy to blame their differences on geography or class, Beth knows those aren't the culprits. Their lives deviated long before Beth left their home state, and besides, Amy lives near Atlanta, where there are probably a dozen kids' yoga studios and where there are enough yuppie mothers to keep a thousand organic-only farmers' markets in business.

When their girls are finished on the seesaw, they come running toward their mothers, elated.

Deep inside the ear is a mazelike structure of bone and pink tissue called the labyrinth, and at the end of the labyrinth is the vestibular system, which governs balance and helps us stay upright. Amy's daughter battles constant inner ear infections and suffers from bouts of vertigo. The little girl falls forward onto her knees and palms. She doesn't cry and she isn't hurt or embarrassed. She stands and continues as if it never happened, though the moment is preserved, temporarily at least, on the traffic camera across the street.

After the park Beth and Amy walk their daughters to Pop-Yop, the ice cream shop, where customers don't pay by the scoop but by the ounce. The cashier actually weighs the cup after you add the toppings. Beth can't help thinking of livestock as they shuffle forward in line. They sit outside in the sunshine as the girls devour every drop of ice cream (Amy's daughter actually licks the cup clean), and then Beth leads them on a slightly circuitous route back to the house, hoping to wear out the wee ones and kill the sugar rush. The strategy is semi-effective. It takes some singing and cajoling and reading, but thirty minutes later, they have the girls down for naps in Beth's big bed.

"I can't tell you how rare this is," Amy says. "She hardly ever takes naps anymore. This is so nice. I feel like I should celebrate. What do you have to drink?"

"I think someone left a bottle of Prosecco here a few weeks ago. You want me to get it?"

Amy nods and so Beth pours the bubbly liquid into two wine-glasses. They sit down on the couch together and appreciate the silence. Spread out across the coffee table there are a series of messy half-finished watercolor paintings. Amy picks up one. The painting is of a red street and a gray building and, behind that, a flat and tall mountain. Beth's daughter painted it. In a closet upstairs there are at least twenty other paintings just like it.

"This is beautiful," Amy says. "She saw it on a vacation or something?"

"No, we've never been anywhere like that." Beth has a few theories about the painting, but she isn't sure what Amy would think of them. Her friend is slumped down in the couch, feet propped up on the coffee table, the Prosecco balanced on her belly button. She looks exhausted. Beth decides to tell Amy everything—about how she occasionally finds her daughter changing all the sheets, collecting all the towels, about how her daughter sometimes insists that she isn't a little girl but a maid in a fancy hotel, a maid with a fiancé who works on a ship and who comes to see her whenever he can.

Amy listens intently. "Huh," she says. "And what do you make of that?"

"I don't know. Maybe she heard it on television."

"Or maybe it's a past life," Amy says.

Beth has often wondered the same thing, but hearing Amy suggest this possibility is a surprise. Amy seems to sense what Beth is thinking. She takes a long sip and smiles before adding, "Don't box me in. You don't know *everything* about me."

When the girls wake up from their nap, thirty minutes later, the Prosecco bottle is empty on the coffee table, and Beth is feeling drowsy and warm and wishing her old friend didn't have to live so far away. Her daughter comes into the room wiping gunk from her eyes and snot from her nose, gazing at them confused and half awake. So much might have transpired to land her little girl in this time and in this place. Beth imagines her daughter tumbling down into her body as some kind of thin mucous light. What she imagines, really, is a kind of fall, a series of them, one life to the next, on and on, accelerating until, velocity achieved, you fell right through the universe itself and were finished. It's an exhausting thought, not to mention a tad New Agey, not an idea she'd dare try and describe to her friend, but she wonders if there's something in it worth holding on to for later, for after this lovely haze has left her.

"Where's my grilled cheese?" her daughter asks, testy, and Beth's fists sink down deep into the couch as she shoves herself upright, the Prosecco purpling her vision. Her body noodles to the left but she manages to lumber through it, crossing the living room with a short laugh, asking Amy if it was possible they'd been overserved, just in case her friend noticed the light-headed wobble.

trans/FALL

In an art gallery that was once a shoe factory, a meager crowd wanders through the exhibits. The white walls are eight feet tall and the dark factory ceiling is at least twice that. It's like wandering through a rat maze. Halfway through the maze there is a room with forty flatscreen televisions across two walls. On each of the screens, a person falls down but in reverse, time slowed, each body emitting a pink and purple light that moves like ripples in water.

"Looks like a music video from the 1980s," someone says.

"Okay, so they're falling up," someone else says. "I guess I get it."

The small crowd takes turns hovering in front of the artist's statement:

Until recently I was strictly a painter. I painted women to look like swans. If you'd asked me why I did this, I couldn't have told you. I painted what I painted. But then an old injury made it extremely painful for me to paint anymore. Years ago I broke my arm and wrist and three ribs in a biking accident. Maybe the doctors didn't set it right or maybe I have tendonitis now. Either way, it got me thinking about the accident. My brother had filmed it and posted it online while I was in the hospital. At the time that pissed me off but then, all these years later, I couldn't stop watching it. I didn't look like myself at all. I could pause it right before I hit the asphalt. I looked both calm and terrified at the same time. Like I'd given in to something. Was this me stripped of all pretense and personality? Was this the actual me? Was this me confronting the void? I showed the video to my wife and asked her what she thought.

She said my face was like Moses' in front of the burning bush—terror and awe.

I started watching other videos. There were so many of them. Millions of people had already clicked on them—and why? Scientists have discovered something called "mirror neurons." A mirror neuron is one that will fire in your brain when you perform an action and also when you watch that same action being performed by someone else. Why we have these neurons is a mystery. Maybe they've helped us become more empathetic. When you see or read about someone else's bad news, maybe a part of you is experiencing it too. It occurred to me that when we watch videos of people falling down, we are waiting for the moment of impact—for a bruise, a hurt, a collision—and that expectation makes us full participants in the event. Every fall we see is our own, and all of us are falling all the time.

I wondered if the same would hold true if I reversed the fall. Would our neurons mirror that rising? Are all of us rising right now? Are you?

—Davy V.

"I don't think I am. I don't feel like I'm rising."

"So it's about sin, right?"

"People falling. Of course it's impossible not to think about 9/11."

"I think it's about how fragile we are. The loss of control. I dropped a pair of scissors once and popped an artery in my foot and almost died."

"Is the artist here? We ought to push him down and film it."

"He's the one over there. In that strange white hat. Talking to that woman."

"Pretty sure that's his wife."

"She looks ten years older than him. At least."

"Supposedly she was his art teacher in high school."

"Let's introduce ourselves."

Tammy is there in the art gallery wearing a black dress and dark lipstick. These days she dyes her hair blond. Not long after her mother died (no ghostly sightings yet), she left the station to start a family. Now that her sons are both in elementary school, she's gone back to work as an editor. She steps forward to examine one of the screens more closely. She's looking at her younger self—that teal jacket, her puffy bangs. Tammy feels uneasy. She's not sure how this video wound up in this exhibit. She watches her body rise up from the pine straw, defying gravity: her dress slides back down her legs to meet and cover her knees, her expression transforms, eyes wide, mouth tight, arms spiraling, and then she is fully upright with her microphone in hand, twisting toward the camera ever so slightly. The video loops back to the beginning and Tammy is on the ground, sprawled, pink and purple lines rippling in the direction of the neighboring screen.

The gallery owner is in the next room talking to a group of people. He is an older man with thinning gray hair, but he is dressed in dark jeans and hip dark-rimmed glasses.

"I want to complain about one of the exhibits," she says to him. "There's a video of me that's being used without my permission."

"I see," the man says. She leads him into the next room and points at the video, her finger only a few inches from the screen. "Oh, I see, yes," he says, looking back and forth at Tammy in person and Tammy on-screen. For a brief moment she interprets his equivocation to mean that he intends to help her by removing the video, but then he gives her a pained look, as if what he has to say next will hurt both of them, and explains that the video, in this context, because it has been transformed—artistically, literally, and otherwise—qualifies as fair use and there's nothing to be done about its appearance in the installation.

"But how did it even get here?" Tammy asks. "Where did it come from?"

His answer to this question is even more perplexing. These

videos, he says, come from all over, from everywhere, and, in a sense, the videos belong to all of us. They are *our* videos, *collectively* ours, not a part of what's commonly called the public domain, per se, but as a part of what could be referred to as the proto–public domain, the substrata of all recorded human experience.

"I could sue," Tammy says without even believing it herself.

"But you've inspired art," he says. "You're the modern *Mona Lisa*."

The Mona Lisa of Falling Down, she thinks. The gallery owner gives her his card. She watches the video loop through three more times before going home to her husband and doing her best to forget that things still exist even when you're not looking at them.

Celebrities Fall Too So Funny—Beyoncé Carmen Electra Simon Punch and More

Years have passed since Marshall was convicted for the murder of Simon Punch. There is no video of the murder itself, but there are thirty-two videos—thirty-two distinct but not wildly different angles—of Simon falling down onstage the week before it happened.

He walks onto the stage in a pair of tight jeans and a loose untucked shirt, guitar already around his neck. The woman in the front row, the one wearing the glow-in-the-dark T-shirt of Simon's face, puckers her lips. For him? He isn't accustomed to that sort of adoration. Until his song got used in the Julia Roberts movie about beekeepers he was never able to book venues this big.

He strums the first chord and a giant screen behind him flashes quick clips from old black-and-white movies and nature shows—frogs, bees, bears. The screen was his label's idea. He smiles back at the woman in the front row before he sings the first verse. The lights change from purple to blue to black to purple again, swishing across the audience and the front half of the stage.

After the first few songs, a band comes out to join him. Simon walks stage left to trade guitars and slips on the spot where one of the roadies set down a bottled water during sound check. Simon's brow hits the floor and gushes blood. He rolls over to look up at the lights. They flash red and orange. The bass player waves two fingers in front of his face. "Seventeen," Simon says, and sits up. They bring him a towel. The audience cheers when he shows off his head wound. "If I forget all the words," he says, "there better be a doctor in the house." The crowd laughs. Probably he will need stitches later. The concert continues.

After the show the woman from the front row finds him backstage. Her name is Susan. She's not wearing her wedding ring. It's on a key chain that tinkles deep inside her purse. She left her husband, Marshall, a few days ago and emptied their bank accounts because, really, the money belonged to her. It was her grandmother that died, not his. Depositing the inheritance in their joint savings was a mistake.

When Susan begs for his signature, Simon asks for her T-shirt. "This one?" she asks. "The one I'm wearing?" She looks around uneasily but strips down to her black bra.

Simon smears his blood across the picture of his face on the shirt. "Better than a signature," he says. She takes the bloodied shirt between her thumb and index finger. A long time ago Simon decided not to sleep with fans, but with this woman, he would make an exception. Her deep blue eyes are wide-set, her face heart-shaped. She seems kind. He can imagine waking up with her and not feeling bad about himself.

"Thanks for this." She doesn't seem to know what to do with the bloody shirt: put it on or continue the conversation half naked.

"Here," he says, and grabs her a tour shirt from a box down the hall. "Sorry, I didn't really think that through. It seemed cooler in my head. I'm on my way to this after-party around the corner. Might be fun. You should come. All the chairs at this club are apparently Fisher-Price."

"As in, the little kids' toys?" The baggy tour shirt swallows her whole.

"Yeah, exactly. A club decorated for kids that's really for adults."

"Sure," she says, smiling. "Count me in."

They leave the concert venue through the back door and walk down an alley wet with rain and full of dumpster-stink. Her high heels echo ahead of them. Outside the club, she digs inside her purse.

"Hold on, sorry," she says. "My sister's calling for like the millionth time. I have to take this real fast, okay?"

BlackBerry flat against one ear and hand cupping the other to block out the traffic noise, Susan walks ahead up the sidewalk, though he can still hear bits of the conversation. "Fine," she says. "I'll call him in a minute. From inside. But you do realize this will only make it worse." She seems upset but, incongruously, turns back to smile at Simon with perfect teeth. "No, of course," she says to her sister. "I'm not trying to make you the go-between." She nods her head quickly. "Okay, yes, love you too. Don't stay up." She drops the phone in her purse and slides her arm through Simon's. "Ready?"

Raindrops clinging to a high gutter splatter down on Simon's neck. A taxi zooms by at the end of the block, sweeping water across the curb. Briefly, he considers running after it. He could go back to the hotel, take a hot shower, stick an ugly Band-Aid on his brow, and fall asleep in front of the television. The night could end here.

The bouncer waves them into the club, and they shove their way to a low plastic table decorated with a plastic flower in a plastic pot and an Easy-Bake Oven. The first round of drinks arrives, in little sippy cups, and then the second and third, and Simon realizes his hand has somehow found its way to Susan's back. His hand is under her loose shirt: warm skin, the soft knobs of her spine. Later, he knows, they will wind up at his hotel—or at her house. He doesn't care which. He downs his drink and opens his phone. She props her chin on his shoulder, asks who it is he's calling. Sometimes he likes to leave himself voice mails—for later, like a diary.

"Hey," he says after the beep. "It's me. It's you. You're with Susan, and she says she wants to paint your naked—what was it, my naked knees?" He laughs. "God, can you hear this?" Susan grabs the phone. "You have beautiful knees," she says, and squeezes his right knee and then passes the phone back to him. "You hear that? Things are going to get weird tonight, man. Oh, shit." He laughs again. "Susan? Okay, Susan just fell over. I repeat, Susan just fell over. It's these stupid chairs. She's all right. Listen, Simon, here's the truth: You're smitten. That's what I called to say. You're smitten. God, what a word. You're smitten with Susan and you're, like, a thousand feet off the ground right now. You've never felt like this. Hey, so I'm booking you a flight, okay? For next week. You're coming back to town. You're taking Susan out." She presses her face to his and shouts into the receiver, "You promised." Her lips so close to his, he kisses her. "This is for real," he says. "Check your email. One-way ticket. You're smitten with Susan, and I just needed you to know it. Also, you're sitting in the world's tiniest chair. That is all. Good night."

Hot Air Balloon
Ride for One

P eople are always asking her if she's *the* F. O. Betts. She's not.
"Then who am I talking to?" The man on the other
end of the phone line asks her this.

She shouldn't have answered the phone. She doesn't know
why she did. She could have locked the doors and been gone an
hour ago. Her boyfriend is probably waiting for her downtown
with an apple martini and a basket of garlic bread.

"I'm the *other* F.O.," she says. "His daughter. Fiona Orlean.
My father was the real F.O." The *F* was for Frank. The *O* was for
Oliver. He taught French and Latin at the high school for twelve
years, piloting trips on the side for extra cash before starting the
F. O. Betts Hot Air Balloon Company. Unfortunately he was also
a sucker for online poker. Fiona officially took over the business
five years ago when they discovered the extent of his debts.

"Is it safe?" the man on the phone asks. "Does it sway a lot?"

"I've been up a thousand times and not one accident," she
says. "And no, it doesn't really sway."

The man says he wants to book a trip for one, please.

"For one?"

"Yes, for one."

"Usually we send larger groups up. Seven. Eight. Twelve. It'll cost extra for just one person," she says.

"I've got money."

"That makes one of us."

"How much for a solo trip tomorrow morning?" he asks.

She names an exorbitant sum, more than she'd usually charge, but he says okay, and she gives him the exact address where they can meet. The next morning, there they are, together in a hazy field at dawn, her tennis shoes and jean shorts wet from the tall grass and morning dew, the hulking balloon taking shape behind her. The passenger watches from a safe distance with his arms crossed. He doesn't like the look of the basket. He asks if he should be hooked in somehow.

"To what?"

He points at the red metal crossbar that keeps the propane tanks in place.

"You'll be fine," she says. "Really."

When they're ready to go, she motions for him, but first he wants to get something out of his car. He digs around in the back-seat and produces a boom box and a small black metal cage. In-side the cage is a green-and-yellow bird.

"What's this about?" she asks.

"This is Magnificent," he says. "The parakeet. I thought she might enjoy the ride."

"We don't usually do this sort of thing," she says, though in truth she has seen and permitted much stranger. She makes good money off the eccentrics. This one time a couple wanted to go up naked and Fiona tried to be funny by asking if she needed to go up naked too, but the couple didn't laugh. They said, sure, if she wanted to, but Fiona stayed clothed and did her best not to look. This other time Fiona let a woman take up her easel and paints and Fiona had expected the woman to produce a beautiful land-scape painting but when she snuck a glance at the work-in-progress, in fact it was a bowl of cherries. The high mountain air, the woman explained when Fiona inquired, was full of good ions and encouraged creativity.

And so, looking at the parakeet, Fiona sees a new business opportunity. The bird will cost extra. Nothing personal, she says. It's an issue of liability, of insurance.

"That's fine." He doesn't even ask how much. He hands her the cage and then the boom box, and then he swings his long legs up and over the lip of the basket even though there's a door that can open. He's in jeans, and his shirtsleeves are rolled up tight around the elbows. He could be an accountant. Small wire glasses hover at the end of his thin, ruddy nose.

When she hits the blast valve, flames and exhaust shoot up the throat of the balloon, and he grips the edge of the basket with both hands. The balloon is a yellow one with blue horizontal stripes that Fiona bought almost five years ago from a company in South Dakota. She has two other balloons but all of them should probably be replaced soon.

Tom is her man on the ground today, her chaser. He has been around since her father ran the company. She gives him the signal, and he lets them loose. The balloon rises up fast into the warm morning air. Tom waves goodbye with a gloved hand. As the chaser, he will follow in the truck. The flame whooshes loudly overhead.

Fiona loves this part, the initial breakaway from the earth, from its interstates and box stores, from its pop songs and headlines with question marks in them, from jorts and jeggings and every other commercial portmanteau. All of it falls away, and you are suspended, divided from it by—well, not much. A little bit of wicker.

According to her mother, Fiona was conceived up here, two thousand feet above the mountains. Counting nine months backward from October would place this momentous event— momentous for her, anyway—in January. She imagines snow on the mountains, her parents' pink hands in gloves, boots on their feet. She imagines quilts on the bottom of the basket, their breath visible in the crisp and chilly air as they come together. The story might not be true. It doesn't matter. Fiona likes it. Whenever she asks her father about it, he says he doesn't remember but he says it with a smile that suggests he remembers every single detail and is just not willing to share. Usually her mother only brings it up when Fiona isn't listening. When she acts far away. When she's got a head full of hot air.

Her passenger doesn't seem to be enjoying the view. He's down in a crouch on one knee talking to the parakeet.

"What are you telling it?"

"It's a she," he says. "And I'm asking how she likes it up here."

He presses play on the boom box, and bouncy notes from a xylophone pop and clink in the air. Each tinkle dissipates a few feet away from the speakers. It sounds like music you hear during a massage. She can almost see the little desk waterfall, the massage table, the crisp white towel. *Atmospheric music*: a joke she probably heard her father tell on some trip.

The man sticks his pinkie finger through the flimsy bars of the cage and wriggles it near the bird. The basket creaks under him as he switches knees. He looks around uneasily, frozen for a moment, and then returns his attention to Magnificent. He whistles to the bird in a secret language.

Fiona is afraid to ask what they're discussing, so she gives him the full F. O. Betts Hot Air Balloon treatment instead. Perhaps he would like his photograph taken in front of the beautiful panorama? Can he believe how pretty the mountains are from this height? Would he like to hear the history of this region? How about an explanation for that bowl-like depression up ahead? Scientists think that it's a crater but she likes to pretend it's a footprint. Maybe he'd appreciate a hot cup of coffee from the thermos? How about a ham biscuit? Did she mention that they also sell videos of the trip? That's right, there's a camera on the bottom of the basket. If he wants, he can buy the video when he gets back to the office and relive the adventure at home whenever he wants, again and again.

"No," he says. "No, thank you."

The balloon is fully over the mountains now. The sun crests the farthest ridge, its bright rays spilling across the dark green canopy in misty light.

"You should see this," she says.

He steps toward her, peers over the edge. "What am I looking for exactly? I just see mountains."

"Okay," she says. "Never mind, then. It *was* the mountains."

Magnificent hops across her wooden dowel with twiggy feet. The newspaper at the bottom of the cage is crusty with dry shit. Fiona will not let his attitude bother her. She can only do so much to make people happy. If floating a thousand feet over one of the oldest mountain ranges in the world doesn't give him a thrill, then what will? She pours herself a cup of coffee and does what she always does when the passengers can't seem to appreciate the experience: pretend to be alone.

"I'm sorry," he says. "It's just that, this trip really isn't for me."

"It's for the bird?"

"No, for someone who couldn't be here. The bird was hers."

"Ah," Fiona says, and now understands completely. She gets this sometimes: the recently bereaved in search of perspective, in search of meaning, fulfilling some promise.

Directly below is Route 91, a two-lane highway that connects with the parkway. She points, thinking that large things made small might make him feel more powerful or important or significant, though it can have the opposite effect too, depending on your mood. You can feel detached too. The earth can appear all at once distant and vast, like all of it was made for *something* but not for you. You are not of it. You are separate. She thinks maybe that's how angels feel: all this creation—this land, this vastness, this lushness, this wildness, this unfolding—all of it for a punier, less deserving collection of organisms. Not that Fiona is a higher form of organism. Not that she believes in angels. She doesn't, or hasn't since childhood. But sometimes aboveness and belowness are more easily expressed and understood using the older modes. We can now measure the distance to the sun, but all the computers in the world can't tell you the weather next Tuesday with 100 percent accuracy, and why is that? What is it exactly that can't be charted, modeled, known?

She is in the wrong mood this morning. The smallness is having the wrong effect on her. She should probably look up instead but doesn't. The passenger peers over the edge of the basket, lips parted slightly. Together they watch a motorcycle scuttle like a cockroach down the highway. A truck slides like a slug. Her passenger now appears to be moved by the smallness, by the aboveness.

She fires off the propane again and the balloon lifts them higher. "You know," she says, "I took a similar trip after my father died last year," and then explains the shape his ashes took when they scattered in the breeze, the way they umbrellaed and then cascaded, the way they disappeared below, how wonderful and heartbreaking that felt, and as she is describing the moment to him, so rich with *letting-go* symbolism, she almost forgets that the story is completely and utterly false, that she has never scattered her father's ashes because her father, F. O. Betts, is still very much alive.

Maybe it's the lonely clack of the xylophone or maybe it's guilt for charging this man so much money for his solo journey, but Fiona wants her passenger to be changed by his hot air balloon ride. She wants him to feel something, be transformed, even if it means pretending that she scattered her poor father over the side. The passenger removes his glasses, scrubs the lenses with the hem of his shirt.

In five minutes, she warns him, they will begin the descent. With the ascent comes the breakaway, and with the descent . . . it's like stepping into a pair of heavy, muddy boots after hours of walking around barefoot and free.

She finishes her coffee and stows away the cup. When she turns around again, he has the birdcage off the floor of the basket. For a moment she wonders if he's about to toss the whole thing overboard. He presses his lips to the bars and whistles again. Magnificent's tiny square mirror pops loose and disappears somewhere around their feet. The bird is lunging and hopping madly. The man opens the cage door and sticks his hand inside. The bird leaps to a high back corner to avoid him, but he manages to grab hold of her. He brings her out. Magnificent looks uneasy out of the cage. The man kisses the back of her ruffled green head, and Fiona can guess what comes next.

"Are you sure you want to do this?" she asks. "Can parakeets even live in the wild?"

He holds Magnificent over the edge of the basket and opens his hand to free the bird. It doesn't explode from his grip the way Fiona expected it might. Instead it just rolls off the end of his fingers. They both move to the edge of the basket and watch it fall, watch it spin, both of them waiting for it to do what birds do. She wills it to flutter and to fight back.

"What happened?" he asks. "I lost sight of her. Which way did she go?"

She points east uncertainly. "I'm pretty sure that way."

The man nods. "Good," he says. "For a split second I got worried her wings were clipped. My daughter never mentioned it, but still. You sure you saw her fly?"

"I'm fairly certain," Fiona says.

Thirty minutes later, the balloon comes to rest in a park west of town, and not long after that Tom arrives in the truck. They pack up the balloon and then give the passenger a lift back to his car.

"What about that video?" he asks. "Do you think it caught her flying away? I wouldn't mind having a copy of that."

"Let me check it." She unhooks the small black box from the bottom of the basket and removes the camera. She pushes a button and taps its side. She holds it up to her ear. She pushes another button. Possibly she's overperforming. The man watches with interest. She doesn't know how to explain it, she says, but the machine malfunctioned. Maybe it has faulty wiring. Or maybe she forgot to press record. She can be that way sometimes: a head full of hot air.

"Shame," he says, but writes her a big check anyway.

That night she visits her father, the real F.O., at his apartment, an out-of-the-way building on the north side of town. The view from his second-story balcony is of a Suds 'n Rinse. He makes spaghetti for them with sauce from a can and spins the noodles tight around his fork. He wants a full report on her mother and *what's-his-face*, his perpetual name for the man Fiona's mother has been seeing for eight years now, ever since the divorce. Her mother and what's-his-face just got back from a trip to Disney World with what's-his-face's grandkids, Fiona tells him. What's-his-face is now busy constructing a pond in his backyard with a black tarp and a garden hose. What's-his-face knows the scientific names of all the frogs in the Southeast, and Fiona's mother finds that just adorable.

"Okay," her father says, "I get the picture."

They're rinsing dishes now. Between the bristles of the scrub brush Fiona sees remnants of scrambled egg. Her father coughs into his armpit and rubs his nose with the back side of his mottled hand.

"How's it up there?" he asks, and nods up to the ceiling, his usual way of asking about the business—and of filling any awkward silence with words.

"It's so-so."

"What's eating you?"

"The business is fine," she says, and then tells him about her morning, about Magnificent, about how strange it was to watch a bird fall like that, to see it swallowed up by gravity. She leaves out the part about his ashes.

They move to the couch in the den. Her father offers her a peppermint candy from the green dish on the coffee table. He props his feet up, the bottoms of his athletic socks brown and threadbare.

"Here's the thing," he says. "Birds are dying every day. There are probably a billion birds in the United States at this very moment. Think about that. You'd think we'd see them drop dead more often. You'd think there'd be bird bodies all over. Where do they go?"

Fiona has never really considered it. She tries to imagine not just one bird falling but a thousand. Then, instead of birds, she imagines people—her mother, her father, the man with the parakeet—all of them twirling down, featherless, naked. She bites down into her candy.

"I only saw it happen once," he says. "It was a bluebird, I think. Your mom and I were on our way somewhere. Dinner, maybe. It hit the pavement ahead of us. It must have fallen from a long way because it popped right open. It was a mess. Came down over my shoulder. I thought someone had thrown it at me, that it was a joke. I actually looked around to make sure it wasn't." He sucks on his peppermint and reaches for the remote. Their plan is to watch whatever movie is on cable, but Fiona can't stay long. She's supposed to stay over at her boyfriend's place tonight. "But it was for real," he says. "The bird really did fall right out of the sky. Your mom was nervous about it. You know how she can get. She said it was a bad omen."

He flips through the channels, looks forward.

"What happened next?" Fiona asks, certain he's withholding crucial details, that there's more to say about this story.

"I don't remember," he says, distracted. "We walked around it, I guess."

More Soon

T he plane landed but his brother wasn't onboard. The woman at the airline counter pouted her lips (sympathetically?) as Bert tried to explain the situation to her over all the commotion, the reunited families crowing, the baggage carousels whirring, the muscular officer hustling by with his skinny brown drug dog.

The woman behind the counter consulted her computer again and then leaned forward to report that, unfortunately, she had no record for a casket on that flight. She asked if Bert had maybe made a mistake. If it was possible that he'd confused the day or the flight number.

He had the correct information. He unfolded all his paperwork across the counter. He could provide her with confirmation codes and receipts and State Department emails—whatever she wanted. She was a small woman with a tight, pink face. No longer pouting (sympathetically or otherwise), she stared down at the mess he'd created on her counter as if willing it to combust and swirl away in a puff of papery ash.

"My brother, Rob Yaw," Bert huffed. "He was supposed to be on that flight. Are you telling me you lost a human body?"

"Hold on," she said, backing away from the counter on ballerina feet. "Let me check with my manager. Stay here."

From his pants pocket Bert fished loose his wife's cell phone—he'd lost his phone for the hundredth time—and dialed Mrs. Oliver. Mrs. Oliver worked for the State Department and had been his primary contact throughout the exasperating process of getting his dead brother back into the country. The department wouldn't be paying for the transit. Apparently that was the family's burden. But Mrs. Oliver had promised to do everything in her power to help.

"They're saying he wasn't on the flight?" she asked. "Interesting. Okay, let me see what I can find out for you. I'll have to call you back. Stay where you are."

Bert hadn't even considered leaving. After all, there was always the chance that his brother's remains would arrive on the next flight, which would land in . . .

"Not until tomorrow actually," the woman behind the counter informed him. She had just returned with her manager in tow, a fat-faced man with small George Bush eyes and a gray soul patch under his lip that he kept licking. The two of them stood shoulder to shoulder in their matching blue and orange airline vests, gazing at the computer, bleary-eyed, somber.

Bert imagined his poor brother's unclaimed casket on a carousel in some forgotten part of the world. A baggage claim mausoleum: no casket, just a body, his brother's skin waxing under the lights of the arrival gate cafés and newsstands, all those people watching Rob, famous for nothing but this, as he cycled around and around with all the other lost bags.

The manager, as far as Bert could tell, was doing very little to help locate the casket, instead only nodding his approval at various mouse click maneuvers. This was no way to run a business! Companies were only as strong as the people it hired, top to bottom. Bert was diligent when it came to hiring for his own business. He'd retired from real estate ten years ago to open his first Pop-Yop, the soft-serve franchise. If all went well he'd be cutting the ribbon on his fourth by the end of the year. None of it would have been possible if he had employees like these two.

The phone rang, and the woman snatched it up, cradling it between her shoulder and ear. Someone was talking very fast and high on the other end of the line, a garbled mess of sound that Bert did his best to decipher from his side of the counter.

"This might be a while," she whispered to Bert after a minute, hand over the receiver. "You can go sit down. We'll come and find you when we have something."

But Bert didn't want to sit down. He refused to sit down. Sitting down was giving up. No matter how much his legs ached, he would stand here, checking his wristwatch, breathing deep. He would hold them accountable.

His wife's phone rang—a chorus of chirping frogs in his pocket—and Bert was relieved to see Mrs. Oliver's overseas number blink onto the screen.

"You were right," she said when he answered. "Rob wasn't on

the plane after all. I'm afraid I have some unfortunate news. They're telling me now that they can't release the body. Not yet anyway."

"Can't release him?" Bert asked.

(Behind the counter the airline employees glanced at each other, clearly relieved to learn they weren't at fault and this was no longer their problem to solve.)

Mrs. Oliver was talking in a rush, her voice low but airy, as if they were connected not by a phone but by a paper-towel tube that spanned the ocean. Each phrase landed in his ear with a thump: security issues, protocol, red tape. She said they wanted to be certain before they risked bringing his brother back into the country.

"Hold on," he said. "Certain of what?"

"Of what it was that killed him."

"I don't understand. I thought we already knew that. I thought the autopsy confirmed the aneurysm."

"It did. Or it almost did, I guess. The bottom line is, they want to do a second one."

"Is that typical?"

"I don't think so, no," Mrs. Oliver said. "None of this is typical. It's a very unusual situation. I'm afraid I don't have much more information for you. They're being a bit cagey about all of it. But you have my word: I'll stay on it. If I have to take this higher up the chain, I will. I'll be in touch, Bert. More soon."

Bert and his wife were eating dinner at an Italian restaurant near the movie theater that night. It was a muggy May evening, but beside their outdoor table a heatless electric fire flickered in a bowl-shaped pit painted a sooty black.

"God, do they think he was murdered?" his wife asked.

"No one's said anything about murder," he said. It was a silly idea, he knew, but, strangely, also a somewhat pleasing one to consider. He didn't wish his brother to have been murdered. Not at all. But it was a new angle for them to discuss. "He wasn't even forty yet, it's true. He was healthier than me. I'm the one who had the bypass. If anyone was just going to drop dead in a hotel pool, it's me, don't you think?"

Ever since getting the news about Rob, he'd been doing his best to avoid that particular image, his brother's chlorinated corpse, the swirl of his brown hair on the surface of the water, his swim trunks bubbled out, floating, floating, floating.

They'd almost polished off an entire bottle of wine, and the food hadn't arrived. Bert was hungry, so hungry that he yelled over to the waitress when she delivered plates to a nearby table whose occupants—Bert couldn't help but keep an eye on such things—had sat down ten or possibly even fifteen minutes later than them.

"Have you forgotten about us?" he called over to her.

"Of course not, sir. I'll check with the kitchen again."

The waitress scurried away, and Delia, Bert's wife, pretended to need something out of her purse, embarrassed that he'd raised his voice in public. She didn't like it when he was ornery with people, particularly with waitstaff. As a teenager, she'd worked summers at a fish camp, serving up fried catfish and hush puppies on newspaper in plastic baskets, and despite the fact that she hadn't worked a single day since marrying Bert, she still professed an allegiance to anyone working in the service industry.

"I'm sorry," he told her quietly. "It's just that this has been such a strange week. What did the girls have to say?"

The girls—his daughters—were not really girls anymore. The oldest was working for a tech start-up on the West Coast. The youngest was a senior in college. Delia had talked to them both that afternoon on the phone while he was at the airport.

"Well," she said. "They hardly knew him."

Her phone chirped. She glanced at the screen and held it out for Bert. It was Mrs. Oliver again. "What's the latest?" he asked, rising from his chair. His black napkin slid from his lap and landed in a heap on the concrete. He darted through the tables to a far corner of the patio where he might be able to hear her better.

"They're telling me now it was some sort of infection. That's what caused the aneurysm."

"What sort of infection? Did they say?"

"That's what they're trying to figure out. That's the next step, apparently."

"Is this something he could have picked up at one of his sites?" he asked. His brother was an exploratory geologist and had worked for a company with mines all over the world. He'd traveled constantly.

"They haven't ruled anything out yet," Mrs. Oliver said. "They put him on a plane this morning. He landed in Singapore a few hours ago, and now he's on his way to Sydney."

She reported all this as if Rob had boarded the plane himself, as if he'd upgraded his seat and was currently knocking back a few complimentary cocktails in business class. None of this made any sense: instead of bringing Rob home, they were sending him farther away?

"Keep in mind," Mrs. Oliver said, "his company is Australian. This is all being done through the proper channels. There's an infectious disease center there that's offered to look into his case. They might be able to figure this out. Okay, more as I have it." The line went dead before Bert could ask any more questions. At that very moment, his brother, poor Rob, was somewhere over the Pacific Ocean in the belly of a plane, very likely sealed up in hazmat bags and labeled with all sorts of biohazard warnings and destination stickers.

When Bert sat back down at the table, his food was waiting for him, a giant plate of chicken puttanesca. Delia had already started nibbling at hers. She ate like a mouse. It was no wonder she'd never struggled with her weight like he had. He discovered that he'd lost his appetite but he still somehow managed to finish most of his meal.

It was a virus. Or at least something very virus-*like*. That is, the culprit behaved similar to and had the characteristics of a virus but was possibly not an actual one. Bert had trouble keeping it all straight as information trickled in over the next few weeks from the lab, via Mrs. Oliver, but Bert's personal theory, one that he offered his wife one night in bed, was that his brother had been exposed to some sort of subterranean flu, a dangerous little bug that had been hibernating in the rocks or the ice for millions of years and that had been released by the mining drills. The earth was on the verge of a pandemic against which it had no immunity, and his brother was Patient Zero.

"Yes, maybe," his wife said. "Or maybe it was the protesters."

"What protesters?"

"The people against the mines. Surely there were protesters. I was reading recently the new blood diamond is computer parts. Our phones and televisions, everything needs these certain minerals, and it's a very nasty business. It was a very upsetting article. Maybe someone read about it and spiked your brother's drink. Maybe he was assassinated. For political reasons."

Bert wasn't sure what to say to that. In truth, he knew very little about his brother's work. They'd never really discussed their careers. They'd never really discussed much of anything over the last few years beyond college football and what to do with their parents when the time came (hospice for their mother; and later, a nursing home for their father). Age was partially to blame for the distance between them. Rob was fifteen years younger, and sometimes Bert felt as though they'd been raised by entirely different families. Their father had already sold his insurance business and retired by the time Rob was out of diapers. Their mother had been forty-nine when she found out she was pregnant again. She'd always treated Rob like some kind of minor miracle. Like something out of the Old Testament. "Just call me Sarah," she used to joke.

Rob had never married—"Too predictable," he'd always said—but he'd cycled through plenty of girlfriends over the years, women he mentioned in passing but rarely brought along to family gatherings. Bert could remember meeting only one or two of them. His brother had dated a red-haired book critic named Monica (that one had really raised their mother's hopes), and then there'd been that hippie girl with the big wire glasses, the one who made soaps—what was her name? Aspen? Bert wondered if there were people out there who wouldn't have seen the obituary in the local paper three weeks ago, people who'd want to know Rob had died, suddenly, tragically, and far away.

Pending the investigation, everything that Rob had been carrying with him while abroad was being held in storage, but that still left his apartment in Atlanta, a place he'd used only two or three nights a month. Possibly he'd kept an address book or a computer with an email account Bert could crack.

"And just how will you *crack* it exactly?" his wife asked him as they drove down to Atlanta on a Saturday morning.

"I could know people who do that sort of thing," he said.

Rob's building was ten stories high, a red-brick behemoth, on a block full of newer stucco condominiums. They didn't have a key to his apartment, so they knocked on the super's door in the basement, hoping she might help. A skeletal woman emerged in a frayed red cardigan, gray wisps of hair like miniature storm systems over her head.

"Yeah?" she asked, and crossed her arms.

"My brother lives here," Bert said. "In 8F. He died, and we'd like to—"

"You're too late," she said.

"Too late?" Delia asked.

"Some people came a few weeks ago. They took all his stuff and sealed up his apartment. Apparently I'm not even supposed to rent it out. They tell you what was wrong with him? They wouldn't tell me. I figured it was pretty serious, for all the trouble it caused."

Bert told her he knew very little. The woman gave them a

disappointed look and retreated into her apartment. Outside again, standing next to the car, Bert counted up eight floors, shielding his eyes from the sun, guessing at his brother's window.

"Well," Delia said, "we tried."

"Wait right here. I'll be back."

"Where are you going?"

He told his wife he had one more question for the super, but back inside the lobby, with its long wall of bronze mailboxes and marble floors that whistled under his loafers, Bert didn't take the stairs down to her apartment. Instead he pushed the button for the elevator. It was a creaking box, barely big enough for two people. He imagined a network of frayed ropes and rusted pulleys on the other side of the ceiling. He'd never understood why his brother had picked such an ancient building. "You never did have any taste," Rob told him once.

When Bert reached the eighth floor, the elevator doors dinged and opened to reveal a long, narrow hallway with beige carpet. Above each door were silver and shiny letters. Finding Rob's apartment was easy. He tried to remember the last time he'd stood in front of this door. Summer before last? Rob had just returned from another trip, and they'd had dinner plans on the calendar for at least a month.

"Oh, that's tonight, isn't it?" his brother had asked coolly, before inviting them inside.

"You need to reschedule?" Bert had asked, not really trying to hide his irritation.

"I guess we should have called to confirm," Delia said.

"No, please, come in. Sorry, I blame the jet lag. Drinks?"

His apartment had always been a museum of his travels, crammed with strange and potentially dangerous artifacts: shadowboxes that displayed shelled necklaces and stringy bracelets and charms of unknown origin, halfway sheathed swords, tribal spears with little notches carved and painted along the shafts; not to mention a surfeit of photographs—of viny temples and lazy brown rivers, of snowy peaks, of mosquito-thick jungles, of smiling strangers Rob never took the time to name or explain—and then of course his stone Ganesha, the knee-high sculpture of the elephantine Hindu deity that sat resplendent beside the sofa, its many waving arms and majestic trunk.

"So is it art?" Delia asked him once. "Or do you, like—what? Meditate in front of it?"

"He's supposed to remove the obstacles from your life. Though he's been known to add them too, in some cases . . . when needed."

"How anyone could believe in something that looks like that, I have no idea," Delia said.

"As opposed to what?" Rob asked. "Besides, he didn't always look like that. His father chopped his head off and to bring him back from the dead his mother had to give him an elephant's head. It's a sweet story, sort of, if you think about it right."

Bert had nothing against his brother's travels, generally, and he tried not to let it bother him that the artifacts represented a part of his brother's life that was, for better or worse, unknowable. But what could be so infuriating was the way Rob seemed to take it all for granted. "Oh, that?" he'd say about the little clay thousand-year-old *whatever* that Delia or Bert had happened to notice on the mantel, as if it were a trinket he'd picked up in the airport gift shop. It was condescending, wasn't it? To feign such indifference?

The door to Rob's apartment wasn't locked today, but when Bert opened it, he discovered a thick piece of translucent plastic had been stretched across the frame and sealed on all sides with yellow duct tape. He pressed his palm to it. Warm, like skin. Probably the air-conditioning was shut off on the other side. Bert wasn't sure what he wanted to do now. He jammed his index finger into the plastic, stretching it until the plastic hugged his knuckle like a condom. He had to claw at the plastic with both hands to actually rip a hole, and when he did, he discovered a second piece of plastic on the other side of the doorframe, small divots left there by his fingers.

He could see through the plastic, barely, the room bathed in milkiness. There was nothing on the walls. He thought of the various tapestries and wall hangings and lamps that had once made this white box of an apartment seem so intimate and homey. Everything was gone now: the furniture, the rugs, the curtains. Probably they'd taken the silverware, the cereal bowls. It was almost like his brother had never been there at all.

Back in the car again, his wife was irate. She couldn't believe Bert had gone upstairs and risked exposure. He'd put them both in danger, and for what? "Truly idiotic," she called it, and rolled down all the windows in the car, as if a little fresh highway air might forestall any disease he'd contracted. When they got home she ordered him into the shower and dumped cleaning chemicals and powders all over his head and back. She scrubbed him, though from a safe distance, with a long rough brush. He endured this without complaint, though the smell of the bleach made his eyes water and his skin itch. That night he broke out in a splotchy rash that his wife was positive had nothing to do with the chemicals. She was certain it was the first of many future symptoms.

"This is crazy," he said. "If they were really worried about contamination, they would have done more than put up a sheet of plastic." Partly, he was saying this to reassure himself. "Trust me. I'm fine."

"For now," she said. "For now you are."

She watched him closely over the next few days, insisting that he sleep on the couch and eat his meals on the back deck. When he still wasn't dead at the end of the week, she allowed him into their bed again.

"Aren't you glad to have me back?" he asked, caressing her leg and sneaking his fingers under her slip.

"No, thank you," she said, and knocked his hand away. "None of that just yet."

"I never should have told you I went up to that apartment."

"Poor baby," she said, and then asked that he please stay on his side of the bed. "For now."

Mrs. Oliver called again, finally, to report that Rob was no longer being held in Australia. They'd moved him briefly to a facility in Russia, where his body had been frozen and sealed in some sort of space-age container (the device had an unpronounceable Russian name), and after that, they'd moved him again, this time to an undisclosed location with heavy security. His brother, it seemed, was destined to be a traveler both in life and death.

"I'm sorry," Mrs. Oliver said. "I know this must be strange for you. But they had to take precautions. One of the pathologists in Sydney, she died."

"God. From the same thing as my brother?"

"It's looking that way, yes," Mrs. Oliver said. "She didn't show up to work. They found her at home in front of the television. They're still not sure how it was transmitted."

Bert hadn't told Mrs. Oliver about his visit to Rob's apartment. The last thing he wanted was to wind up in some sort of quarantine.

"Am I ever going to see my brother again?" he asked.

"The honest answer," she said, and sighed, "is that it's looking less and less likely. Basically, at this point, he *is* the disease, you know?"

So, it had come to that. His baby brother, the disease. His baby brother, the human infection.

Rob hadn't been the easiest person in the world to get along with, but surely he didn't deserve this sort of treatment, being frozen and shipped all over the world as a scientific curiosity.

Mrs. Oliver was saying goodbye when Bert asked again about his theory, about the chances that Rob had contracted a long-dormant disease while down in one of the mines (a theory that, if true, would surely implicate the company to some degree). Mrs. Oliver, her voice deep and warbled, said, "Mr. Yaw, please, we just don't know. You'd be astounded by how little we know. By how many theories there are! It's a very sensitive case. It's not for nothing that we want to keep this out of the news."

All along Bert had understood the need for discretion. According to Mrs. Oliver, her updates were hinged on him not passing information along to anyone. She trusted him, she said, to keep this confidential, though exactly how confidential she never specified. That left him in a difficult position with friends who'd met his brother over the years and who sensed that Bert was withholding crucial details about Rob's death. He was never quite sure how much to reveal to people. It was a concern, however, that Delia didn't seem to share.

"They've got him on ice," she told some of their friends over wine one night. "He's contagious. No one can go anywhere near him."

"Contagious with what?" their friends asked, impressed by the drama.

"Bert thinks it's some kind of Jurassic flu," she said, turning to him. "Right?"

"I have no idea what it is."

"What will they do with the body next?" the friends asked then.

"What will they do?" Delia asked Bert.

"Your guess is as good as mine."

She looked at him, flustered. "Anyway," she said, "it makes it hard to get any closure. The least they could do is burn a finger or a toe, and send us some ashes. Then we'd have something to bury and pray over. Wouldn't that help, Bert?"

Bert wasn't sure if that would bring him any peace. He

thought of his parents' graves. They were buried near their church in one of the greenest and most immaculate cemeteries Bert had ever seen. "They only keep it like this," his brother had once noted, "because they really do think all these bodies will get raised from the dead someday. They really think everyone will come popping out of these perfect little graves. To meet Jesus, I guess." It was an unappealing idea, Bert admitted, your soul like a nice clean hand jammed back into a dirty wet garden glove. It was one thing for Jesus to bring back Lazarus after only a few days in the tomb, but say you'd been dead for a thousand years, say your ashes had been dumped into the sea and swallowed by tuna and served up as sushi. What then? Sure, Bert could imagine a scenario in which all the elements that once constituted a body were instantaneously re-formed into the original body-shape, but what about the fact that atoms got recycled over time? No doubt his own body contained more than a few atoms that had already belonged to previous souls, and so who would have dibs come Judgment Day—the first claimant, or the holiest? It was a silly question, of course, but that was the problem with believing in anything too *specific*. Bert had long ago dropped his parents' church for his wife's uncharismatic Episcopal one, a church whose priest counseled people not to focus too much on the machinery of it all.

As far as Bert knew, Rob had not belonged to any religion at all when he died. "Quickest way to figure out a church," he remembered Rob saying once. "Go to their website and Control-F for the words *inerrant* and *infallible*."

Delia took another long sip of wine, eyes flicking back and forth between Bert and their friends. She was still waiting for him to respond. "Would it help if they sent you a toe to burn?" she asked again. "Though I guess it's not like y'all were especially close."

"We were close enough," Bert said.

"News to me," she said, then, "Sorry."

Bert stayed quiet and sullen for the rest of the night. Delia had said too much about Rob's condition, but he didn't want to let on in front of their friends. She glanced over at him every so often, her eyes half closed and soft, her way of trying to communicate an apology.

"Don't act like it's top secret," she said in the car on the way home. "It's not. You haven't signed anything. And frankly I think it's a little odd how you're suddenly so insistent that you and Rob were such bosom buddies."

"Brothers don't have to talk on the phone twice a week to be close," he said. Delia was on the phone with her family constantly.

"Listen, there's no need to play this game with me," she said. "We both know what your brother was like. He was an asshole, okay? Don't look at me like that. I'm sorry, but he was. Your parents let him get away with everything. Remember when he wrecked your Jeep and almost killed that stupid girl he was dating, and what did your parents do?"

"I was working by then. I didn't need their help paying for another car."

"Sure, of course, but that didn't mean they needed to buy *him* a new car that same Christmas! Just because he's dead doesn't mean you have to be nice or lie," she said.

They were almost home now. He was tired of fighting with her and was ready for bed. Plus, she was right.

My baby brother, the contagion, he almost said aloud. No one could say that Rob had ever been boring. No one could possibly say that.

Rob had been dead for almost four months when Mrs. Oliver started emailing all her updates. Bert didn't mind this shift, though her written messages did tend to be short and cryptic.

FROM: MARISSA OLIVER

DATE: SEPTEMBER 29, 2014 08:33:02 EST

TO: HUBERTYAW@POP-YOP.COM

SUBJECT: R

> ANOTHER RESEARCHER DEAD. IN RUSSIA. FROZEN R JUST
>
> AS DANGEROUS!–MO

FROM: MARISSA OLIVER

DATE: OCTOBER 2, 2014 08:16:59 EST

TO: HUBERTYAW@POP-YOP.COM

SUBJECT: R

> R ON CONTAINER SHIP.—MO

FROM: MARISSA OLIVER

DATE: OCTOBER 4, 2014 08:42:28 EST

TO: HUBERTYAW@POP-YOP.COM

SUBJECT: R

> SHIP ON THE ATLANTIC!!! MUCH DISCUSSION OF WHERE HE GOES
>
> NEXT. NATSEC ISSUE, AS YOU CAN IMAGINE, YES?—MO

FROM: MARISSA OLIVER

DATE: OCTOBER 15, 2014 09:14:22 EST

TO: HUBERTYAW@POP-YOP.COM

SUBJECT: R

HAVE YOU HAD A MEMORIAL YET? IMPORTANT TO GRIEVE, I THINK.—MO

FROM: MARISSA OLIVER

DATE: OCTOBER 18, 2014 23:01:13 EST

TO: HUBERTYAW@POP-YOP.COM

SUBJECT: R

THINKING OF YOU TODAY. NO WORD ON R. SORRY.—MO

FROM: MARISSA OLIVER

DATE: OCTOBER 20, 2014 12:30:56 EST

TO: HUBERTYAW@POP-YOP.COM

SUBJECT: R

TIBETANS SAY BODY IS EMPTY AFTER THREE DAYS.

(MY AUNT IS A PRACTICING BUDDHIST!)—MO

FROM: MARISSA OLIVER

DATE: OCTOBER 31, 2014 11:44:08 EST

TO: HUBERTYAW@POP-YOP.COM

SUBJECT: R

CONTAINER SHIP FOUND!!! MORE SOON.—MO

Bert hadn't realized that the ship had ever been lost, but he was glad to know that Mrs. Oliver had located it again. When he told Delia this bit of news, she only nodded. They hadn't been talking about Rob as much lately.

"Is this ever going to end?" she asked him. "I never would have guessed it was possible, but your brother's turned out to be more of a pain dead than alive."

"I think that's going a bit far," he said.

"I'm going to tell you something I've never told you," she said. "Six years ago, the Christmas after your dad died, your brother walked in on me as I was stepping out of the shower."

Bert waited for her to continue. "And?"

"*And,*" she said, "*and* he didn't leave right away."

"How long?"

"I don't know. I can't remember. It felt too long. Nothing happened, other than that, but he just stood there, looking at me. Like a little reptile. And I could just . . . tell."

"Tell?"

"Tell what he wanted."

"Did you cover up?" Bert asked.

"Of course, yes," she said. "What kind of a question is that?"

But he couldn't help but wonder at the speed of that covering-up. Delia was a good-looking woman, and Rob had been an attractive younger man.

"Why are you telling me this now?"

"Because," she said, almost pleading, "Rob is not worth . . . all this energy."

But Bert wasn't sure. He'd read once in a magazine that even the Neanderthals, more than a hundred thousand years ago, had buried their dead, arms folded, panther bones and stone points scattered around the body. That this practice had been going on for so long, Bert figured, was significant. It was important to treat the body, no matter how irritating its former occupant, with a little respect.

Maybe, Delia joked once, instead of his having a tombstone as a memorial, the scientists studying him could simply name the disease after Rob. Bert relayed this to Mrs. Oliver, explaining that Delia had never been his brother's biggest fan, that she'd been troubled by the way Rob treated people, specifically women. (And incidentally, he asked, surely they'd already ruled out the possibility of a sexually transmitted disease? *Ha ha ha,* Mrs. Oliver wrote back to that.)

His exchanges with Mrs. Oliver were an escape from the frozen-yogurt deliveries and the management trainings and the accounting, a little bit of international intrigue delivered right into his otherwise lackluster in-box. Perhaps it would continue this way forever, these reports on his brother's never-ending itinerary, updates that conjured up an image of Rob standing at the bow of a ship, its prow slicing forward through a sea of churning gray waves on its journey to the end of the earth.

FROM: MARISSA OLIVER

DATE: NOVEMBER 2, 2014 10:16:12 EST

TO: HUBERTYAW@POP-YOP.COM

SUBJECT: R

    R MOVED ONTO A NEW SHIP. CDC VISIT PLANNED.—MO

FROM: MARISSA OLIVER

DATE: NOVEMBER 4, 2014 09:52:40 EST

TO: HUBERTYAW@POP-YOP.COM

SUBJECT: R

    CDC ON SHIP WITH R TODAY. HOW YOU HOLDING UP?—MO

FROM: MARISSA OLIVER

DATE: NOVEMBER 4, 2014 16:16:28 EST

TO: HUBERTYAW@POP-YOP.COM

SUBJECT: R

> R CAN'T BE CREMATED OR LIQUEFIED OR ANYTHING ELSE. TOO
> DANGEROUS, THEY SAY. NEW OPTIONS BEING DISCUSSED.
> MORE AS I HAVE IT.—MO

FROM: MARISSA OLIVER

DATE: NOVEMBER 19, 2014 12:02:14 EST

TO: HUBERTYAW@POP-YOP.COM

SUBJECT: R

> TWO MORE PEOPLE ON SHIP CREW DEAD!!! MUCH REVIVED TALK
> OF WHAT TO DO WITH R.—MO

FROM: MARISSA OLIVER

DATE: NOVEMBER 20, 2014 21:40:04 EST

TO: HUBERTYAW@POP-YOP.COM

SUBJECT: R

> MOST RELIGIONS SAY ZERO PERCENT OF SOUL REMAINS IN BODY
> AFTER DEATH. COMFORTING, YES? R WILL NEVER NEED THIS
> VESSEL AGAIN, I DON'T THINK.—MO

FROM: MARISSA OLIVER

DATE: NOVEMBER 25, 2014 23:01:21 EST

TO: HUBERTYAW@POP-YOP.COM

SUBJECT: R

> R HAS BEEN DECLARED A BIOLOGICAL WEAPON. WILL CALL
> WITH MORE AFTER THANKSGIVING.—MO

.   .   .

Bert was checking in on one of his Pop-Yop franchises (his busiest location, at the outlet mall) when he got the call. He took his cup of lemon tart soft-serve outside to an empty stretch of parking lot to walk the white parking space lines like tightropes as he snacked and listened.

"First," Mrs. Oliver said, "I'd like to retract part of my previous message. The part about your brother being a biological weapon."

"So he's not, then?"

"Let's just pretend I never said it. Can you do that for me?"

"Okay," Bert said, and raised the little pink spoon to his mouth.

"But here's the good news. In a few days his ship will come within a hundred miles of Norfolk. Any chance you could get to Norfolk?"

Bert stopped walking. Norfolk was a six-hour drive. "Maybe. Why?"

He could almost hear her smiling as she detailed the bureaucratic magic she'd performed on his behalf. She'd appealed to the right people, she said, and made them see how cruel it was to deny Rob's family the right to properly grieve. So, when the ship passed close to Norfolk—that is, if Bert was up for it—they were going to put him on a helicopter.

"So I'll get to see my brother then?"

"See your—" she said. "Oh, no. Bert, you can't step foot on that ship. But they're going to fly you over it. It's the best I could do. Under the circumstances, I thought you'd be happy."

He *was* happy, he assured her. She was very kind to have made the arrangements. She'd gone above and beyond what was required of her, he had to acknowledge that, but still, he'd need the night to consider. He drove straight home to talk it over with Delia, who was elated at the prospect. "Of course you're doing it," she said. "It's not even a question. You'll do this and we'll be finished. Goodbye, Rob."

They left the house a day early, before dawn, with fresh coffee in the thermos and turkey sandwiches in Ziploc bags. They had reservations at an inn in Colonial Williamsburg and arrived before check-in time. While Delia shopped, Bert strolled up and down the cobblestone streets, stopping to watch women in bonnets churn butter and make candles. That night Delia and Bert had dinner at a tavern and talked about their kids, about Pop-Yop— about anything but Rob.

The next morning they were up early again. The radio news station crackled and died in the tunnel under the Chesapeake, and when they emerged again on the bridge, the sky was a dazzling blue pocked with flapping gulls.

Bert switched off the radio so Delia could read the directions to the base. Once there, a man at the front gate checked a clipboard before waving them through, and then, as instructed, they parked in front of a beige brick building not far from the entrance.

"You ready for this?" Delia asked, pulling her purse over her shoulder.

Inside the building was a small waiting room with white plastic chairs and a low table full of magazines with old fashions. The uniformed man at the front desk scanned Bert's and Delia's driver's licenses and passports and then printed them both sticker badges. He pointed them toward the empty chairs, saying it wouldn't be more than fifteen minutes or so before departure.

"So," Delia said, "when do we meet the mysterious Mrs. Oliver?"

"I don't think she's coming," Bert said. "At least that was my impression."

"Shame," Delia said, digging a book out of her purse.

They had been in a helicopter once before together, many years ago on their honeymoon in Hawaii. The helicopter ride was an expensive excursion that had taken them over an active volcano. Rob had been thirteen years old at the time of the wedding, but, at the insistence of their mother, he'd acted as Bert's best man, his cummerbund so loose that it smiled below his waist. "Please tell me you already tested the goods," Rob had said before the ceremony with a dumb teenager's grin, braces shiny and sharp. (His brother, the biological weapon.)

Armed men arrived to escort them to the landing pad. Together they hustled outside and crouched low to pass beneath the giant whooshing blades of the aircraft. Delia struggled to contain the swirling mess of her hair. The pilot, an older expressionless man with aviator sunglasses over his eyes, twisted around in his seat and gave them a thumbs-up. Bert helped Delia with her buckle before working on his own. They were both given headphones that clapped over their ears and muffled the noise. The helicopter was about to lift off when another woman came galloping toward the craft. She was wearing jeans, a T-shirt, and flat yellow shoes. Her hair was slick, short, and red.

"Sorry," she shouted to no one in particular, then tried to smile at Bert and Delia. She was pretty but pretty like a model: flat-chested and vaguely androgynous. She strapped into a seat across from them. Soon they were in the air and headed for the coast, the city sliding away beneath them.

Their headphones crackled. "This won't take too long," a gravelly voice said. It was the pilot. Bert realized that they could talk to each other, thanks to the headset intercom system. The new passenger stared down at her cell phone and a wad of mascara-stained tissue. Presumably she was out here for the same reason, to say goodbye to someone, to another one of the infected victims. She looked up and caught Bert studying her.

"Kind of an odd way to meet, isn't it?" she asked him.

Bert nodded.

"You don't look much like him," she said. "Just a little bit, around the mouth maybe. Chin, too."

Bert didn't say anything.

"I'm Cecilia," she said.

"Have we met?" Delia asked.

"No, but I just assumed—" She looked at her hands, then back at Delia. "I guess it makes sense. You weren't that close, were you?"

"Did he tell you that?" Bert asked. "That we weren't close?"

Cecilia made a face like she might cry. She fidgeted in her seat. "No, sorry," she said. "It was just my impression. What do I know, you know? I didn't mean to—"

The helicopter banked left, and Bert felt his stomach drop. The sky was cloudless. Below he could see whitecaps spitting and foaming.

"Almost there," the pilot said.

A long gray metal ship was coming into view. It was a tremendous boat, the size of a football field and stacked high with containers of all colors: blue, red, purple, orange. As the helicopter descended and spun around the ship, Bert spotted another, smaller boat, tethered to the container ship by bulky cables that dropped beneath the water. The big ship was towing the smaller one.

"That's it," the pilot said. "The little boat. That's where the bodies are."

"Bodies?" Cecilia asked. "As in, plural? As in, more than one?"

"That's correct. I think we're at five now."

"Shit," she said, appealing to Delia and Bert. "Fuck, can you believe any of this? It's unreal." She dabbed the corners of her eyes with the tissue. "I'm not sure if this trip was a good idea or not."

"I'm sorry," Delia said, "but I have to ask. Were you . . . *with* Rob?"

She nodded. "Off and on. Mostly on. Before he left for his last trip, on."

The helicopter circled the smaller boat a few times.

"I don't see any people on deck," Delia said.

"They're keeping the bodies isolated," the pilot said. "No one living is allowed on board."

Bert had a clear view down to the boat. He could see a metal ladder leading up to a small, empty captain's deck. He could see a metal door with a crusty porthole. The sunlight glinted off the metal and the water with the same blinding sparkle that made it difficult to look down for very long without his eyes watering. The pilot advised them to say their goodbyes if they hadn't already because they were about to head back to the base. In truth, Bert felt no closer to his brother's death out here than he had back on land. But he needed to let go. His brother's story would have to end here at sea in the belly of an unmanned boat. The helicopter pulled away from the ship and the water, and Cecilia craned her neck to keep sight of it. "That's it?" she asked, frustrated. "What happens next?"

"Nothing," the pilot said. "Nothing happens next."

"I thought we'd get a little closer," she said. "I don't under-stand. It's not like they can keep him out here forever."

The pilot nodded. "This is only a temporary solution. Until they figure out a better one."

Cecilia closed her eyes. "It's almost like I can feel him," she said. "It's, like, this terrible feeling that he's trapped out here."

Delia reached for the woman's hand, but the straps con-strained her to the chair. Bert wondered if Cecilia really did feel Rob's presence, if there was something closed inside of him that prevented him from feeling it too. He twisted for a final view of the two ships, memorizing all the details he could, the rust and corrosion and salt stains, the antennas, the arrangement of the containers. He was constructing a reliable image that he could refer to months from now, when this helicopter ride would no doubt begin to seem more like a dream than a memory.

"Goodbye, Rob," Cecilia said, and tossed a piece of paper out the window.

"What was that?" Bert asked her.

Cecilia was looking out the window, watching the paper twirl and disappear. "I've met someone else." She turned to them and grimaced. "Is that awful of me?"

"Well, it's been half a year," Delia said but didn't say whether she thought that a long or short amount of time.

"This is it for me," Cecilia said. "This has to be it. It's not healthy to dwell on this for too long."

Bert nodded and Delia said, "For us too. Absolutely. This is goodbye. That's what I keep telling Bert. We have to move on. Right, Bert?"

"Right," he said. "Yes."

The helicopter banked left, and they fell forward into their seat belts. For a moment Bert feared the pilot was trying to toss them, but then the craft evened out, and they were on their way home.

His oldest daughter was visiting from out West the day three large cardboard boxes showed up on the doorstep. They contained some of his brother's belongings, the tapestries and photographs from his apartment, the stone Ganesha. He paraded it into the kitchen, where his wife and daughter were boiling water for tea.

"No," Delia said. "Absolutely not. Not in this house."

"Oh, he's not so bad," his daughter said, holding it under its lowest arms like a toddler. "He'd make a pretty good doorstop, I'll bet."

"I'm taking him to work," Bert said to Delia. "You won't have to ever look at him again, I promise."

"You'll scare off all the customers," Delia said, pouring water into mugs. "People will lose their appetites. The business will go under."

It had been almost a year since their helicopter ride, and in that time he'd scrapped plans for a fourth Pop-Yop franchise and sold his third location to its manager, a nice young girl who, he had to admit, deserved most of the credit for its recent success. Bert wasn't ready for retirement, not yet, but he could feel himself losing steam. He had plenty of savings. He and Delia had even talked about traveling more, possibly on a cruise, in the Caribbean or in the Baltic or, eventually, both. He imagined himself standing on the lido deck with a cigar and seeing, in the gray distance, his brother's ship. Wouldn't that be something, brothers on tandem ships.

Rob was out there, somewhere. Mrs. Oliver, who'd been emailing him less and less frequently, sometimes wrote Bert notes that included only GPS coordinates. To keep track of his brother's movements, he bought a small world map that he could fold and keep in his wallet. He recorded Rob's route as a series of dots across the latitudinal and longitudinal lines. His brother traveled south across the Atlantic, around the Cape of Good Hope, and then east across the Indian Ocean, where he was transferred to a military plane and flown to an undisclosed location off the Australian coast. He was there for a full six months before details surfaced that he was on the move again, this time north to a research facility off the coast of Japan.

There, they dipped and froze Rob's body in a mixture of gelatin and water and then cut the entirety of him into wafer-thin sheets. Each slice, only a millimeter thick, was scanned and digitized. Scanning one layer meant obliterating the previous one, and by the end of the process, Mrs. Oliver explained, there was nothing left of him, as he'd been ground up into a fine and invisible dust, neutralized and vacuumed into nonexistence.

God forbid Rob should ever rise from the dead: Bert wrote this to Mrs. Oliver with a glint in his eye, as a joke, but after pushing Send, he realized it was no joke at all. Some part of him really did wonder if there was something to it, to the idea of a physical resurrection, of the roaming spirit's future need for its body.

Mrs. Oliver never addressed that particular concern, not explicitly, but she did say that she didn't want Bert to worry. In fact, she saw no reason why Bert shouldn't get his own copy of the slides. His brother was computerized now and, as a digital entity stored on a number of servers, he would quite possibly outlast them all.

And so she began transmitting his brother electronically as a tremendous file that contained over two thousand high-resolution images. The software that assembled them did so in real-time, and over the course of an afternoon Bert watched his brother load onto his computer, the layers stacking into a familiar shape—toes, feet, ankles, legs, knees, all of it adding up to . . .

. . . to what, exactly? Entire parts, he realized, were missing: an arm, a section of shoulder, his mouth, an eye. Though Bert could flip through his brother's body like the pages of a book, could click down through the pale skin, could rotate each bone and navigate the world of his organs, Rob remained an incomplete specimen, a redacted document. When he let Mrs. Oliver know this, she was embarrassed to admit that she hadn't yet secured the rights to certain slices, the scans of which were currently on lockdown for reasons she couldn't disclose.

To Bert, this latest—and possibly final—hiccup was so absurd he considered breaking off communication with Mrs. Oliver altogether. He printed out his brother's incomplete naked body on his office printer and called up Mrs. Oliver. "You've done all you can," he told her. "And I'm grateful for that."

"We'll get the clearance," she said. "Eventually. I promise you that."

The stone Ganesha was on the shelf above Bert's desk, and he stood up from his roller chair so that he was eye-level with it. "And I don't doubt you," he said to Mrs. Oliver, cradling the hot phone between his ear and shoulder so that he could fold up the printout of his brother and stick it under the statue. It was off-balance now and seemed to lean forward. Bert stepped back and bounced the floor to make sure the statue wouldn't come tumbling off the shelf. It seemed sturdy enough.

Mrs. Oliver was still on the line, reiterating how committed she was to securing the rest of the files and completing the process. She would be there for him, she said, almost pleasantly. She would continue to work on his behalf with the powers-that-be. "More as I have it," she said, and hung up.

Hall of Small Mammals

The zoo, finally, was going to let the public see its baby
Pippin Monkeys.

"I bet we won't be able to get very close," Val said.
Like always, he had on his blue backpack, the one that contained
what I understood to be his novel-in-progress, plus his supply of
granola bars, arrowroot cookies, popcorn, and insulin injections.
The water bottle clipped to the side of the backpack was metal
and shiny in the cloudless afternoon heat. Val was my girlfriend's
twelve-year-old son, and I wanted him to like me.

We were at the back of a very long line that began near the
Panda Plaza and wound all the way around the Elephant House.
Nobody was very interested in the elephants or the pandas at the
moment. Everyone was at the zoo for the baby Pippins. If just one
of the three Pippin Monkeys survived to maturity, it would apparently be a major feat for the zoo, since no other institution had
been able to keep its Pippins alive for very long in captivity. The
creatures came from somewhere in South America. They were

endangered and probably would go extinct soon. But before they did, Val wanted to see one up close: the gray fuzzy hair, the pink face, the giant empty black eyes. Val wanted to take a picture to show his friends.

"I can turn off the flash," he said, messing with his camera phone. We had just passed a sign that banned all photography once we were inside the Hall of Small Mammals, where the Pippins were on display for one weekend only. "No one will notice," he said.

"Just be covert about it," I said, though I didn't really approve. Generally I don't condone rule-breaking of any kind. I've always been this way. At the airport, when there's a line roped off for the check-in counter, I will walk the entire maze, back and forth, even if I'm the only one there to see me do it. If my car barely protrudes into a nonparking zone, I will drive for miles in search of another spot.

Val tapped his sneaker on the asphalt, steaming from the earlier spray of the sprinklers. By this point we'd been waiting for almost an hour and had not even passed the Elephant House. I tugged my shirt off my sticky back to let in some air. Directly behind us in line, a man with a comb-over fished around in his neon green fanny pack and produced two Wetnaps, one for himself and one for his wife, a somber-looking woman in a zebra-print dress that I gathered she had picked out specifically for this excursion. I watched them unfold their antibacterial napkins with care and scrub every inch of their hands—palms, fingers, creases, wrinkles, even up past the wrists. Watching them groom was exhausting. All of this was exhausting.

I was ready to give up and go home, but, ever since seeing the color photo of the Pippins in the magazine insert of the Saturday newspaper, Val had talked about little else. It would make him so happy, his mother had said. Val had studied up on Pippins and knew all there was to know about their tool-making intelligence and diet, about the destruction of their leafy forest home in wherever-it-was, about the mysterious malaise that overcame captive Pippins and made reproduction difficult and rare. Frankly, I didn't want to hear any more about the godforsaken Pippins.

"So," I said, trying not to sound bored, "tell me about your novel." Val looked up at me like I'd just asked him to squash the family hamster.

"First of all," he said, "it's not a novel. It's a screenplay."

"Oh," I said. "Sorry, I was under the impression it was a novel." I didn't tell him that his mother had more than once referred to it as *Val's not-so-secret secret novel*. "What's it about?"

The boy sighed. "Okay," he said. "So what do you know about sensory deprivation?"

I admitted that I knew very little about sensory deprivation.

"Well, you probably won't get it, then," he said, and writhed loose from his backpack straps. He took out a granola bar and his insulin kit and then handed me the pack like I was his personal valet, which in a way I suppose I was. "I need to go do this now," he said. "Don't get out of line. I'll be right back."

I watched him waddle off toward the bathrooms taking big bites of the bar. Maybe it was his flat dry hair or his tube socks or his white hairless legs, but Val already had the look of a middle-age government employee. I saw nothing of his mother in him, so he must have resembled his father, a man who lived in the same city but whom I'd never met and never would. I'd been dating

Val's mother for only a few months. She worked in the same building as me but for a separate company. Her department did something that involved cardboard tubes. The tubes were different sizes and lengths and colors. They leaned against all the walls and desks on her floor. She didn't enjoy discussing her work. "That's not *who* I am," she'd say. By the time we broke up, not long after my visit to the zoo with Val, I still hadn't figured out if her company shipped the tubes or received them or made them or what.

The couple behind me in line was getting impatient.

"This is ridiculous," I heard the man say. "They have a responsibility to keep the line moving, don't they? How much time do you need in there? One look and go."

The woman examined her zoo map, did some calculations on it with a pen from her purse. "We started here and now we're here," she said. "That's about two hundred feet. Divide by the time, and we're moving at a rate of"—she scribbled—"three feet per minute."

"And," the man said, "so what?"

"That means we should be there in"—she scribbled some more—"seventy-two minutes. At this current rate, I mean."

"Is that supposed to make me feel better?" the man asked.

I had to agree with the man. Seventy-two minutes was a lifetime. I checked my watch as we shuffled forward. The zoo would close its gates in two hours. The sprinklers came back on outside the Elephant House ahead of us and large misty clouds floated over the ferns along the walkway, giant ferns with long, sweeping fronds that knocked against the shoes of the few people on their way to see the elephants. I searched Val's backpack for some hard candy. He had some peppermints and half a bag of peach lozenges, and I helped myself to a handful of those. I also couldn't resist looking at his screenplay. I suppose that's why, really, I'd opened the bag in the first place. Just to have a quick peek. I didn't have to take out the pages to read them. Somehow that made it feel like less of a violation.

The title page said *Prehistory X by Valentine Creel*, and it had his home address at the bottom. The story was about time travel, that much I could see right away. Val's hero was the son of a famous scientist, who in the first scene turned up dead in her lab. I gathered that by using a sensory deprivation tank the hero's mother had figured out a way to move through time with her mind. Soon, using his mother's copious notes, the hero was whipped back to the Bronze Age, a scary place populated by gruesome men with painted faces and women with large "cannonball" breasts. Miraculously everyone spoke English. The villain was some sort of tribal chieftain who was holding the mother captive. Yes, she was still alive. I no longer remember how Val explained it scientifically but I think it involved a disembodied mind, forever lost in time.

"Give me some skin," the villain said at one point, spear raised. The line stuck out because it was something I often said to Val, ironically, palm raised for a high five, though of course in the context of this scene, the line must have had a different, more ominous meaning. *Prehistory X* was not very subtle in its intentions. I had no trouble working out what was going on. The villain was me, clearly, and I was probably going to die before the end of the movie. I should have hated the script, I suppose, but partly I was honored to be included at all.

"I think the pace is picking up," the woman behind me said, and when I looked up, I saw that she was right. We were really moving now. I could see the entrance to the Hall of Small Mammals, its brown double doors open wide to receive us. But where was Val? I scanned the crowds. Had I been wrong to let a twelve-year-old go off on his own at a public zoo? I was beginning to suspect that I'd made a poor decision. My experience with children was and is fairly limited. I have two nieces that I rarely see in person, though my fridge is plastered with their childhood photos and printed emails. My older brother, the girls' father, once said that being a parent is the most important thing he's ever done with his life. I've never had the nerve to ask him what that says about my life.

"Here we go," the woman said. "I can't wait. I'll bet they are so adorable. I wish we could touch one."

I stepped out of line and gazed back at the man and woman and all the people behind them. I didn't see any sign of Val. He'd been gone for more than twenty minutes.

"Would you mind holding my place?" I asked the couple.

The woman said of course they wouldn't mind, but my request agitated the man. He rotated his fanny pack from right to left hip. "Well," he added, "we can try."

I set off for the bathrooms with Val's blue backpack over my shoulder. Children streamed by eating cotton candy and peanuts and hugging plush animal toys—pandas and giraffes and hippos. Before the Elephant House, I turned left up the paved path to the Hall of Great Apes, just in case Val had gotten distracted. Overhead, along cables that connected the Ape Hall to what looked like a cell phone tower, an orangutan bounced up and down on the lines. Long sinewy muscles, pouting mouth, thin orange hair—the orangutan had the look of an aging body builder, a creature long past his prime but presiding over the crowds from his cables. He tracked my progress toward the door.

With everyone in line for the Pippins at the Hall of Small Mammals, I was alone with the bigger apes. In the first room, behind a wall of glass, five well-mannered chimpanzees played sluggishly in stooped fake trees. They regarded me coolly. In the next room, I discovered the Gibbon Monkeys, white and shiny coats, all of them silent and unblinking. In the final room were the Orangutans. Three sat in some straw on the concrete floor, shoulders hunched, a semicircle. Had one of them thrown down an Ace of Spades and said, "Read 'em and weep," I wouldn't have been much surprised. From a shaft at the top of the enclosure, a fourth orangutan descended on a network of metal crossbars. He was the one I'd seen outside, and sure enough, he sat apart from the others, chin jutting out, eyes recessed in his wrinkled face, cheek pads gray, cracked, and bulging. He wasn't staring right at me. It was more unsettling than that. He was more like someone you see out at dinner one night whom you almost recognize, the person who keeps sneaking glances at you over the wine menu, a don't-I-know-you-from-somewhere expression on his face. One solitary creature regarding another, I guess you could call it.

I didn't linger. I couldn't. Val was not in the Hall of Great Apes. My detour had been another bad decision. I was beginning to panic. I imagined the boy in the trunk of a kidnapper's car, red brake lights across his helpless, tear-streaked face. I imagined him convulsing on a stretcher in the back of an ambulance, the oxygen mask over his mouth. I walked faster. Maybe the zoo was going to have to make one of those announcements over the loudspeaker that has shamed so many parents over the years, but in the end, Val was the one who found me.

"What are you doing?" he asked. He'd run up behind me, his glasses slightly skewed, hair wet in front.

"I was looking for *you*," I said. I was relieved but also a little irritated to see him again.

"Just great," he said. "Wonderful. I leave you alone for ten minutes. Was I not clear enough? Didn't I tell you not to get out of line?"

I admitted that yes, those had been his instructions, but I'd had my reasons for disobeying. He was only twelve after all and as his guardian for the day, my first responsibility was his safety and not holding his place in line. Hearing this sent Val into a rage. He called me useless. He called me hopeless and worse. He spoke with such authority that I almost believed he was right. When he grabbed his backpack from me and started back toward the Hall of Small Mammals, I fell into step behind him.

"Actually," I called up to him when I remembered it, "someone is holding our place." If Val heard me, he gave no indication. His blue backpack was flush against his neatly pressed short-sleeve checkered shirt. He stomped ahead, resolute, tight pink corpuscle fists at his side, thumbs jammed through his belt loops. When we got to the Hall, the couple holding our place had already gone inside. Val was two seconds behind me in putting it together. I had no idea what to do next, and Val despaired.

"You do realize this is a limited-time exhibit?" he said.

Not for the first time Val's obsession with these creatures was beginning to bother me. What was so fascinating about them?

Even if they all died out one day, we still had plenty of other monkeys to admire—Spider Monkeys, Squirrel Monkeys, Marmosets, and Howlers. I found it difficult to care much about an animal with so little regard for itself and for the survival of its own species that scientists had been forced to extract semen from unwilling males for insemination in the unwilling females. I wasn't going to miss the Pippins when they disappeared from the earth. But I suggested to Val that we get back in line. Maybe the zoo would stay open late to accommodate all the extra people. He was doubtful but agreed that we should at least try. We turned to walk, and just when I thought I'd finally brought him around to my side again, a zoo official in khaki duds came out of the Hall of Small Mammals. He was a short, plump man with messy dark hair. He counted off twenty people—"One, two, three," his finger pointing—and then announced that everyone else was out of luck.

"I'm sorry," he said over the groans and complaints, "but that's the way it is."

The crowd began to disperse, grumbling. Val was not dissuaded. He got in line behind the twentieth person.

"Sorry, buddy," the official said to him. "Only these twenty. Line has to end somewhere."

"Right," Val said, "and it ends behind me."

Perhaps assuming I was the one in charge here, the zoo official appealed to me for help. *Do something about your kid,* his face said. But I had no intention of getting involved. I didn't budge or say a word.

"Listen," the zoo official said. "I get it, kid, I really do, but you have to understand that I just turned away a hundred people. If I break the rules for you, then where does it end?"

"With me," Val said, arms crossed, mouth so tight and dense it exerted a gravitational pull on the rest of his face. He was even bold enough to meet the man's gaze. They locked eyes and stood there, two angry mannequins.

The official was the first to look away. He turned sideways and scratched behind his red ear. I thought maybe he'd given up, but he hadn't. "No," he said, and stepped into line ahead of Val. "The line ends here."

"Get out the way," Val said, and tugged at the man's arm, and for the first time in this exchange, he gazed over at me. I could see how upset and desperate Val was. He seemed to be on the verge of tears, though whether or not those tears were strategic, I wasn't entirely sure. Anything was possible with this kid. But I sensed an opportunity. Maybe the tribal chieftain wouldn't have to die at the end of Val's movie after all. Maybe he wouldn't even have to be the bad guy.

If you'd asked me then why I cared so much about what happened with Val and why I wanted him on my side, I probably would have lied and said I didn't care one iota. It wasn't as though I was in love, and I certainly didn't have plans to stick around for the long haul. Val's mother was beautiful though a bit uptight and officious. I recall one night, especially, when she insisted on supergluing back together an entire stained-glass lamp we had accidentally rocked off the nightstand, a project that required hours of Zen-like concentration on her part and bored me enough to turn on the television. Plus, I'd never dated a woman with a kid, and she was reluctant to leave Val with a babysitter for more than a night or two a week, which seems more admirable to me now than it did at the time. I was suspicious of Val's complete lack of interest in me. I worried he was bad-mouthing me when I wasn't there. That's why I'd volunteered for the zoo trip, of course.

I've long been something of a serial dater, I'm the first to admit that, and I do have a bad habit of giving up at the first hint of difficulty or complication, but I don't believe in regret. I believe it's important to face forward. And yet, sometimes I do find myself thinking about Val and his mother, curious about the course of their lives after I moved on. What are the chances that Val, wherever he is, still thinks about our day together at the zoo?

"Now, wait a minute," I said to the official. "Wait. Can we talk for a minute?"

He pretended not to hear me, but a few other people ahead of him in line turned to see what all the commotion was about. I slipped my hand into my back pocket and felt for my wallet but didn't take it out yet. "We'll follow the rules," I told the official, "but first just talk to me. Okay? Just hear me out."

"What do you want to talk about?" he asked.

"Talk to me over here," I said. "Please."

Reluctantly he stepped out of line and toward me, one hand in his pocket, the other scratching his red ear again. I wondered if it was infected. "You need to get a handle on your kid," he said quietly.

"I know," I said, wallet out of my pocket. "You're absolutely right. But listen, the thing is, he's not even mine. He's my girl-friend's kid, and I won't lie to you. He can be a real pain in the ass, okay? The other night I caught him spitting in my red wine. He hates me, okay? But listen, he's got to see these monkeys. If you don't let him—" I handed him two twenties. "If you don't, I'll never hear the end of it. Please, help me with this."

The official shoved the money back at me. "No, no, that's not what this is about," he said.

"Then what is it about?" I asked.

"It's about respect. He doesn't have any."

While that was true, I wasn't going to say so to this guy.

I needed a different approach and quickly settled on pity. "This isn't his fault," I said. "I'm the one who lost our place in line. No need to punish him, right?"

The official didn't say anything.

"The kid has problems, okay?" I continued. "He's a sick kid. Check his backpack. He has to carry around his medication. He has to give himself shots, all right? I'm pretty sure that's why he wants to see these baby monkeys. I think he relates to them on some level."

The official's ear was so red I thought it would burst open. He stopped scratching it and considered this new information.

"What's wrong with him?" he asked.

As far as I was aware, diabetes was the extent of it, but I told him it was lots of things, that I couldn't say exactly what it was because his mother didn't like for me to talk about it, but it was bad.

The official shook his head back and forth, his mouth a rigid line. "Regardless, he needs to apologize," he said.

"Yes, of course," I said. "Definitely."

We walked over to Val, who had never abandoned his place in line.

"Val, apologize to this gentleman," I said.

Val was about to say something—something offensive, I was sure of it—so I made a face that I hoped he would understand, my eyes wide, lips pursed. He fidgeted with his backpack straps, uncertain. "Okay," he said, and looked up at the official. "Sorry. I am. I was just excited."

The official nodded and said, "You can't just go around doing whatever you want to do. That's not how life works."

Val didn't respond. This was a lesson that he probably needed to learn, and now, because of me, maybe he never would. He looked up at both of us with the same cool stare, waiting to see if he was going to get what he wanted, and of course he did.

"He can go in," the zoo official said, then turned to me. "But just him. You'll have to wait outside."

"Why?" I asked. "We're together."

"Take it or leave it," the man said. "I'm only letting in one more person. You or him. Up to you."

Val looked up at me victoriously, apparently not doubting that he'd be the one to go inside. That's the way it is with kids, I suppose: they take it for granted that the last cookie on the tray is for them. I told the guard thank you, though I suspected this was all his way of clinging to the little bit of authority he had left. He was being petty, but I let it slide and took my place beside Val. A few people tried to join the line after that, but the official shooed them away. He brought over an orange cone and dropped it directly behind us. Val watched that procedure closely, happy of course to be on the right side of it. If the boy had any new respect for me, he certainly didn't show it.

"I'm glad it's working out," I said, and raised my hand unconvincingly for a high five. But Val didn't want to meet my hand up high. He stuck his palm out low, and when I tried to slap it, he snatched it away at the last second.

"I'm still sensing some hostility," I said, trying to be funny, and, in the absence of any laughter, mine or his, feeling more upset. "To be perfectly honest, I wouldn't mind a little more appreciation, pal. I just got you into this party."

"Thanks for that," he said. He was such an easy kid to dislike.

He got out his phone and double-checked that the flash was disabled. We were quiet until, finally, it was his turn to enter the Hall. Inside I could hear a movie presentation about the Pippins, the narrator's British accent. Cool air gushed out of the dark hall in powerful and pleasant waves. It felt wonderful and inviting. I still had no love for the poor baby Pippins, but I wouldn't have minded seeing what all the fuss was about.

The zoo official was holding open the door with his back, his hand on the horizontal bar, ready to swing it shut behind Val. Without exactly intending to, I'd come very close to the entrance. For a moment I wondered if he was actually going to let me pass as well, if maybe he had forgotten or no longer cared about this part of our agreement. But as I approached, he shot me a hard look, almost daring me to take another step, and I knew that if I pressed forward, he would stop me, or possibly even the both of us. Val shoved his backpack in my direction as though to prevent me from trying.

"Don't lose this," he said. I watched him go forward, hands deep in his pockets, and then pass through the door alone. He didn't turn back to say *Thank you* or *I'll see you on the other side* or anything else. He acted like I wasn't even there, like he'd already forgotten me.

We of the Present Age

To prevent the newest discovery from winding up in yet another showman's dime exhibit, we decided to send one of our own to bring it back for safekeeping. Tall, cheerful Dr. Anders was the first to volunteer for the trip, though among the naturalists in our Academy interested in vertebrate fossils, he was by all accounts the least qualified. The young doctor had recently caused a stir by mistaking an adolescent mastodon jaw as proof of an entirely new genus and species. A laughable idea. But what Anders lacked in credentials, he made up for with his unwavering enthusiasm—and (it need be mentioned) with his political connections. By luck or by connivance he had become engaged to a woman from one of the city's wealthiest families, and that family, thanks to Anders, had made significant contributions to our esteemed Academy. Those kindnesses considered, we could find no reason why it shouldn't be Anders we sent to procure what was rumored to be the most complete specimen yet unearthed.

On the morning of Anders's departure we accompanied him

to the station, the trains steaming and hissing all around us as we clapped him on the shoulder and wished him well. "You won't be disappointed," he said, confident. "Because when I return, I will come bearing gifts millions of years in the making." Prepared remarks, no doubt. It was winter and we stomped our feet to keep out the cold. "Very well," we told him, and watched his train crank away and disappear into a gauzy rain.

He traveled twenty hours south to a provincial town called Newton, where we had arranged for his transfer to a stagecoach. Unfortunately the promised coach did not manifest (its driver, we later learned, had fallen down drunk and been trampled by his own horses), and Anders was forced to finish the journey on the back of a mule cart that happened to be on its way to the town of Golly, his final destination. If not for this setback, perhaps history would have been quite different for Anders, for our Academy— and for science.

These events transpired many decades ago, before we had a name for many of the fossilized creatures that once populated our planet, before we even had a name for their particular field of study; in the days before we'd completely mapped the wilds between East and West; before Mr. Morse sent his first electrical message whipping across two miles of wire; when a young Mr. Darwin was still filching finches for his sketches in the belly of HMS *Beagle*. The world was on the verge of a great transformation, to be sure, a scientific awakening, and we were the agents of that coming and necessary change.

Before his journey south, Anders professed to share this belief. He was an ambitious and adventurous man. In the years before he received his formal medical training, he had worked as a ship's surgeon aboard a vessel called the *Holy Wonder*. During one of its southern voyages, the *Holy Wonder* had been inundated by a powerful storm, and Anders had slipped on deck and broken his leg. Despite a months-long convalescence in a Buenos Aires hotel, the injury had not properly healed and was, all these years later, still easily inflamed. It was for this reason that his ride to Golly on the bumping and bouncing mule cart was such an unfortunate development. When he finally reached the town late that night, he could hardly walk at all. Two men had to carry him into the boardinghouse, where a special room was prepared for him on the first floor so that he could avoid the unnecessary punishment of the stairs.

Anders's recovery required two full days of bed rest, and it was during this time that a delegation working for Dabney Dubose slipped into town and purchased the bones for the showman's infamous traveling museum.

This was not the first time that our efforts had been thwarted by someone as nefarious as Dabney Dubose. All varieties of huckster, scoundrel, thief, and hype-man had been busy snatching up every new fossil find. Some of the bones were shipped to Europe for exhibits in London and Paris. Others were fashioned into parlor furniture and sold for small fortunes.

Mr. Dubose called his personal bone collection *Monsters from a Darker Age*, and it constituted one of the chief attractions in the Dubose Brothers Traveling Museum, a caravan of oddities and curiosities that rattled from town to town on creaking wooden wheels, charging poor dupes at every stop for the chance to see its Gander of Six-Headed Geese, Rumpkin the All-Seeing Seer, the Infinity Box, the World's Smallest Preacher, etc., etc., etc. To claim his newest acquisition, his entire caravan now turned south for the town of Golly.

Workers had discovered the bones by accident while blasting for a new well on a farm on the western edge of town. For their protection, the bones had then been transported to a nearby barn and nested in bales of hay. Dr. Anders, unaware that he'd already failed in his mission, visited the farm on his third morning in Golly to make the acquaintance of the property owner, a knobby man with two buttons missing from his work shirt.

"You've come too late," the man said.

Anders was shocked. That the sale had occurred only the previous afternoon, as he lay in bed recuperating, only worsened the blow. He had traveled so far and, it seemed now, for nothing. If he returned home empty-handed, what would we say? What would we think of him?

"Can I at least see them?" Anders asked. "Would you mind if I catalogued and sketched them?"

The farmer scratched at his bristled chin with a jagged dirty fingernail, perhaps looking for a reason to say no. They were standing in front of the man's miserable one-room house. A strange animal skull hung on a nail above the open door. "You want to draw them, is all?"

"If you don't mind, yes. I'll stay out of your way. I assure you."

The man shifted from right foot to left. "All right, then," he said at last. "But if you try and run off with—"

"I wouldn't dream of it," Anders said.

He followed the farmer across a long frosted field that stretched behind the house. His leg still aching—a sharp stabbing pain that radiated from hip to toes—Anders hobbled along on an ivory-handled walking stick obtained for him the previous evening by the town doctor. The cane left a trail of small divots in the hard soil. When they reached the barn, the farmer threw open its tremendous doors, and dusty sunlight spilled across the compacted straw floor. Both men's shadows stretched long and distinct ahead of them. Anders coughed, a handkerchief over his nose and mouth. The farmer motioned at the hay bales and said that so long as the bones didn't leave the barn, there wouldn't be any trouble. He gave Anders a final appraising look before spitting in the straw and leaving.

From his bag Anders removed his pen, ink, journals, caliper, and measuring rods. He was thrilled to find, among the bones across the bales, dorsal and caudal vertebrae, a partial pubis, distal ends of the right radius, the left femur, and the proximal end of the left tibia, ribs, and, best of all, the entire lower jaw. The farmer and his friends had done an adequate job of chiseling away the rock, though some pieces were still embedded. This was no mammoth or mastodon, of that Anders was quite certain. (Our museum already had in its possession a nearly intact mammoth skeleton.) It was not an ancient horse or deer or sloth or cat either. It was much larger, and very likely reptilian. He catalogued the bones in his journal. A truly remarkable find. That it now belonged to Dabney Dubose, of course, was a travesty.

By no means was Anders an accomplished illustrator, but with help from the Academy he had improved upon his shading, crosshatching, and stippling techniques. He endeavored to make his drawings as scientifically accurate as possible. One day, he hoped to include the figures with the papers he aimed to publish.

Anders was engrossed in his drawing of the jawbone when he

heard the squeak of wood overhead. He glanced up and saw that a wild-looking creature with long twisted hair and ruddy cheeks had climbed into the rafters. The creature—a boy, Anders decided— stared down with deep brown eyes, his toes hugging the splintery edges of the beam upon which he crouched.

Anders returned to his drawing and said, "You're welcome to join me. No need to hide."

The boy didn't say anything.

"My name is Dr. Anders," he added.

The boy thudded down into the straw, kicking up more dust. Anders stood to greet him with an outstretched hand. The child shook it uncertainly. His shirt was soiled with dirt and sweat and probably a thousand messy meals.

"You can sit with me if you'd like," Anders said, making room. "I don't mind."

The child, noiselessly, fell into a cross-legged jumble at the scientist's feet. He watched Anders's pen dance across the page, as if the transference of the ink was a minor miracle.

"How does it look?" he asked, and the child shrugged.

"Your name?" Anders asked.

"Temp."

"Temp," Anders repeated. "Short for what? Temperance? Or temperature? Or temporary?"

"Tempest." The child's eyes darted from bone to bone. "I'm told it was my mother's family name."

As Anders drew, he told Temp of his own childhood, about his mother's death in a fire, about his minister father, about their lonely years with a congregation in a town much like Golly, about his early fascination with the Creation story and, in particular, with a tantalizing verse in the Book of Job that described a behemoth with a tail like a cedar and bones like bars of iron.

Temp gazed at the jawbone, fascinated. "So it's a monster from the Bible?"

"Well," Anders said, "that depends on what you mean by *monster*. Certainly it was of a monstrous *size*. By my calculations, this creature stood at least ten feet tall. I believe it was bipedal. In other words, it walked like you and me. Upright. On two feet." He stood to demonstrate, shifting his weight to his good leg. He snarled at the boy playfully and smiled. "But I don't care for that word, *monster*. Calling it a monster implies that it was a wholly unnatural creature. In its time, this was no more a monster than any other animal that currently walks the earth. Including you and me, by the way."

"But," the boy said, somewhat alarmed, "how'd it get *here*? On my daddy's farm?"

"Same way as you and me. The evidence suggests there were multiple Creations before our own. You've heard of Noah's Ark? The Flood? Well, before the Flood, there was a different set of creatures here on earth. And before them, there was an altogether *different* set of creatures that were wiped out by a different and earlier Flood. Each catastrophe makes way for the next Creation, you see, and each Creation is a little better than the last. We're the latest. And hopefully the last."

The child ran his hand along the jaw, hard and gray as stone, bits of rock still clinging to it, and asked what the creature would have eaten and what it might have looked like with the skin attached, and Anders—though aware that to make such physiological inferences was well beyond his expertise—guessed that it ate both plants and animals and that it might have had the smooth, scaly skin of a snake. "Yes," he said, "I'm very sure that it did. It stood upright like us, ate plants and animals like us, and when it craned its long neck skyward it saw the same yellow sun as us."

The child looked up into the rafters.

"Ink, please," Anders said, and Temp scurried toward the satchel, already proving himself a useful assistant.

The morning that Mr. Dubose arrived in town to collect his prize, Anders was out on one of his early peregrinations. His walks were imperative. In addition to his leg injury, Anders suffered from poor circulation and a weak heart, and a strict routine of exercise was of vital importance. After his walk, he took a bath—always cold with two tablespoons of castor oil over his head. His delicate system demanded that he ingest only a simple breakfast of water and plain whole wheat bread. Butter was a gross injustice to the constitution.

Mrs. Lang, the owner of the boardinghouse, didn't care for his diet. "But wouldn't you like some fruit, Doctor? I have all these lovely apples. It's such a waste," she said, eyeing his crusty bread. She was a beautiful if odd red-haired woman who insisted Anders take all his meals with her in the dining room.

"I'm afraid the fruit would upset my system," he explained. "But thank you."

She couldn't understand why he'd only munch on hard bread when her cook had prepared them such an elaborate breakfast. She ate the apple with a fork and knife and dabbed the corners of her thin lips with a fresh white linen napkin. Mrs. Lang had traveled to London and Paris as a small girl, and Anders gathered that her childhood had been full of such luxuries—trips abroad, new dresses for every season, tutors. It seemed her father had played a minor role in brokering the Louisiana Purchase, a fact that somehow found its way into more than one conversation. (Mr. Jefferson, it should be noted, was an early member and supporter of our Academy. During Jefferson's administration, one room at the White House was dedicated entirely to the fossils collected by Mr. Clark on his famous western expedition!) But since those days, Mrs. Lang's family had come down in the world. Their fortune had been lost in poor investments, though she was hazy on the particulars. Her parents had all but arranged her marriage to a businessman with roots in Golly, but now, fifteen years later, both her parents and her husband were dead, and Mrs. Lang lived alone, childless and perhaps a bit lonely. She took in the occasional lodger, she said, for the company and not for the income.

"Forgive me," she said, "we never even blessed the food."

"I don't mind, really," Dr. Anders admitted, but she grabbed his hands anyway and bowed her head, waiting for him to speak. After a considerable pause, he muttered a succinct but sufficient blessing. She released his hands slowly.

"Oh, thank you," she said. "Will you be visiting that barn again today? I suspect so, but I'd hate for you to leave town without seeing what else Golly has to offer besides a dirty old barn. Have you seen the waterfall down at the end of Dempsey Road? It's a very nice place to take a lunch."

"I don't doubt it."

"But you want to look at those bones."

"That's correct."

"What's so interesting about those bones? They probably just came from a big old buffalo. They used to roam all the way to the Atlantic, isn't that so?"

Anders smiled. "Perhaps, but these are not buffalo bones. They belonged to a much more fascinating creature than that. If you study the Old Testament in the original Hebrew, you will find many clues that the world is very old and very vast. In the beginning, it was filled with gigantic animals that would have towered over us. These bones are the proof of that."

"Interesting," she said. "You know, my father used to tell me stories about the Cyclops. Do you know about the Cyclops? Well, my father would make up his own silly stories and tell them to me before bed. He told me that the Cyclops's name was Figaro, and that he was very lonely giant. Poor Figaro wanted a mate, but there were no female Cyclopes on his island. There were only the normal, two-eyed variety, and these women wanted nothing to do with Figaro. They thought he was so hideous. And big. And malodorous.

"One day Figaro got a grand idea. He picked the most beautiful woman on the island and used a slingshot to knock out one of her eyes. It was very gruesome, and she was utterly depressed, as you can imagine. She had to wear a patch over the hole. People no longer called her beautiful, but it was all she'd ever known how to be. She threatened to throw herself off a cliff. But then Figaro showed up with his one giant eye. He called her beautiful. He said he loved her one blue eye. She saw no other options but to run away with him. So they married and moved into his cave. She was embarrassed about all of it. She imagined her old friends laughing at her misfortune. That night Figaro lifted her into his big bed. He had to be careful he didn't crush her, but—" Mrs. Lang blushed a little, but pushed ahead with the tale. "Well, let's just say, after *that* night, she no longer cared what anyone thought about them."

"It's been a while since I read my Homer, but I don't believe I'm familiar with this particular myth," Dr. Anders said. "And your father told this to you as a little girl?"

"Something like it. So is it a Cyclops in the barn?"

Anders assured her it was not.

"Shame," she said, and blinked across the table. "By the way, I meant to tell you, your little assistant is downstairs waiting to speak with you."

"Temp is here? In the house?"

She nodded with a quick stab of her chin.

"For how long?" he asked, irritated she hadn't mentioned it sooner. He had instructed Temp to come and retrieve him upon the arrival of Mr. Dubose.

Temp had been downstairs, she said, ever since Anders had returned from his morning stroll. He excused himself and dropped his napkin on his chair. The child was waiting for him in a plush red chair at the base of the stairs, hands folded in his lap. He sat there frozen like a museum exhibit, perhaps overwhelmed by Mrs. Lang's home, its fine white curtains and vases with fresh-cut flowers and crystal figurines and oil paintings in gilded frames. Seeing Anders on the stairs, he stood like a soldier at attention.

Dabney Dubose had arrived, Temp reported in a rush, and now something strange was under way in the barn.

. . .

"I could use someone like you," Dabney Dubose said to Anders outside the barn. He was a dough-faced man with icy blue eyes, his dark hair receding but wild and curly where it did grow in tufts. He seemed amused by Anders. By everything. "I'm told you've been examining the bones over the last few days? I'm curious to hear your thoughts on them. Until now what we've seen has been so . . . preliminary. Bits of this, bits of that. I never knew what to make of it. I couldn't *see* it. And as a man who prides himself as a visionary, that's quite an admission. But what we have here, well, now. It really is spectacular. I can almost imagine it."

Frustrated, Anders scratched his cane in the dirt. His leg throbbed. In the distance stretched long fallow fields, gloomy and brown. It felt like it might snow. The barn doors were shut, but a commotion of hammering and sawing and the clink-clink-clinking of a chisel escaped between the gnarled slats.

"Let me buy the bones from you," Anders said. "Please. For our museum."

"I'm afraid that won't be possible," Dubose said. "Not even for a good price." The bones, he explained, were going to become his main attraction. Using wood, papier-mâché, plaster, and anything else necessary, he would present the world with the first fully reconstituted Monster from a Darker Age, a three-dimensional model constructed from the bones themselves. Never before had anyone seen something of its kind. For a few coins, you would be able to view the creature up close, stand in its towering presence, rub its hairy hide.

"I don't think it had a hairy hide," Anders said. "I believe that it belonged to a Tribe of Ancient Lizard."

"And that's precisely why I need your help. You can be my scientific advisor. Help me make the creature as real and accurate as possible. Accuracy is crucial. I'll give you full oversight of my crew."

Anders was aware of course that a compact with such a man was not a wise decision, that Dubose's intentions were very likely anathema to science. Science eats the dark. Fear not that which is illuminated. Science names the nameless—megalonyx, mammoth, mastodon, megathere. Fear not that which has a name. Science excavates; it makes the unfamiliar familiar. Science knows all; it demystifies. Dubose was an author of mystery in the world, not its unraveler.

"Think of it this way," Dubose said. "This is your chance to educate the public. To open minds. Most people won't believe in something unless it's right in front of them. You've got to wow them. Shake them up."

"Yes, but," Anders said. "But you have a responsibility to—"

"Of course, a responsibility," the man said solemnly.

Anders, we are sad to report, proved himself susceptible to the showman's false promises and logic. This will come as no surprise to anyone who has examined Anders's notebooks from this period (now in our archives). The pages are marred with all sorts of revealing marginalia; with fanciful sketches of creatures inspired by the bones he'd long admired in the cabinets and display cases of our Academy's museum; with his wild questions too: Had the creatures leathery skin? Could they have been pink and soft like us? With long tangled hair or short fine fur? How about feathers? Did their eyes bulge like a fish's? Did their claws rip and grip like a bird's? How big or lean were their muscles?

And so it was that Anders agreed to help Mr. Dubose with his project. Elated, the showman clapped his hands together. There was no time to waste. The rest of his traveling museum would arrive in mere days, Dubose said, and after the monster's debut in Golly, it would go on the road, winding its way north to New York, where he was in the process of building a more permanent home for his entire collection. Beyond that—who knew?—perhaps he would ship it to Paris and London. Anders could not imagine how Dubose planned to transport a ten-foot-tall creature, but in the barn he discovered that at least some of the hammering and sawing had been in the service of a massive cart with giant wooden wheels. It would take a team of horses to pull it. The bones themselves had been placed at intervals across the straw floor.

"It's going to take longer than three days," a man with frayed blond sideburns came over to report.

"This is my architect, Mr. Gustafson," Dubose said to Anders. "Mr. Gustafson, you're in luck, we have a scientist here who has extensively studied the creatures. He has even published papers on the topic."

Anders did not correct the showman regarding his publication history, despite the fact that he had not published a single paper on vertebrate fossils (or, for that matter, on any other topic zoological).

"Expert or not," Mr. Gustafson said, "I'd like to see *him* try and fit the pieces together."

Anders's knowledge of nonhuman anatomy was, to put it delicately, incomplete, but at the boardinghouse he had with him a number of engravings from the Academy's holdings. He sent Temp for his books, and when they arrived, he opened each to various illustrations—of mammoth molars and giant sloth skulls—looking desperately for any correlations between those figures and the dark gray chunks cast about the straw. Gustafson and his team had chiseled away more of the rock, though not with any precision. Some of the fossils now had small fissures, cracks, and chinks. About this Anders said nothing.

He shuffled the bones. He traded one toe for another, experimenting with angles and directions. The spiky horn: Was it a feature of the tail, of the foot, or of the head? The rib cage he arranged and then rearranged. Temp watched from his perch in the rafters as Anders spun the femur like a windmill blade, around and around until it paired with the tibia. As for the *other* tibia, the missing one, they'd have to make it from plaster. They'd have to form much of the skeleton from plaster, Anders slowly realized.

The men who'd been busy building the cart and freeing the fossils now leaned back in the hay with straw between their gray teeth, murmuring and laughing as Anders hobbled around on his cane, exhaling loudly whenever something failed to fit, which was most of the time.

The spine, Anders eventually decided, was the best place to start, and so he began all over again, this time focusing on the vertebrae. But which were the dorsal and which were the caudal and what was their order?

"Where's the head?" one of the men asked. "It's got a head, right?"

Anders didn't answer him. Other than the lower jaw, there was no skull.

"Looks like a giant horse to me," another man said, and Anders saw that the way in which he'd laid out the spine did make it appear rather horselike.

At the end of the day, Mr. Dubose reappeared in the barn and asked the men to lift him into the air so that he could get a better view of what he called Anders's *diligent scientific study*. They hoisted him up and sat him on their shoulders, his waist squeezed between their heads. He loomed over all, barking at them to move backward, then forward. Clearly he was displeased with his new scientific advisor's progress. He didn't try to hide this fact. The skeleton on the barn floor was messy and incomplete and not at all terrifying or impressive. The showman closed his eyes and then popped them open. "What about those over there?" he asked, and pointed to all the bones not yet utilized.

"Tomorrow," Anders said.

"Tomorrow," Dubose said, "it gets a head. I want to see its head."

Mrs. Lang's dinner table was more crowded and livelier than usual that night. Mr. Dubose and his representatives, it seemed, had been hard at work drumming up enthusiasm for the project in the nearby towns. Word had spread and people were arriving in droves for the chance to see it on Saturday, when it would be unveiled for the paying public.

"Is it true that the jaw is longer than my arm?" the man sitting across from Anders asked. He was gnawing on a fatty piece of beef. "Gracious God!" he said when Anders nodded vaguely. "How many animals do you think it crushed?"

"Crushed?" the woman to his left said, eyes wide. "This is like something from a horrible dream. Somebody pinch me. I'm afraid if I see it once, I'll see it everywhere I go. I'll never be rid of it again. It will be there—and there and there—hiding behind every house and tree."

"I suspect it wouldn't be very good at hiding behind trees," the man said, "or anything else."

"You know," another man said, tugging at his wiry gray chin beard, "I've heard Indian stories about beings that used to stalk this continent. They say that their ancestors were giants, just as big as the buffalo and lions that lived here. They say everything was bigger back then, including us."

"I doubt that very much," Anders said. "Every creation is an improvement upon the last. We in the Present Age are God's most perfect creation. Everything that came before us, God destroyed for a reason."

"But giant men. Can you imagine?"

"Is it a form of crocodile?" the woman asked. "That's what I heard."

Anders explained that though the bones indicated certain lizard qualities, it was not a crocodile but a distinct and unrelated species, heretofore undiscovered and unknown.

"Heretofore undiscovered and unknown," the man across from Anders repeated, his squirrel's tail of a mustache shining with roast beef grease. "Now you sound like Ol' Dab."

"Dabney Dubose," Mrs. Lang said. "You know him, then?"

"My whole life, just about. Been all over the world with him.

London, Calcutta, Constantinople. No place that man hasn't traveled to. If anyone can figure what the monster is, it's him."

"To be well traveled hardly qualifies him for this," Anders said.

"Not the travel," the man said, and formed two fingers into prongs that poked away from his eyes. "It's this that qualifies him."

"And what is that, exactly?" Mrs. Lang asked.

"Sight," he said. "Insight. Outsight. Pastsight. Futuresight. Take your pick of the sights."

"Well," Mrs. Lang said. "I for one think we should defer to Dr. Anders's authority on these matters."

Anders nodded gratefully in her direction—though he couldn't help wondering if she was right to do so.

Across town, at that very moment, a behemoth was being born.

Dabney Dubose was not a patient man, and he had doubts about having his show ready in time with Anders at the helm. Perhaps another naturalist from our Academy might have been better suited to the task, it's true. But then again, no other of our naturalists would have dared partner with such an unscrupulous man. As Anders was feasting on beef and potatoes and then later as he dreamed in the big white bed set up for him on the first floor of the boardinghouse, Dubose and his crew continued their work by the light of lanterns hanging from barn nails.

"Make it bigger," he instructed his team. "Do what you have to do. Put cork between the joints. I want it on all fours. That horny spike there—I want that on the head."

Mr. Gustafson, reinstated as architect, started with the feet, connecting tarsals and phalanges and claws with wires and rods. As the beast began to take shape on its wagon pedestal, Dubose clapped and cheered. Rough plaster molds were made to fill in the missing sections. When the rib cage collapsed, Gustafson had them insert wooden dowels where the organs would have been. Bones were attached to bone, even when they did not properly join. Unnecessary parts were tossed aside. With all four legs on the ground, the spine sagged in the middle like a toothy smile. The tail pointed skyward at the tip. At the other end, the neck craned up and forward, as if the animal had just been caught in the act of feeding on a fresh carcass.

The creature they were building of course bore no resemblance to what the physiology of its bones actually suggested. Dubose brought in his tailor to measure the beast and test various fabrics that might serve as a skin. They tried cotton and silk and wool but ultimately decided on a thin pounded leather, which they could ornament with layers of iridescent flakes. Dubose wanted to leave the top ridge of the spine exposed as proof that that their monster contained the actual bones. The tailor worked from the bottom up and, when he reached the spine, suggested that he glue on horsehair, dyed gray and blond, to resemble a scraggly mane. "Do it," Dubose said. As the tailor's assistants stitched the silvery flakes into the hide, the creature began to shimmer under the burning lamps.

By midmorning, when Anders returned, he was stunned by the overnight transfiguration of the creature. What had been scattered and flat across the straw now towered overhead, twelve feet tall and at least thirty feet long, atop the cart bed. With its sparkling scales and hideous mane, the headless chimera was like something out of the Greek myths. Never in his wildest dreams had Anders imagined the behemoths as such.

"As you can see"—Dubose stepped toward him—"we took the liberty of continuing your work last night. Your guidance was crucial."

"This is all wrong," Anders said. "You need to strip it back down."

"As for the head," Dubose said, undeterred, "do you have any ideas? I suppose we'll need to dream up something, won't we?"

"Dream up?"

"Yes, since we don't have those bones."

"But if we dream it up, then how will it be accurate?"

"I take your point, but people will be let down if it's headless. Just give me a rough idea. Do you think it had tusks like the mammoths? That would be interesting, wouldn't it? I have a few in my collection that we could include."

"No, I don't think it had tusks. We can't know what it had. You . . . you might as well make it a Cyclops. That's how little we know. Why do we need to provide a head? Put up a sign, explain to people that the head has not yet been located. People will understand."

"Yes," Dubose said, nodding. "Yes, I suppose you're right. We'll figure something out, I'm sure. You will be coming to the show on Saturday, I hope? Your admission will be complimentary, that goes without saying."

He escorted Anders out of the barn and shook his hand amicably. "See you then," the showman said, and returned to his project. In a daze Anders wandered back in the direction of the ramshackle farmhouse, his toes so cold and numb in the tips of his shoes that he had to subtract them from the idea of his feet. It was a drizzly day, the earth and sky washed in gray. Temp appeared on the horizon as a peachy dot, moving toward him at a run. As the distance closed, Anders was surprised to discover certain changes in his assistant. Temp's hair had been brushed flat and parted neatly down the middle. Not only that, the child was wearing an oversized dress with a white ruffled collar and a dusty toolong hem. Temp, he realized, was a girl.

"You like it?" she asked, pulling the loose fabric tighter at the hips. "I didn't want it, but my daddy said it was time I dressed right."

Anders didn't know what to say. That he'd so grossly miscategorized a member of his own species was no doubt distressing. How could he understand a creature that was thousands of years behind him, if he couldn't make sense of the world directly in front of him?

Temp smiled politely and held out a small gray bone. "There's a whole pile of these in the barn," she said. "The ones they couldn't get to fit right. I don't think anyone will miss it."

Anders accepted the bone. It was one of the creature's ribs. "Did they see you take it?" he asked, already tucking the bone into his jacket pocket.

"I doubt it," she said. "They're very busy."

Of all those forms now passed into extinction, the Gollysaurus, *as I have dubbed it, is the most impressive and inspiring.* Anders's letter, composed later that afternoon in his room at the boardinghouse, reached us far too late to be of any use. Contained therein was what he called "a serious attempt at objective description despite his overwhelming excitement." Only in his conclusion did he reveal to us his failure to procure the bones, and Dubose's scheme to use them as an exhibit for his *Monsters from a Darker Age*. But through other sources we had been kept well apprised of developments in Golly and our representatives were already en route to try to repair the situation.

When Mrs. Lang knocked on his door for supper that evening, Anders shouted that he wasn't hungry and was in bed with a headache. Alarmed, Mrs. Lang let herself into the room to make sure that her guest was comfortable. Did he want food brought to him, perhaps? Could she prepare a wet cloth for his forehead? Did he want the windows open or closed? Anders wanted only to be left alone. He wanted to sulk. But Mrs. Lang refused to abandon him in his time of need. "It could be a fever," she said.

She dragged a chair to the edge of his bed and sat with a book while he pretended to sleep. Afternoon sunlight through the window danced violently, orange and red, inside his lids. When the room went dark, he opened his eyes and discovered that Mrs. Lang, by candlelight, was watching his chest rise and fall.

"I'm feeling better," he said.

"It was the bones that did this to you."

"No," he said, not mentioning the bone under his pillow. "That's not possible. Sickness comes from the air. From unhealthy vapors. It's been proven."

"Was it bad air that killed off the monsters, then? Maybe some of that bad air got trapped down there in its grave." She grabbed his hand. "Now we'll all get sick, everyone in town."

Anders assured her that she was mistaken, that the monster posed no real threat, at least not to her *physical* health. "If you say so," Mrs. Lang said. He asked her to retrieve the paper and pen from his bag. When she brought it to him, he thanked her for taking such good care of him. "I'll be fine," he said. "You can go to bed now. Really."

She hesitated at the door but, seeing him put the pen to paper, left the room. Anders was writing a letter to his fiancée. In it, he likened his love for her to a bed of flowers blooming in unison. He wrote that he was her moon, forever loyal in his revolutions.

My trip hasn't gone as planned, he confessed, finally, and told her of Dubose and the bones and their upcoming unveiling, and of Temp, the girl he mistook for a boy, and then, curiously, of his own misgivings regarding our scientific mission. *Some part of me fears,* he wrote, *that the world as we know it only exists as a set of shared beliefs, which change and grow according to our needs and intellects. Meaning, the world becomes more complex as we do, forever outwitting and confounding us. In the beginning, perhaps all that was needed to sustain us was the idea of a small garden, a plot of land bordered on all sides by nothingness. The earth formed around us as we explored it, the stars burst into light when we looked up. Microorganisms might have only sprouted into being the first time we gazed through a microscope. The sun might have revolved around the earth until the very moment we needed it to be otherwise. Did we dream the fossils into the ground? If enough of us believed it possible, maybe Dubose's monster would walk right out of the barn and destroy us all. I fear we're on a wall that can't be scaled, one we climb with one hand while we build it higher with the other. If that's the case, we might as well stand back and just paint pictures across the stones—one-eyed monsters, cataclysmic floods, the universe as imagined by a caveman or a carnival barker or a wild-haired prophet.*

Forgive me, my darling, he concluded. *Perhaps I shouldn't have been napping with a fossil under my pillow.*

His disturbing and faithless letter is stored in our archives to this day along with Dr. Anders's other personal papers, all willed to our collection at the time of his death.

The Dubose Brothers Traveling Museum arrived on Saturday morning. Sitting on the front porch of the boardinghouse after his cold bath and simple breakfast, Anders watched people stream into town on foot and on horseback, entire families crammed onto rattling carts. Anders's ears burned from the cold. Mrs. Lang emerged from the house in a long brown jacket over a frilly apple-green dress.

"Are you sure you won't join us?" she asked.

Anders had decided to skip the event. "I'll be fine here. Go ahead."

Slowly the boardinghouse emptied, and Anders was alone. Across the street the shop had closed its doors for the day. A billy goat with a white sagging neck and two short horns hopscotched down the street and stopped abruptly to consider Anders rocking on the porch. It stepped toward the gate that divided them. But Anders had no scraps for it.

One day, after the next Catastrophe, the town might look like this, empty and abandoned to the billy goats. In his notebook, Anders sketched his own skeleton embedded in the stone beneath

the boardinghouse porch. He imagined his gray bones on a pedestal, the identifiable fissures in the right femur that would make
him a particularly interesting specimen. If his skull was missing,
some future showman would stick some other animal's head
there, a skull disproportionate to his own body, a fox head perhaps, its long, thin, haggard mouth with sharp hanging incisors,
eyes on the side of its head. A monster for a brighter age. They'd
give him a glittery hide, a demon's horns.

"Aren't you going to see it?" It was Temp. She was wearing
her dress again. Over her shoulder she carried a bulky burlap sack.
It clattered when she dropped it at Anders's feet. "The rest of the
bones," she said. "If you want them."

Anders uncinched the top and peered inside. There were
probably thirty bones and fragments in the bag, none bigger than
his forearm, but still: thirty bones for the Academy's collection—
or maybe even for his own. He took the bag inside and deposited it
under his bed. When he came back out onto the porch, buttoning
up his coat, he said, "You lead the way. I'm ready to see the monster." The billy goat skittered away, the bell around its neck clang-
ing, when Temp kicked open the gate and stepped into the street.

What Anders didn't know was that some of us were already
there on the farm, waiting and touring the exhibits.

The Infinity Box, we discovered, was a room full of old frac-
tured mirrors. Inside a wagon lined with puffy red fabric sat
Rumpkin the All-Seeing Seer, a man with a long drooping white
mustache that he twisted and twisted between his fingers before
offering his vague prognoses of life, love, and death. The museum's Gander of Six-Headed Geese had already flown south for
the winter. The caravan curved snakelike through the farmer's

fallow brown fields, and the well-dressed crowds stepped carefully over the rutted earth. The smell of spiced meats and stewed apples wafted over the open land, and people lounged on quilts with their plates and drinks.

At dusk, the World's Smallest Preacher emerged from the barn. He was three feet tall and dressed in a black robe, his thin dark hair combed neatly. In one hand he gripped a tremendous Bible. When he stepped forward, three bonfires burst into flames, blue, then red and orange. Men wearing Indian headdresses paraded out on white horses. We heard drums and a trumpet fanfare. The World's Smallest Preacher, his voice strained, yelled out the name Dabney Dubose, and the infamous showman emerged from behind the barn door to massive applause.

"Before Jesus, before Moses, before Noah . . . a million years ago a monster roamed these ancient forests and devoured any poor animal that crossed its path," he shouted to an enraptured audience. "It was the scourge of the world! More terrible than a tiger! Bigger than an elephant! Ladies and gentlemen, using the latest scientific methods available, and with the cooperation and approval of a prestigious scientific Academy, we have exhumed and rebuilt the animal. Ladies and gentlemen, for the first time in the history of man, the behemoth returneth!" One barn door creaked open and a line formed. "Have your fifty cents ready, please," the preacher added, as if it were an afterthought.

Needless to say, our Academy had given no such approval to Dubose and had not cooperated with him in any way. That can't be emphasized enough. It was Anders who had done these things, and certainly not as our dutiful representative. Those of us present resolved then and there to take a vote at our next meeting—to oust Anders, no matter his backers. We could not allow this exhibition to besmirch our good standing in the wider scientific community. We went in search of Dubose to demand he apologize publicly for claiming such an affiliation. If he refused us, we were resolved to destroy his creature by any means necessary, even if it meant setting fire to the barn.

We found Anders before Dubose. He was exiting the barn, along with Temp, a dazed look on both their faces. "So you've come," he said when he saw us striding toward him. We didn't like how pleased he seemed by all of this, by the music, by the celebration. When we informed him of our plan, he said, "Yes, well, I expected you might try something like that."

We ordered him to take us to Dubose.

"He's in there," Anders said, and pointed back to the barn. "With his monster." Every single crack between the dark wood slats exploded with yellow and orange light. We told him we had absolutely no intention of setting foot inside that barn. We wouldn't give Dubose the satisfaction of gazing upon his creation. "Suit yourselves," Anders said, smiling now. "But if you want to find Dubose tonight, if you want your apology, you'll have to go in that barn. No other way."

When he moved to leave us, leaning forward on his cane, we grabbed him by the arm. We asked why he couldn't go into the barn and drag Dubose out to us.

"Something has occurred to me," he said, shaking us loose. "If you made Dubose a member of our Academy, the bones would, in a certain sense, be ours too, would they not?"

He was talking nonsense. We told him so. He shrugged and disappeared into the crowd along with the girl.

We were divided on what to do next, but a quick vote decided our course: we would take our place in line. They were admitting only four people at once, and the line moved at a snail's pace. By the time we reached those immense barn doors and reluctantly dropped our coins into the preacher's jangling bucket, night had fallen and the only light was that provided by the lanterns. Inside, the straw was soft beneath our feet. We saw no sight of Dubose. We were told to keep moving. Smoke danced through the rafters of the barn, and there, up ahead, illuminated by a ring of red and blue glass lanterns, like something plucked from a nightmare, was the creature, lurching toward us with rows of sharp teeth and two long curving tusks, its chest puffed with breath, a single knowing blue eye at the center of its giant apish head. We were very, very quiet.

Ba Baboon

For a long time they do nothing but hide and wait. Very little light creeps in under the pantry's double doors. Brooks examines the cans on the shelf level with his head: beans, corn, soup. This pantry does not belong to him—or to his sister, Mary. They are in someone else's home. Mary has her eye pressed to the door crack.

"Do you have to breathe so loud?" she asks. "I'm trying to listen."

The pantry is small but not coffin-small, not so small that Brooks can't stretch his arms wide like a—well, like a *what*, exactly? Like a scarecrow on a pole. Okay, a scarecrow, sure, but where did that image come from? From the muck of the way back when, no doubt. "Your long-term memory seems to be hunky-dory," Dr. Groom has told Brooks more than once, jubilantly.

Sure enough, a student theater production from almost thirty years ago bubbles up fresh, unbattered: the out-of-tune piano at the end of the stage, the hard crusts of chewing gum under the seats in the auditorium, the flattened cereal boxes cut into rectangles and painted to look like a road of yellow bricks. Fourteen years old, Brooks nearly landed the coveted Scarecrow role in *The Wizard of Oz*, coveted because of the beautiful blond-haired fifteen-year-old playing Dorothy Gale, a girl who later, according to three munchkins, gave it up to the Tin Man in the janitor's closet. It could have been Brooks she gave it up to if he hadn't screwed up the song in auditions and been cast instead as a member of the dreaded Lollipop Guild.

"If I only had a brain," Brooks sings.

"That's not funny," Mary says, and looks over at him. "I really wish you wouldn't say things like that. It's upsetting."

Say things like what? Oh, the bit about the brain. Brooks gets it now, why he's thinking about the mindless scarecrow after all these years. Somewhere up in his head is the Old Brooks, that asshole, and he's poking fun at this moodier, slower version of himself. *If you only had a brain,* Old Brooks is singing, a malicious smile on his chubbier face, his brown hair combed over neatly and not cropped short with scabby scars across the scalp.

"You might feel irrationally angry sometimes," Dr. Groom has said. If he's feeling agitated, Brooks is supposed to ask himself why, to interrogate his agitation, but God, does he want to punch something right now, anything, the angel-hair pasta boxes or the cracked-pepper crackers, the clementines or the canned chickpeas, so many chickpeas, a lifetime's supply of chickpeas. He could punch the peas into a mash and lick his knuckles clean. Brooks has lost all sense of how long they've been hiding in this pantry. He plops down onto a lumpy dog food bag beside his sister.

"I don't hear them anymore," Mary says. "They might be up-stairs. Maybe they're asleep."

Brooks nods, then lets his eyebrows scrunch. He can feel his sister studying him.

"Have you forgotten why we're in here?" Mary asks. "Have you forgotten about the dogs?"

The events of the afternoon float and constellate in his memory: a turkey sandwich, his sister's Taurus, a small brass key from under a rock, a tiled kitchen floor, two snarling dogs. It's like standing inches away from a stippled drawing and being asked to name the subject. And the artist.

Mary gives him one of her pity smiles, where her upper lip mushrooms around her bottom lip, consumes it. She is a compact, muscular woman, still a girl, really, with a body for the tennis court, not the sort of person you could knock over easily.

The dog food pebbles crunch under his sharp butt bones when he shifts. He's lost weight, probably twenty pounds since the accident. Brooks doesn't remember anything from that night, but according to the police (via his mother), he was alone at the time, unloading groceries from the back of his car on the street in front of his townhouse. Someone smashed the left side of his head with a brick. A brick! The police found it down the street in some bushes, along with bits of Brooks's skull. The assailant took the car (which still hasn't been recovered and probably never will be) and his wallet. "A random act of violence," his mother called it. "A totally senseless thing." Unnecessary qualifiers, he sometimes wants to tell her, as the universe is a random and senseless place.

"I need to go," he says.

"We can't."

"Go, as in pee."

"Right," Mary says. "Of course. I'm sorry. Let's just give it a few more minutes. Just to be safe. The last thing we need is to go out there and get bitten."

He squirms.

"Here," she says, and offers him a third-full bottle of organic olive oil. "You can pee in this."

You can pee in this. Mary feels like one of the nurses. Brooks is staying with her for a month, and that means she is responsible for his meals, for his entertainment, for getting him to all his appointments.

Yesterday they had to wait forty-five minutes for the doctor to return to the examining room. Brooks was a broken record while they waited: "Pencil box screen door pencil box screen door." Dr. Groom was to blame for this. One of his memory games. The doctor often began his checkups by listing a random series of words for Brooks to later repeat on command, a test of his short-term memory. Before leaving on her month-long adventure to Bread Island, Mary's mother warned that Brooks might attempt to scribble the words on his hand when the doctor wasn't looking. Brooks, her mother had explained, wanted his independence back almost as much as they wanted to give it to him. But that wasn't possible yet. He still had what she called "little blips." He could be coherent and normal one minute, and the next . . . well.

"Pencil box screen door pencil box . . ."

"You don't have to remember it anymore," she said. "The doctor already asked you, and you got it right. You already won that game."

That didn't stop him. He hammered each syllable hard, except for the last one, *door*, to which he added at least three extra breathy *o*'s. He ooooohed it like a ghost or a shaman might. Maybe he *is* a shaman. Who can say? What the doctors call hallucinations and delusions—maybe they are something else entirely. Mary read an article somewhere online explaining that people with brain injuries sometimes report unusual and even psychic side effects. There was a stroke victim who said he could read a book and be there—actually be *in the book*, tasting the food, smelling the air. A teenager in a car accident lost his sense of taste but said he could feel people's emotions. It had something to do with unlocking previously unused parts of the brain.

Watching her brother clumsily tap his fingers on the shiny metal table, Mary wondered if it was possible he was in communication with something larger than both of them: a cosmic force, the angels, Frank Sinatra, anything. She doubted it. Her poor brother could barely button his shirt. And as for those words, the skipping record, maybe he'd fallen into some sort of terrible neural feedback loop. He seemed to be saying it involuntarily now.

She was almost ashamed by how much she wanted to slap her brother. Her whole life, Brooks had been the one looking after her—and so what right did she have to be irritated now? When things got rough with her boyfriend Tommy after college, it was

Brooks who drove all the way down to Atlanta and helped her pack. It was Brooks who defended her to their mother when she quit her job with the real estate company. It was Brooks who wrote her a check to buy the Pop-Yop, her soft-serve franchise.

She worried that it would never be that way between them again, that the balance had forever shifted, and then she felt selfish for worrying about such a thing. Brooks needed her. It was her turn.

"Your pants, Brooks," she said, and handed him his khakis.

He stood there beside the exam table in his white underwear and a wrinkled blue shirt, holding the khakis in front of him like a matador's cape. Mary was supposed to have ironed his shirt for him before leaving the house that morning, and that she hadn't fulfilled this duty was a source of some anxiety for her big brother. He could no longer tolerate creases—in clothes, in paper, in anything. Watching him step into his pant legs, she worried that he was about to bring up that morning's ironing debacle again, but he tucked the shirt and zipped his pants without comment.

His crease intolerance was one of many changes that had come with the accident. A longtime smoker, he now said that smoke made him feel sick. A closetful of dark clothes that these days he deemed depressing. In fact, his new favorite article of clothing was a tight bright pink and purple sweater that they wouldn't let him wear outside the house because it wasn't his but their mother's.

When, finally, Dr. Groom returned to the room, Mary stayed seated in her little plastic chair, eyeing all the instruments, the cotton swabs and tongue depressors in the glass jars, the inflatable cuff of the blood pressure device, the trash can with the metal step-lid, biohazard stickers plastered across it, all of it highly unadvanced medical paraphernalia, stuff you might have seen in a doctor's office a century ago. The bigger, more impressive machinery was somewhere else, in another building. The nurses had trouble keeping Brooks still in those machines. Apparently he got antsy.

A frail smile formed on Dr. Groom's face. His eyes were large and blue behind a pair of fashionable glasses. According to Mary's mother, he was the best traumatic brain injury doctor in the state.

"Pencil box screen door," Brooks blurted, all trace of shaman gone from his voice.

"Very good, Brooks," the doctor said, and then leaned back against the table to explain the scans, how they were looking fine, better than expected given the nature of the accident and Brooks's age, which was forty-four. Of course, he said, it wasn't *all* about the scans. The scans wouldn't show any shearing or stretching, for instance. But Brooks was doing well, that was the bottom line. He wasn't slurring his words. His headaches were less frequent. Even his short-term memory was showing signs of improvement. A fuller recovery, the doctor said, might very well be possible.

Brooks is not sure how possible it will be to pee, cleanly, into a third-full bottle of organic extra virgin olive oil, especially given the tiny circumference of its plastic top. The tip of his penis will not fit into that hole. The bottle is a little slippery. He pops off the black top that controls the outward flow of the oil and hands that to Mary. He turns away from her and unzips.

"I've got this can of Pirouette cookies if you run out of bottle," Mary says.

"I just need you to be quiet." He concentrates—or, doesn't. What's required is the absence of concentration. That should be easy, shouldn't it? He's a pro at that now. He sees a yellow brick road. The urine comes in splashy spurts at first and then streams steadily. The bottle warms. The urine pools in a layer above the olive oil, all of it yellow. Thankfully, he doesn't need the cookie tin for overflow. Mary hands him the top when he asks for it and tells him job well done.

Bottle plugged, they decide to store it under the lowest shelf, out of sight for now. He plops back down onto the dog food bags. If he had to, he could sleep like this. He checks his wristwatch with the shiny alligator leather strap, a gift from a long-ago girl-friend. Which girlfriend, he couldn't say.

"We've been in here for an hour," Mary says. She stands and peers again through the crack in the double doors. "Maybe we should just go for it. I don't see the dogs."

Her left eye still at the crack, she crouches down for a new angle on the outside world, her small hands on either side of the white doors for balance.

"Let me," Brooks says, rising. He grabs the brass knob near her left temple. He shoves the doors open, outward into the house, and Mary slides away to let him pass. He emerges from the pantry. To his right, through another open doorway, he can see a kitchen with high white ceilings and recessed lights. To his left a long un-familiar hallway unfolds, hardwood floors with wide dark red planks, at the end of which a cantankerous grandfather clock ticks.

"Not that way," Mary says when he starts down the hall.

He hears a distant clacking of nails, a jangling of collars.

Never has such a tinkly sound seemed so ominous. Mary is behind him now, tugging at his shirt, his arms, pulling him back into the sepulcher of the pantry. The dogs are approaching, their stampede echoing down the hallway. When his back collides with the food shelves, two fat cans drop and roll at his feet. Mary pulls the doors shut again. Seconds later, the dogs galunk into them. Their bulky, invisible weight shakes the flimsy wood of the door so hard Brooks wonders if the hinges might pop. Mary holds the brass knobs tight, as if worried the dogs are capable of turning knobs. The dogs growl. It's hard to think straight over that noise.

"I'm sorry," she says. "I shouldn't have let you go out there. That was dumb of me."

"What are they exactly? What breed?"

"Rottweilers? Dobermans? I don't know what they are, but they're freaking huge. Biggest dogs I've ever seen. Genetically modified, maybe. Wynn would do that. Order a bunch of genetically modified military dogs. That would be so him. There are two of them, Baba and Bebe. Wait, let me try something. I think I just remembered it." The dogs are still clawing at the pantry door. She sticks her lips to the crack and says, "Baba Ganoush." The dogs don't stop their attack. "Bebe, Baba, Baba O'Riley. It's something like that."

"What is?"

"The safe command. Oh, Goosie, I'm sorry I got you into this."

Goosie. When was the last time she called him that? Back at his townhouse, in the drawer to the right of the stove (his mind still has *that* power at least, the power to conjure up images, to see things that aren't directly in front of him), he must have a hundred thank-you cards addressed to Goosie. Thank-yous for the loan, the money that helped Mary buy the soft-serve place that she had, until then, only managed. The golden egg, she called his loan. Him, the goosie.

"The safe command will make them docile," she says.

"Remind me again who Wynn is to you," he says.

"A friend," she says quickly. "He's out of town for a few days, and I agreed to feed his dogs and bring in the mail. He gave me the safe command before he left. I should have written it down."

"Could have just told me. I would have remembered."

She smiles.

"Let's just call someone for help," Brooks says.

"I would if I could. My cell is out in the car."

Brooks fishes around in his pockets.

"Yours is in the car too," she says.

"Well, that's bad luck. What should we do now?"

"When they settle back down again, we'll go together. There's a door in the kitchen. That's, what? Like, thirty feet from here?"

Brooks isn't sure but nods. The dogs are no longer scrabbling at the doors but whining. They walk in circles, with clicking nails, outside. Mary reaches over Brooks's shoulder for a bag of pistachios. She rips open the plastic at the top and offers him some. "We missed breakfast," she says.

He doesn't want any nuts. He sits down on the dog food again, his head back against a shelf. His medication can make him groggy. He needs to rest his eyes.

If only she had poison. Mary imagines Wynn coming home and finding both dogs dead. She imagines him cradling their bodies and weeping. No, Wynn wouldn't weep. He'd probably just buy two more dogs, recycle the names, and move on with his life. Mary has never killed an animal as big as a dog. She veered her car in order to hit a squirrel once and regretted it for two days.

She eats another pistachio. She forgot to put out breakfast this morning because her mother called early from Bread Island for an update.

"How's my boy doing?" she asked.

"He's still asleep. He made dinner last night for both of us. He dropped an egg, and he freaked a little. But mostly he was fine. Good report from the doctor yesterday." Mary did her best to repeat the doctor verbatim.

"Did you ask him about the morning headaches?"

"I forgot, I'm sorry. But Brooks hasn't mentioned them since you left."

Her mother sighed. "I'm going to cut my trip short," she said. "I don't like not being there."

"Mom, you don't have to do that, really. We can manage. Are you staying warm?" Mary pictured her mother layered up in animal furs like one of the Arctic explorers of old, posing at a pole, her cheeks red, the fuzzy dark hair on her upper lip frozen, seal blubber on the bottom of her shoes.

"It's three in the afternoon. We keep the woodstove burning all day, and we've got electric heaters too, but Lord, my butt's been numb ever since I got here. You can take a southerner out of the South but you can't—well, you understand. The point is, don't take her out. Just leave her be. But Cora has been great with me here, she really has. This morning she convinced me to visit one of the mining camps with her. She was doing her interviews. I didn't understand a word of it, of course. All I can do is hold the micro-phone steady."

Cora was her mother's "roommate," a term they'd used around town for years, with a wink, of course, since they owned separate houses. Cora was a sociologist at the university and had recently won a Fulbright to study the few people who lived on Bread Island, a mostly wild and rocky dot in the ice-cold Baltic Sea. Besides the miners, the only other inhabitants were a small indigenous popula-tion that kept to themselves. Mary's mother, who had never even been outside America before she met Cora five years ago, was on the adventure unofficially as an assistant. Internet access was limited and, because of the time difference, so were phone calls.

"Did you get the pictures I sent?" her mother asked. "Of the frogs?"

Yes, Mary had seen her mother's photos of the snow frogs, slimy and shimmering on the edge of a half-frozen pond. The frogs, while strange, had been a nice change. Mostly her mother just wrote to complain—about the temperature, about the long days, about all that white, white, white, as far as the eye could see. She said it was like the inside of a crazy person's head. They found white skeletons in the snow. The wolves ate the musk oxen. The polar bears ate the seals. Everything ate something else. Probably she would be eaten too.

But the frogs, she wrote, were a real inspiration.

"Their eggs are neon-blue in the lake behind our cabin," her mother said. "The eggs actually glow. It's amazing. When I'm feeling sad I go down there. Then I remember that everything will probably be all right."

"Be all right?"

"Didn't you see my picture of the frogs hugging? Okay, not *hugging* exactly. The gentleman-frog hitches a ride on the lady-frog's back, and he fertilizes each egg as it comes out. Cora says they stay that way for months if they go into hibernation together. Romantic, isn't it?"

Two nasty, clammy frogs squeezing each other for weeks on end in the middle of some frozen field? *Romantic* was not the first word that hopped into Mary's mind, not at all, but then again she understood what her mother was getting at, she really did, two otherwise lonely creatures conjoined, clinging to each other, not giving up on each other, swimming into the dark and watery deep, down to the cold, cold bottom of things where nothing else lives. There was, if you disregarded certain details, such as the sex itself, something beautiful about it . . .

"What's the matter?" her mother asked. "I can't tell if you're crying or if the connection's gone bad. Are you crying? Did I say something wrong?"

Mary apologized. It was nothing, she said, just something silly. "Stupid boy stuff."

"Tell me."

She had kept her mother out of the loop these last few months because of everything that had happened with Brooks. She hadn't wanted to bother her mother with any of her own troubles. But now that her mother was far away and free, she didn't mind unloading, at least a little bit. She told her mother about Wynn—about Wynn's chin, his blue eyes, the perfect gray streak in his long windswept hair, their weekend at the house in Myrtle Beach, and then about his crazy wife, the pediatrician, who was hardly ever around.

Her mother was silent.

"Come on, you can't judge me. You used to be *married*," Mary said. "To a *man*."

"I'm not judging you. And for the record, I wasn't married when I met Cora. In case you've forgotten, I was alone for almost eight years after your—"

"None of this matters anyway," Mary said. "I broke up with him. I didn't love him. I barely even liked him."

"So what's the problem?"

Mary sighed. "I did some things I'm not proud of."

"What sort of *things*?"

"He liked to—this is embarrassing—make movies."

"Oh, Mary."

"I know. It only happened once. He says he taped over it—but still."

"Don't provoke this man," her mother said, meaning what? Provoke him how?

"Just don't do anything you'll regret," her mother said. She thought the best and wisest course was for Mary to let it go. To move forward with her life. To just forget the tape.

He is halfway in a dream when his sister announces that it's time for another escape attempt. The dream is about fishhooks. Well, not *about* fishhooks, but it involves them. He is looking for one in the bottom of a tackle box. Brooks hasn't gone fishing in more than a year, probably not since his last trip to Nicaragua. His company, which he started with a friend a decade ago, manufactures medical devices and has a factory outside Managua. The last time he was down there, Brooks took a few extra days and chartered a deep-sea fishing boat out of San Juan del Sur. He caught a striped marlin, though it was the captain who did the hard work, setting up the rod, finding the right spot. All Brooks did was wait and take orders, reel when the captain yelled to reel. Going deep-sea fishing is, actually, kind of like how he lives now. Sure, he can fry a few eggs, but only if there is someone there to help him, to keep him on task, to clean up the mess when his hands fail him, to calm him down when he loses his temper, to reel him in.

"You have gunk on your face," Mary says, and wipes it away with a wet thumb. "I think it's old soy sauce."

"Are you sure we should go for it again?" he asks. "How long will the owners be away? We could survive in here for days."

"No," she says. "I got us into this mess. I'll get us out."

Brooks knows this is the truth, that his sister is to blame, but he can't let go of the feeling that he should be masterminding the escape. After all, he's the big brother. He's always taken care of her. That's just how it is. His former self, the Old Brooks, up there somewhere, would know exactly what to do in this situation. Old Brooks sees a solution, surely, but he's keeping quiet about it. He's enjoying all this confusion. "Try not to think about who you were *before* the accident," Dr. Groom has said, "and concentrate on who you want to be now. Accept the new you." Sometimes Brooks wants to toss Dr. Groom out the window.

Mary opens the pantry doors and peeks out into the hall. "I don't see anything," she says. "Maybe they've gone upstairs."

He follows her to the kitchen entrance. She turns, a finger to her lips, but he has not made any sound. He watches her inch into the kitchen. To his right is a refrigerator. Photographs and appointment cards attached to its white side with magnets. In one of the photographs are two children, an older boy and a tiny girl, on a seesaw. Across the bottom someone has written, *What goes up* . . .

"Stop moving," Mary whispers, at least forty feet of tiled floor left between her and the exit.

But Brooks sees something on the wall, something that might help them: a cordless phone. Mary can just call her friend and get the safe command, and all this will be over. He reaches out for the black phone with the glowing blue screen, unhooks it from its cradle. When he turns to show it off to Mary, he realizes that she has come to a full stop at the entrance to the living room. "Easy," she says.

Through the door he sees them, the dogs, heads low, tails stiff, coarse black fur Mohawked up along their backs. Is it possible that the dogs have set an elaborate trap for them?

Mary inches backward. The dogs growl. "Baa, baa, black sheep," she whispers. "Bibi Netanyahu."

Brooks could probably make it safely back to the pantry. But not Mary. She's too close to the dogs, too far from the pantry. Behind him, on the stove, is a grimy cast-iron skillet. He grabs that. "Top of the fridge," he says.

"What?" Mary sneaks a look over her right shoulder. The dogs come at her with their clicking nails and soggy growls. She lunges at the fridge. She tries to use the ice dispenser as a foothold, but the freezer door swings open. She slams it and scrambles up onto the soapstone counter, knocking aside cookbooks and an old Mr. Coffee pot that shatters across the tiled floor. From there she pulls herself up onto the fridge. Brooks is two steps behind his sister. Phone in hand, he flings himself onto the counter, belly first. He feels like a spider with all its legs ripped out. He reaches for a cabinet knob. One of the dogs locks on to his ankle, and he screams. He writhes, swinging the phone back and forth. When the phone connects with the dog's head, he loses his grip on it and it goes clattering to the floor. But he's free now. He's able to clamber up beside his sister.

They have to crouch on the dusty fridge-top or else their heads will touch the ceiling.

"You're bleeding," Mary says, bending down to his ankle.

"Don't bother with it now." He looks down at the dogs, at their giant stinking faces. One dog is on the floor whimpering, and the other is pogo-ing up and down the front of the fridge, knocking loose all the photos and appointment cards. Its back paws come down on the phone and launch it sideways.

"I dropped it," Brooks says. "The phone. Sorry. We could have called your friend."

Mary is prodding at his ankle unscientifically. "Don't worry about it. That wouldn't have worked anyways."

"Why, he's out of the country or something?"

"Well—"

"He doesn't know we're here," Brooks says, surprising even himself.

His sister looks at him as if she were the one with the dog bite.

The night Wynn first brought out his video camera they were in Myrtle Beach at his family's beach house. Mary listened to the waves through the open window as Wynn fiddled with a tape. Then he told her to start playing with herself. Already she could anticipate the regret. Maybe that was part of the fun. Her friends had warned her about Wynn. They'd heard strange things about him. Perverted things. According to a guy who used to work with him, he cheated on his wife constantly. He'd been with a hundred women. Probably his dick was contaminated, her friends joked. At least make him wear a condom, they said.

Did she enjoy making the video? A little bit, sure. For the newness of it. But not for the sex itself. It didn't even feel much like sex to her. It was like something else. She was a planet, way out in space, out of its orbit, and he was an unmanned spaceship, taking measurements of the atmosphere. She was not suitable for habitation. The pillowcase smelled like potato chips and sweat. She wondered if he'd even washed them, if maybe this was one of the kids' bedrooms. He smacked her bottom, and she almost laughed. It wasn't risqué, it was silly.

She broke off the affair a few weeks later when he proposed a new video, this one in his bathroom at home. His wife was at work and the kids were at school. He already had the camera out.

"Do you ever watch these later?" she asked.

"Not really," he said. "It's not about that. Making them is what's fun. It's fun, isn't it?"

She was in a white towel, examining the shower. There was blond hair swirled around the drain. His wife's, no doubt. One of the drawers was halfway open, and she could see hair products and cotton swabs and a box of tampons. She opened the medicine cabinet and found three different kinds of antidepressants.

"Not mine," he said. "Let's start with you in the shower. You ready?"

She was not ready. She slipped back into her underwear and told him it was over.

"I don't understand," he said.

"I want the tape," she said. "From the beach."

"I erased it. I always tape over them."

She left him half naked in the bathroom. Later she wondered if she might have gotten the tape from him then if she'd only been a little bit more persistent. She thought about it constantly. At work, ringing people up, she lost track of the numbers. She spilled a box of rainbow sprinkles, and what should have been a ten-minute cleanup took her almost thirty.

"You've got to get the tape back," her friends said. "What if he puts it online?"

Online! She started visiting pornography sites, just in case. There were so many sites, so many categories of sex. She couldn't believe all the categories: Mature, POV, MILF, Amateur, Ex-Girlfriend. How might Wynn have categorized her?

She called him and demanded the tape.

"I already told you," he said. "It doesn't exist anymore."

"I'll call the cops."

"Listen, if I had it, I'd give it to you, but I don't. You can't just call me like this. I'm at work."

She imagined a locked desk drawer in his home study, a hundred tapes, each with a label, her name on one of them, the date, the location, the positions, the noises made, all of it charted out and diagrammed.

This was her situation to fix. Wynn kept a key hidden under a rock on the back porch. She remembered that. All she had to do was wait for the right day, the right moment . . .

"And so you think he has the tape here," Brooks says. "Somewhere in this house? And that's why we broke in?"

She nods.

"You could have just told me earlier," he says.

"You would have judged me."

"Sure, but only a little."

"Would you have gone along with it? If you'd known we were breaking into someone's house?"

"No, of course not," he says. "I would have waited in the car."

She smiles at him, and he is relieved to see that it's a real smile, without a trace of pity. "So where is Wynn now?" he asks. "How much time do we have?"

"A few hours, maybe. They drove up to Chapel Hill for the day. His son's looking at colleges." She knows this because Wynn shares so much of his life online. When she was with him, he was always typing something into his phone.

"If I had a sex tape, I don't think I'd keep it in the house for my wife to find."

"You don't know Wynn."

The dogs have stopped barking. They sit patiently at the foot of the fridge. Brooks's ankle throbs. He doesn't know what to do next. If only he could curl up on top of the fridge and take a nap. But the dogs will never give up. They are trained to attack intruders, and that's exactly what he and his sister are: intruders. Brooks has broken into someone's home. He needs a brick. Where's his brick? Give him a brick.

Brooks jumps—not over the dogs and toward the door but to their left. He lands on both feet and sprints back down the hall. The dogs follow. He's the distraction, the bait. "Find it!" he yells back to Mary. He passes the pantry. Ahead of him is the grandfather clock. A blue Oriental rug shifts sideways as he turns left at the end of the hall. He runs up a wide staircase, hand on the rail, and at the top he sees that there are doors, three of them. They look the same. It's like a terrible game show. He grabs the knob of the middle door, but his fingers won't grip right. "Some things will get better and others won't," Dr. Groom says, and Brooks will have to accept that.

But it's not his fingers, he realizes. The door is locked. He slings his shoulder into it with all his weight. Thankfully the lock is cheap and the door pops open.

Closing it behind him, he finds himself in a room with hot pink walls decorated with gruesome movie posters. A stereo and a television barely fit on a small white desk beneath the window. In the dead gray television screen Brooks can see his own warped reflection staring back: his terrible haircut, his skeletal face. Overhead the ceiling fan spins. The bedspread moves.

Moves? A tiny wiggle at the corner of his vision. An almost imperceptible change in the arrangement of wrinkles in the blanket. Like a scene from a horror movie.

In the months after the accident Brooks experienced what he now knows were mild hallucinations. At the hospital he became temporarily convinced that a family of goats had taken up residence under his bed. They had gray coats and wet black eyes, and at night they came out to lap water from the toilet. If Brooks called for help, the goats would scatter in all directions. They would duck for cover and hide. Dr. Groom explained that Brooks could no longer implicitly trust everything he saw and heard. What Brooks needed, he said, was a healthy dose of skepticism. If goats were ransacking his room, he was supposed to remember that it would be very tricky for a goat to somehow get past the hospital front desk and take the elevator to the third floor. If the coat rack asked him for a grilled cheese, Brooks needed to remind himself that coat racks did not typically require human food, especially not grilled cheeses. If the bedspread sprang to life . . .

He steps toward the bed. There are pillows piled at the head and foot. In the middle, under the bedspread, is a person-sized lump. He watches it closely. It might be rising and falling, but then again—

"Who's under there?" he asks.

The lump is very still.

"I'm trying to leave," he says. "So don't be afraid. All of this was a big mistake. Us being here, I mean. We know your dad. We got trapped. By your dogs."

The lump doesn't move.

"I'm Brooks. I'm not sure if you're actually under there. Maybe I'm talking to nothing. I can get a little confused. I haven't always been this way." He steps toward the desk. "I'm moving your desk so I can go out the window. Your dogs want to eat me. So I'm going out the window. Sorry." An apology to a ghost.

He slides the desk toward the closet, everything on it rattling. A water glass topples over and the liquid rolls. He grabs a soccer sock off the floor and sops it up before it touches a closed laptop covered in pink monkey stickers. "I spilled some water," he says, "and I had to use one of your socks. Sorry. Your laptop is fine, I think." He gets the window open and pops out the screen, which lands below in some holly bushes. He sticks one leg out and straddles the sill. It's a long way down but not so far that he will necessarily break a bone. Still, this is probably going to hurt.

"Ba baboon," the lump says.

"I'm sorry?"

"Say that to the dogs and they won't attack you."

"So you're really under there?"

The lump doesn't answer.

"Thank you. That's very kind. I'm Brooks."

"Yeah, you said that already."

"Aren't you supposed to be off with your family or something?"

"I got out of it. Please go now."

"I hope you're not just in my head," he says, and goes to the door. "Because that would mean *ba baboon* is total nonsense, and I'm about to get bitten again." The lump doesn't answer. He's about to turn the knob but stops. He walks back over to the bed. "By the way, just in case this ever happens again—"

"God. Why haven't you left yet?"

"I will. I'm about to. But next time this happens, you should really consider calling the police—or at least your parents."

The lump is quiet.

"Just an idea," Brooks adds.

The lump sits up fast, the bedspread transformed into a mountain. "Look, my mom, like, stole my cell, all right? I told you what to say, now go. Just get out of here."

Brooks isn't sure what to say. He considers apologizing again.

"Actually, I lied," the lump says. "I did call the police. They'll be here, like, any minute. You're going to jail."

"Okay," Brooks says, hand on the door. "Okay, I'm going."

When Mary climbs down from the fridge, part of her just wants to leave and forget the tape. But she can't do that. Brooks could be hurt upstairs. He could lose his way. He could trap himself in the linen closet and, in the dark, lose himself entirely.

Until her brother's accident, Mary never gave much thought to the idea that personalities may be not only malleable but also divisible from the self. There has to be more to us than memories and quirks that can get smashed away so easily. This raises questions of accountability. What part of her is accountable for her decisions if all that stands between Mary being Mary and not someone else is a simple bump on the head?

Wandering down the hall in search of her brother, she finds a room with a computer on a mahogany desk and a leather chair on a clear plastic mat over the carpet. Wynn's camera is in the chair, and in a metal tray beside the computer she finds a stack of small gray tapes. She can't sort through them here. She'll just have to take them all with her. She dumps out a bag of tangled cables, connectors, and start-up discs and loads the tapes into the bag. Then she adds the camera, just in case.

The hallway is quiet. Brooks is upstairs, somewhere—and the dogs? At the bottom of the stairwell she hears their nails. "Get out, Brooks," she yells, and runs back the way she came, down the hall, past the grandfather clock and the pantry, into the kitchen, all of it so familiar now. She goes out the back door and runs out into the yard, the sunlight on her face, a stultifying whiteness. One day she will forget everything, and there will be nothing left of her except . . . This. Whatever *This* is. Total erasure, maybe.

She wanders around the perimeter of the house, searching for any sign of Brooks up in the windows. She sees a popped-out screen in the bushes—but no Brooks. On the front porch she leans into a narrow window beside the door with her hands cupped around her eyes. Through the thin white curtain she can barely make out a table in the foyer, a painting on the wall above that, and the base of the wide staircase. She rings the doorbell three times, hears it echo in the house. She is about to abandon the porch when, through the window, she sees feet on the stairs, then knees, then a torso. Brooks is striding down the stairwell like he owns the place.

The dogs follow him, no longer vicious at all, their heavy dumb tongues lolling over sharp, crooked teeth. Her brother has tamed the beasts. The dead bolt clicks open, and there he is, framed in the doorway: her big brother.

The dog bite isn't deep enough to warrant a trip to the emergency room. "No more stitches," he says. "Please." Back at Mary's, he takes a hot shower and lets the water trickle over his wound. Blood swirls around the drain. He towels off and wraps his ankle with gauze and then falls into a long nap on top of the covers. When he wakes up again, it's dark out. He does his exercises at the foot of the bed and checks his email.

His mother has sent more pictures of the frogs. He scrolls through them: big-eyed blobs in the white snow, their neon-blue eggs like a thousand eyes under the freezing water. The final photo is of his mother and Cora crouching. Seeing his mother this happy in such a bleak landscape makes him smile.

He prints the picture to show his sister and heads downstairs. In the den, the blinds are drawn and the television screen casts a blue light across all the furniture, the plush couch and ottoman, the wall of framed photographs from Mary's semester abroad in Rome—her black-and-whites of the Colosseum, the Circus Maximus, so many gardens, basilicas, crumbling stone baths. On the den floor stacks of gray tapes surround a video camera tethered to the television by a long cord.

Brooks sits down cross-legged and brings the camera into his lap. He can hear Mary in the kitchen, pots rattling, a dinner being prepared. The tapes all look the same. He picks one and pops it into the camera. When he pushes play, he keeps his finger on the button, just in case he's presented with something no brother wants to see.

Two lines squiggle across the screen, and then a patio appears, a concrete space bright with sunlight. The camera is bouncy in someone's hand. Two kids are on the ground, dyeing Easter eggs in red Dixie cups. The boy, maybe twelve years old, gives an egg to his younger sister. Holding it between two fingers, she dips it in the cup.

"Hey, didn't know you were awake," Mary says, striding into the room. When she sees what he's watching she sighs and sits down beside him on the floor. They stare up at the television together. It's been years, Brooks thinks, since he last saw this tape, but it's all coming back to him now: their dye-stained fingertips,

Easter eggs buried in the pine straw, the smell of the azalea bushes, his mother lounging in the yard with her Bible and *People* magazines.

"Seems like yesterday that was us," Mary says.

The little girl on the screen knocks over the cup, and colored water spills all over her dress, the blue dye splashed up across her chest. She faces the camera bewildered, looking for help or reassurance maybe, and begins to cry.

"We shouldn't be watching this," Mary says, and grabs the camera from Brooks's lap. "It's wrong. Do you think I should try and return all this stuff? I feel awful about it. I guess I could leave it all on the doorstep."

As she's saying this, a woman Brooks doesn't recognize rushes onto the screen with a handful of paper towels for the little girl's dress, and only then does he fully understand that this isn't their patio or their Easter or their mother. This isn't their childhood at all, and it never was. "Stop clinging to the Old Brooks," Dr. Groom likes to say. "And guess what? You'll still be you."

He looks over at Mary, her finger poised on the Stop button. But she doesn't press Stop. She doesn't pull the cable from the camera or gather the tapes back into the crinkling bag either. She is watching the boy, on screen, as he holds up a perfect egg and then runs out of the frame. The little girl crashes into her mother's lap and cries into her shoulder. The scene ends and cuts to another. The kids are off searching for the eggs—in tree limbs, desk drawers, mulch beds, and, improbably, under a doormat. "Not there," Mary says aloud. "I mean, really."

When that video ends, the room is dark, and they are quiet.

Brooks waits a few seconds before sliding another tape to her across the floor under his hand. Mary's eyes dart up his arm and to his face, his ears and nose and forehead and scalp, her expression so serious he wonders if she's really allowing herself to see him for the first time since the accident. He mushrooms out his upper lip, imitating her pity smile, and she rolls her eyes.

Then she loads the next tape.

ACKNOWLEDGMENTS

Thank you to all the editors and staffs at the magazines and journals who gave many of these stories a first home: Ralph Eubanks, Roger Hodge, Laura Isaacman, David Leavitt, Cressida Leyshon, Paul Reyes, Evelyn Rogers, Randy Rosenthal, Deborah Treisman, Allison Wright, and more. A special thanks to Mike Curtis for many years of encouragement and advice.

To my teachers. At Wofford College: John Lane, Deno Trakas, Mark and Kerry Ferguson, Mark Byrnes, Ellen Goldey, Bernie Dunlap, Paige West (by way of Columbia University), Larry McGehee, and so many others. To the MFA faculty at UVA—Chris Tilghman, John Casey, and Ann Beattie—for every bit of guidance, for every note, for letting us invade your homes. Thank you to my fellow workshoppers: I've included you here with my teachers for a reason.

For her enthusiasm and ideas and patience, a big thanks to my editor, Laura Perciasepe. Also to Jynne Martin, Katie Freeman, Geoffrey Kloske, and all the other wonderful folks at Riverhead.

To my agent, Jin Auh, whom I should really be naming here twelve or thirteen times, thank you for everything that you do. Also to her assistants, Jessica Friedman and Nina Ellis, and everyone else at the Wylie Agency.

Thank you to my early readers. To my friends, new and especially old. Thank you to my family: Jesse, Corinne, Lily, and River Luckett; Charles Thomas and Leslie Cayce; Meg and Richard White; and my parents, Mickey and Nancy Pierce. And finally, a huge thanks to the two most important ladies in my life: my wife, Catherine, and daughter, Eleanor.

A note/confession: The line "Let the mind enter itself" in "Grasshopper Kings" was lifted, more or less, from Theodore Roethke's "In a Dark Time," a poem that could have served as an epigraph to this collection.

ABOUT THE AUTHOR

Thomas Pierce was born and raised in South Carolina. His stories have appeared in *The New Yorker*, *The Atlantic Monthly*, *Oxford American*, and elsewhere. A graduate of the University of Virginia creative writing program, he lives in Charlottesville, Virginia, with his wife and daughter.